Also, by Michael P Brawn

Pangur Ban
Flaming Margarita
TENSE
The Wollemi (Book 1 of the Wollemi Trilogy)
Killara

WOLLEMI
DREAMING

BOOK 2 OF THE WOLLEMI TRILOGY

MICHAEL P BRAWN

Editing Louise Brawn. Cover photo and design, Louise Brawn.
Copyright © 2023

Published 2023

First Printing 2023

ISBN 978-0-6480912-7-1

Published by Ashbourne Publishing

Ashbourne.publishing1@gmail.com

DEDICATION

This book is dedicated once again to my lovely wife, soulmate, partner, and guide, as well as my editor and chief critic, Louise. It is hard to write a sequel. It is even harder to inveigle one's nearest and dearest into reading it. I must also call out my dear friends, Kellie Blackall and Marie Basset Inglot, for their feedback and support.

CONTENTS

INTRODUCTION

In writing this sequel, 'Wollemi Dreaming', I have come to the understanding that what I am attempting is a kind of Australian magical realism. I am aiming to convey the sense of infinite magical possibility that I feel whenever I look down from Hawkins' Lookout across the great sweep of Hawkesbury River and the apparently endless forest beyond. It always seems to me that almost anything could be hidden in that endless primeval forest, and probably is.

DREAMTIME

Emma awoke to the sound of her own screams. The dream memory of Max's voice saturated her awareness. The feeling of being over-whelmed, sucked in, and assimilated, of her entire self being squashed into nothingness, left her retching. The salt taste of warm blood clogged her mind.

A door slammed nearby. Images of the other world dispersed like smoke from a snuffed candle drifting away on the early morning breeze. Her bedroom window was open, just a little, for fresh air. It was cold and still dark outside this time of year. It would be light soon. Her breath steamed in the still air, visible as a slight blur against the bar of light coming from under the bedroom door. Aine was up, no doubt wakened by the sounds of her mother's disturbed sleep. The door opened a crack. A small, slim girl poked her head in.

"You all right, Mum?" Aine stepped into the room. "Another bad dream?"

"Yes, I think it was a really nasty one."

'You were talking loudly in your sleep, arguing with someone."

'It was Max, I think, or someone speaking in his voice."

"Who else could speak in Max's voice except for Max?" Aine, an innocent in a world of empaths, born and brought up since the Event, could sense every nuance of her mother's fear, confusion, and pain.

"You think it might have been someone else?" There were times when Aine could be like a dog with a bone. Her life's goal, if she could be said to have had a life's goal at that age, was to be happy. And she would have been happy had not some innate sense of purpose-driven her. She was meant to do something or to be something. She had no idea what that something might be. Frustrating.

Emma pushed the heavy quilt aside and swung her legs over the edge of the bed, placing her bare feet firmly on the cold floorboards, savouring for a moment the bracing chill of early morning.

"Who do you think it was then?" Aine was not to be diverted.

"I don't know." Emma stood up and grabbed her dressing gown from the hook on the back of the door.

"I understand that you don't know," Aine persisted, "but who do you think it *might* have been?"

"I swear to God." Emma's frustration broadcast loud and clear for all to sense, "Things were so much easier in the old days."

Aine stepped close, slipping her arms around her mother's waist and snuggling. She realised that she might have pushed a bit too hard.

"It felt a bit like the OneMind."

Aine disentangled herself and stepped back.

"Do you mean you dreamed the OneMind was speaking to you in Max's voice, or do you mean you think it was the OneMind?"

Emma shook her head, "I don't know. I'm not sure. Sometimes, very late at night, when all the world's asleep and there is no empathic background noise, I think I can hear it thinking or dreaming. And some-times I fancy I can hear a little voice somewhere at the back of my mind talking to me." Aine stepped back, evaluating her mother's words, comparing what was said with what was felt. Feeling for a discrepancy. There was none.

"I'll put the kettle on." Aine turned and walked from the room. Extraordinarily innocent and, at the same time, wise beyond her years, and a powerful empath, it seemed at times that Aine's gift bordered on telepathy. Tommy, their mongrel cattle-dog-staffy cross, looked up for a moment from his rug by the range. Perhaps realising that he was un-likely to be fed at that time of day, he grumbled once and went back to sleep.

Emma found her slippers and padded into the kitchen. Through the window, the first hint of grey revealed, in broad outline, the world out-side. Although it was not yet light at that moment, there would be daylight soon. A kookaburra started up in the big old mountain gum that dominated their small backyard. The world was waking up, but there was probably still half an hour of peace before the emotional backwash of humanity dispelled even the memory of the visitor in the night. Aine pottered about making the tea.

"The OneMind is gone. The Wollemi are gone."

Emma held her peace. She knew Aine was right, but still.

"But you're not absolutely sure of it, are you?"

"No." Emma's voice was firm, "I was a part of the OneMind for the whole of the End Game. I was at one with the Wollemi. The One-Mind is subtle and cunning. The OneMind is not tame. It has not been… domesticated. Aine placed a piping hot mug of tea in front of her mother on the old kitchen table.

"There were layers," Emma continued, "depths where I was never able to venture. The 'I' that was Emma Hexenkriege, temporarily ab-sent, subsumed in the vastness of the one single mind. I sensed but never plumbed the oceans of thought that moved with slow deliberation across the world." Emma stared absently through the kitchen window. From the vantage point of distant memory, she peered into the early dawn of another new day. She could still recall the scintillating gestalt formed by the millions of individual minds that comprised the one great Mind. The greatest intellect ever seen on Earth, the OneMind of the Wollemi. Emma shuddered. *Just the nip of early morning,* she told her-self. Aine could feel the truth in her mother's voice. She could feel the wonder and the doubt. And something else. Something indistinct as yet, part formed.

"Can we go to the cottage for the weekend?"

"Why do you love going to the cottage so much?

"I love the total absence of humanity. I love the freedom from humanity's moods. It's like paradise. I just love it deep in the forest."

Emma nodded. It was Aine's happy place. Aine, being the more closely attuned to the empathic outpourings of humanity, suffered more than Emma from the constant noise.

"OK", Emma took a sip from the steaming mug, "We'll head over there after I finish work."

The two 'women', Emma, and her precocious eleven-year-old daughter, sat in silence, sipping tea. For the moment, quiet and at peace with the world and the silent multitudes who slept. The noiseless susurration of their unconscious feelings formed a slow, steady purr, not unlike that of small waves upon a pebble beach.

At last, it was fully light. Aine's phone rang. It was her grandma. Well, her step-grandma, Emma's step-mum. Kaitlin's voice came from the tiny speaker. It was weird how she always seemed to know when Emma and Aine were awake.

"I knew you'd be awake." Kaitlin never explained *how* she knew these things, and Aine had learned not to ask. Emma's stepmother had acquired an extensive knowledge of the obscure and arcane over a lifetime as a practising shaman and witch. Asking her how she knew something would either be met with silence or with a very long, typically incomprehensible, explanation. Suffice it to say, Kaitlin knew.

"Are you well, pet?" Kaitlin kept a weather eye on her step-granddaughter. "Are you working hard at school?" Kaitlin's overdeveloped protective instinct jarred with Aine's rebellious side.

"Yes, Grandma." Aine smiled. The ritual grilling was about to start.

"Yes, you're well, or yes, you're working hard at school?"

"Yes"

"Don't get smart with me, young lad. I've a thousand things to do today. Now put your mother on."

Aine giggled and passed the phone over to her mother. She loved Kaitlin, but it irked her when Kaitlin's compassion and generosity slipped towards martyrdom.

"Hi, Kaitlin, what's up?"

"You've been having those dreams again, haven't you?"

"Yes," Emma didn't bother to ask how she knew.

"Your dad and I are going fossicking this weekend. He says he knows a spot."

Jack always knew a spot or said he knew a spot, and he usually delivered the goods.

"Where?"

"Somewhere in the Wollemi Forest."

"Gold?"

"Yes, what else would it be?"

Emma knew. If it wasn't gold panning, it was sifting for opal or scratching around dry riverbeds for sapphires and emeralds.

"I'll drop by on Monday. For a chat."

"About my dreams?"

"Yes"

"What about my dreams?" Katlin could be maddeningly vague. If Emma were to think about it, she would probably conclude that Kaitlin had raised vagueness to the status of an art form. It was pretty much her modus operandi. Emma was never vague. Emma made a point of being as strong and competent as possible.

"Monday. Love you. And love to Aine." The phone went dead.

Monday it is then, Emma thought, *nothing I can do about that.*

APOLLO 11, SERIOUSLY?

Colonel Tom Olsen, US Marines (retired), stared across at 'The Dish'. There was something archetypal about the ageing radio telescope. Silent, brooding in the dawn chill. Parkes was bloody cold in winter. NSW was cold in winter. Who knew? The last time he'd been here, it was summer, and it was damned hot. It had been more than twenty years since his first visit, and Colonel Tom was in Australia somewhat incognito this time. He hadn't yet dropped in on the Hexen-kreiges to say 'hi'. He had not announced his arrival to any of his old comrades. This was a private visit, at least for now.

Colonel Olsen was back in Australia, determined to get some answers. One question above all pressed in on him, demanding satisfaction. Why had the powerful but enigmatic HARP device ever been developed? What on Earth had prompted DARPA, NASA, and the Centre for Disease Control to develop such a formidable, inscrutable device? And what, if anything, did it have to do with maintaining the veil? Tom, ferreting around the archives of the NSA where he had been a special liaison officer before retirement and where he could still pull a few strings, had found a link, albeit tenuous, to 'The Dish' in NSW and the 1969 Apollo 11 moon landing. There was a scan of a handwritten note torn from a notebook. 'Something unexpected' had been detected high in Earth's atmosphere as Apollo 11 passed through the Van Allen Belts. Something out-of-this-world, or perhaps not *of* it, had, for a split second, revealed itself.

Tom had come to the Parkes observatory to meet someone. The car slowed. The GPS had found the spot. As instructed, the vehicle pulled over on Telescope Road at the northern edge of the facility's permitter fence. A man wearing a hooded sweatshirt approached, walking towards him along the little service road that led to the facility's maintenance block. The man opened the passenger door and climbed in.

"Drive" His voice was somewhat muffled by a scarf draped around his neck and the lower part of his face. Tom turned off the autopilot and started the engine himself. They headed north, away from the Observatory. He pulled right off Telescope Road proper onto a dirt road and stopped. The two men sat in silence for a moment. Tom, an intelligence veteran of many years, waited. The man spoke again.

"You're the first person to come asking. It's been nearly twenty years since I made the report, but I always knew someone would come." Strong emotions roiled around the man. Anger and relief vied with fear and righteousness.

"I brought you a coffee from the roadhouse. It should still be warm. Damned cold around here this time of year." Tom controlled his emotions, emanating calm and confidence. His informant was safe. It was all going to be all right. The man took the coffee and sipped. Tom waited as the warm sweetness calmed the man further.

"Why don't you start at the beginning? What was your role on the mission?" After a couple more sips, the man began to speak.

"I was a junior radio engineer. My job was just to monitor the equipment. I had to check the signal strength and report variations. I also looked after the Rad. I was only included at the last minute as the automatic signal strength monitor turned out to be glitchy." Tom didn't interrupt. Explanations could come later. The man sipped his coffee, settled back in his seat, and continued.

"I was twenty-one years old. First job out of uni - seems like a lifetime ago now. I suppose it was." Tom didn't interrupt. The man was speaking. Let him speak.

"It was very early on in the mission. I reported a slight fluctuation in signal strength. It was small, below the tolerance threshold where it would cause concern. I should have kept my mouth shut."

"Why is that?" Tom focussed on generating feelings of concern. He had not grown up in a world in which all humans were empaths. He still had to control his emotions to avoid broadcasting what kids these days called 'backwash'.

"I wasn't part of the team. I was a Johnny-come-lately and a fresh-man. I wasn't trusted. At best, I was tolerated."

"What happened?"

"I was told to shut up. Keep to the protocol."

"And then?"

"And then the Rad spiked. Not quite off the scale but damned near."

"The Rad?"

"That's what we called it. Short for Radiation Spectrometer. It's a device designed to measure the power distribution spectrum of a source. The incident radiation generates a signal that allows us to determine the energy of the incident particle. Apollo 11 had one fitted. I was monitoring its signal."

"I see.' Tom didn't. Not at all. He allowed his bafflement to be perceived. The man sitting next to him laughed briefly.

"Sorry. I've spent my life around these things. Everyone's a geek here."

"Did you mention the spike at the time?"

"No. I should have, of course, but I was still smarting from the dressing down I'd been given a few moments earlier. I wrote the incident up later. In the flight logbook - a paper logbook kept in the control room. That's how we did things back then."

"What caused the spike?

"Well, that's the funny thing you see; I had no idea. At the time, I mean. We were only just coming to grips with the Van Allen Belts, what they were in fine detail, and how they formed and were maintained. We were just starting out, really."

"And now?" Tom persisted, "Now you know, or I expect you have a theory."

"Yes. More than a theory. Strangely, it was the Event that gave me the answer."

"The Event?" Tom was trying to make the connection between the first moon landing and the world-changing 'Event'.

"Well, think about it." The man was animated now, fully engaged. His earlier reticence had evaporated. He was in his element. "All those learnéd articles published after the Event by the world's leading scientists, anthropologists, evolutionary historians, and the rest, none of them asked the crucial question except one. Only one asked the critical question. Critical to me, I mean."

"And what was that?" Tom leaned in, genuinely absorbed, "What was the essential question?"

"Almost all the scientists were talking about the nature of the barrier, the veil between the worlds. Linguists and historians were scouring ancient texts for some insight. The physicists were talking about phase shifts, quantum non-locality and the like. But there was this old-school guy, a Russian physicist from way back. Cherenkov or something like that."

"What did he say?"

"It's not so much what he said, but the question he asked." Tom shifted in his seat, unable to prevent his frustration from leaking out.

"Sorry. Cherenkov asked how wide or thick the veil was and how far out into the Earth's atmosphere it stretched."

"And that was crucial to you? That question?"

"Yes. You see, the veil was not, is not a universal phenomenon. It is local. It has to be. There isn't an entire parallel universe duplicated on the other side of the veil. It is a bubble."

"A bubble?"

"Yes, and Apollo 11 broke through it."

"That was the spike?"

"That was the spike. And by going back and checking the flight logs later and the output trace from the Rad, I was able to calculate how high above the Earth the veil extends and its thickness."

"Wow."

"Yes, wow. I filed a report and sent a copy to NASA and the CSIRO."

"What happened?"

"Well, nothing, actually. I got a note back from the CSIRO thanking me, but I was and am an engineer, not a scientist. They probably binned it."

"And from NASA?"

"Nothing at all."

The two men sat in silence. It had become full daylight, and the bright bleak sunlight of the NSW winter beat down on the car. It was getting hot inside. Eventually, Tom thought to ask the obvious questions.

"Um, how high up is the veil then? How thick is it?"

"Bear in mind I didn't have precise measurements, and the monitors back then were a bit flaky."

"Ok."

"Well, I calculated that the veil is coterminous with the magnetopause."

"Sorry?"

"The altitude varies. Imagine the veil like an enormous soap bubble surrounding the Earth at the point where the incoming solar winds are exactly balanced by Earth's magnetic field."

"Why there?"

"Well, I think the veil may be sustained by the energy of the solar winds."

"How does that work?" If true, this was amazing. He would have to tell the others.

"It's only a theory, but the energy of the solar wind is soaked up in the magnetosphere. I think the veil is self-sustaining. It harvests as much of that energy as it needs to sustain itself."

"So, it doesn't need any support from the OneMind? It's not maintained psychically as we all thought?" The OneMind had lied. That was a thought that had never occurred to him before.

"I guess not. I never thought about that."

"So, the veil is solar powered. And I thought we humans invented that." Tom was trying to make sense of this new information. Everything that the OneMind had said about the veil and the reason it had weakened was untrue, he realised. The apparent imminent collapse of the veil had been manufactured by the OneMind itself to trigger a reaction from humanity, a specific, carefully worked-out reaction. To deploy the HARP. His informant detected Tom's amazement, but he was unsure of the cause.

"But plants have always been solar powered. Chlorophyll and all that?" Tom brushed aside the man's comment.

"How thick is the veil, by your calculations?"

"The outer edge of the phase shift, you mean. Maybe a few hundred microns. The spike appeared and disappeared within the detector's minimum unit of time. Less than 100th of a millisecond."

"Wow."

"Yep, if I had blinked, I would have missed it."

"Can I see the flight log? Do you think you could get it for me? I don't want to take it away. Just take a photo of a couple of pages."

"No. I'm afraid not."

"Look, it's just for historical interest. I…"

"It's nothing like that," the man cut in, "the book's gone."

"Gone?"

"Yes, it disappeared a while ago. I checked if it had been sent to the archive, but it hadn't."

"You think someone took it?"

"Nah. Most likely, someone stuffed it into a desk drawer. It'll turn up someday."

Tom entertained a different theory—one he chose not to share. A thought occurred to him.

"How come you're still here?" he asked. "How come you're still working at the Dish? You must be passed retirement age, right?"

"Yes indeed. I should have retired a while ago, but I couldn't bring myself to leave. They keep me on now as a sort of maintenance man. I'm about the only person who can remember how all the mechanical stuff works." The man smiled. He'd made his life here. This was his place.

"Well, I can't thank you enough for taking the time to meet with me. Where do you want me to drop you off?"

"I was happy to get to speak with someone about it, to be honest. I'll get out here and walk back."

"You sure?"

The man nodded. He and Tom shook hands. The man stepped out of the car and trudged back along the dirt road towards the observatory. For a long time, Tom sat and mulled things over. He was perhaps one step closer. He may not have found out what had prompted NASA to develop the HARP, but he was a little closer as to its purpose. One thing had become clear to him, though. It had nothing to do with maintaining the veil. But what exactly the OneMind need it for remained unknown.

At last, Tom reached under the seat, turned off the voice recorder and slipped it into his pocket. He still had a fair way to travel before evening. Tom checked his phone for the correct address and keyed it into the navigator. He had only typed a few words before the address popped up in the dropdown. The OneMind museum was a place of interest. Tom clicked on the proffered address and said 'Drive'. The engine started, and Tom settled back for a snooze. He'd be there by lunchtime.

THE ONE-MIND MUSEUM

As usual, Alice Whalebone was the first person to arrive at the Wisemans Ferry 'OneMind Museum and Visitors Centre'. As Chair of the Board, she felt it was her responsibility to model the behaviour she expected of her people. Not that she thought they should always come in early, but they had always to understand that she would, that she cared and took responsibility. She expected her people to take responsibility, and as CEO of Red Earth Mining, she felt and acted in precisely the same way. Alice was a natural leader. More than anything else, that was what defined her.

But she had arrived at the Museum early this morning because she wanted to check something out before anyone else arrived. This was something for which she wanted privacy. Strange things were afoot, which was not, in and of itself, an enormous surprise. The environs of Wisemans Ferry and its hinterland did tend to throw up weird and wonderful stuff from time to time. But what she had come to check on was odd. Alice found it a bit creepy, more than merely strange it was just plain bizarre.

Alice let herself in, turned off the building alarm and headed for the glass atrium at the centre of the purpose-built visitor's centre. She unlocked the small glass access door and stepped into the wilderness, or what the visitor's centre gardeners had managed, through clever planting, to present as wilderness. It was pretty spectacular. She had to admit that. The undergrowth was too dense for visitors to see from one side of the atrium to the other. The effect was as though someone had captured a piece of the Wollemi Forrest and encased it in glass.

Alice picked her way to the centre of the display. To a spot invisible to the passing multitudes. Here she had, on a curious impulse, done something unexpected. At the centre of the atrium, Alice had done a bit of planting of her own.

More than two decades had passed since Alice had led her people into the forest to rescue Emma. Since that time, the full gamut of scientists, archaeologists, and anthropologists had trampled all over the Wollemi Forest. Many strange finds had been turned up, and no doubt much remained to be discovered. A good deal had been learned about the 'Wollemi', the ancient humans who had lived there, hidden behind the veil. Amongst the ancient artefacts that had been found was a worn wooden staff, later discovered to be a relic from an ancient almond tree. It was a curiosity, nothing more, and after lying around various labs for a year or two, it had been donated to the OneMind Museum, where it lay in a glass case for many years. A local clergyman had named it 'Adam's walking stick', a reference to the branch from the Tree of Knowledge of Life and Death that Adam had supposedly taken from Eden. The name stuck and had even been written on its display case.

Sometime later, another similar staff had been found, in a cave near the Pagoda Lookout, overlooking the Cudgegong River. Perhaps inevitably, this one had been called 'Eve's walking stick', this time a reference to a branch said to have been taken by Eve from the Tree of Life.

Walking past their display case one day, Alice had, to her great surprise, noticed that the two long-dead objects had burst into life. Although it was winter, they had begun to sprout tiny roots and leaves. Perhaps the warmth inside the museum and the strong lights had triggered them.

She had had the display case moved to her office where, over the following weeks, she had watched them grow still further. One moonlit evening, on impulse, she had taken the two relics and planted them in a tub at the very centre of the atrium. They were merely curiosities, she told herself, and anyway, she couldn't just sit back and let living things die. Now she had returned to check on them.

To her amazement, the sight that greeted her was of two small leafy trees. They had sent out shoots towards each other which had grown together, creating the illusion of a single tree with two trunks. That this was somehow symbolic, Alice could see straight away, but of what precisely it was symbolic, for the time being, eluded her. Kaitlin knew about these things. She might be able to fathom it. Alice took a couple of snaps on her phone and headed back to her office. People would be arriving soon. As she walked into the office, her phone rang. It was Tom Olsen.

"Oh my God," Alice was surprised to hear from him. It had been quite a while, "to what do I owe the honour of a personal phone call." She could hear Tom laughing on the other end of the line.

"I've been out at Parkes. I'm heading in now. I'll be there in a few hours."

"What are you doing all the way out there? How come you're even in Australia?"

"I'll tell you when I see you. How're you doing?"

"Good. I have something to tell you too. Well, something to show you. I'm hoping you may be able to shed some light."

"Sounds interesting."

"It is."

"See you soon. I should be there around lunchtime." The phone went dead. Alice sat behind her large modernistic desk and flipped open her computer. She said the word 'search' and the word 'listening' appeared on the screen, announced by a tiny 'ping' sound. Alice waited, but the anticipated search words evaded her. She had at her disposal the combined, AI-curated knowledge and wisdom of humanity. All she had to do was ask. But nothing seemed to come to mind.

Glancing over at the now empty glass display case, Alice's eye happened to rest upon the small, typed label. The words 'Made from a branch of an almond tree' jumped out at her. What did that mean, she wondered? What was the mythological significance?

"Search for staff made from almond tree." A moment later a snippet of text appeared on the screen.

"Almonds, in general, and specifically rods and staffs made from almond wood, play a significant part in the Aramaic religions. Adam was said to have been given a staff or walking stick in the Garden of Eden made from almond wood. Both Moses and Aaron were also said to have been given magical almond wood staffs. The Jewish symbolic candlestick, the menorah, is said to have been inspired by almond blossom."

This is Kaitlin's area, Alice thought. Alice herself was an Elder of quite a different tradition. She picked up her phone and sent the two photos she had taken in the atrium to Tom and Kaitlin.

Let's see what they have to say, she thought.

Some time passed. The Museum and Visitors Centre staff began to amble in, going to their allotted posts or setting up their areas. The faint hum of human activity began to fill the place. Alice checked her messages and set up a few meetings. Her phone rang. It was Kaitlin.

"Hi, Alice. So, what's with the photos? Have you developed a green thumb all of a sudden?"

"Something like that. Are you guys at home?"

"I'm with Jack at one of his 'undisclosed locations', panning for gold."

"Figures. How are you two going?"

"Fit as fiddles, the pair of us. And yourself?"

"I'm good, thanks, but I need to talk to you. It's about the photos."

"Well, fire away. Jack's stomping around in the shallows sifting small pebbles. I'm supposed to be making tea."

"You remember the two almond-wood staffs that the CSIRO donated to the visitors' centre?"

"Yes."

"Well, they've sprouted."

"Sprouted. Do you mean they are alive? Growing?"

"Yes."

"What did you do to them?"

"Nothing. Well, nothing to make them sprout. They'd been in their case for at least fifteen years."

"What have you done with them now, then?"

"I planted them."

"You planted Adam and Eve's staffs? Why didn't you call in the CSIRO?"

"Should I have done? Yes, I suppose I should. To be honest, the thought never occurred to me."

"How are they doing?"

"They're doing fine. Well, they're thriving. You can see from the photos."

"Have they joined up? Are those root things interconnected?"

"Yes, I think they've grown together, like clones. Like the Wollemi Pines."

"You're kidding? I'll come and take a look as soon as we get back."

"OK, but do you have any idea what it might mean?"

"Mean? What are you getting at?"

"Is it, you know, significant?"

"You're thinking symbolically? Like, what might it mean symbolically?" there was a slight pause while Kaitlin thought about it. Alice was a bit freaked, and that wasn't typical for her. Not at all. Kaitlin continued.

"Look, it's probably nothing, but…."

"But what?" Alice's tone suggested she didn't want to know. Kaitlin was reviewing the recent series of unusual events. Perhaps this was connected.

"But if it were to symbolise something, given where they were found and all that, it could potentially be some kind of message."

"From?"

"Well, maybe the OneMind."

"The OneMind? You really think so?"

"It's probably just a coincidence. Maybe we should check with the CSIRO. Maybe this is not all that unusual."

"Coincidence? What coincidence? What else has happened?"

"There are a couple of things I need to run past you." Conversation faltered for a moment, neither woman certain which way to go.

"But best to avoid a snap judgement. Could mean nothing at all." Somehow neither woman truly believed that.

"Tom will be here soon." It just came out. Alice wasn't sure why she had mentioned it. It wasn't a secret, but she'd gained the impression Tom wasn't broadcasting his presence.

"Tom, who? Not Tom Olsen?"

"Yes, Tom Olsen. He's here for a visit."

"He didn't mention anything to me or Jack." Kaitlin's tone was matter-of-fact. There was nothing implied in the comment. Alice could not have detected any emotional nuances over the phone in any case.

"Something's up." Kaitlin continued.

"What makes you think that?"

"Intuition? Emma's been having those dreams again. She and Aine have gone to the cottage for the weekend. Now Tom's arrived unexpectedly. Jack and I had a feeling something was going on, and the OneMind may have sent us some kind of message."

"You think it's back?"

"Don't know. Maybe."

"I'll call you when Tom arrives if you don't mind. I think we need to put our heads together."

"No worries. I'd better make the tea." In the background, Alice could hear the soft whistle of an old-fashioned kettle.

"OK. Talk soon."

FOSSICKING

Jack splashed his way out of the shallow riverbed holding up his battered old pan. He'd been at it an hour or so, and his back had begun to ache, but he wore a huge grin.

"Take a look at this lot." Jack brandished the pan under Kaitlin's nose. Kaitlin smiled.

"Sure, I'd expect nothing less." At the bottom of the pan, there glittered a few tiny specks of gold. Jack smiled, feeling acknowledged. Gold was gold, no matter how little, and this little lot was for free. Old habits die hard.

"Alice is growing walking sticks."

"Of course, she is. CEO of a mining company, chairperson of a museum and Aboriginal Elder, what else would she be doing?"

"No, really. I want to swing by on the way home and take a look."

Jack shook his head and focused on chivvying the tiny glittering specks into a small clear glass medicine jar.

"What do you mean, she's growing walking sticks? What is she actually doing?"

"She's planted the Adam and Eve walking sticks at the museum. They started sprouting."

"They sprouted before she planted them or after?"

"Before."

"That's impossible."

"Here are the photos she sent me." Kaitlin held out the phone towards Jack.

"See."

Jack leaned in.

"Have they grown together? They're like clones. Like the pines."

"Yes, looks like it. Oh, and Tom's here."

"Which Tom? Tom Who?" Jack had on his impatient, 'stop talking in riddles' look, his frustration a palpable force emanating from him.

"Olsen. Tom Olsen is over for a visit."

"He never told us he was coming, did he?"

"No. It's a surprise visit."

Kaitlin finished making the tea. The intrepid pair sat themselves down on a large flat rock and contemplated the world. The sounds of the forest settled in around them, a reassuring blanket of small hums and resonances.

"And Emma's been having those dreams again. I spoke to her first thing this morning."

Jack withheld immediate judgement, seeking instead some kind of pattern.

"She and Aine are going to the cottage for the weekend."

Kaitlin noticed Jack's pensive look. She could feel the slow, steady cogs of his mind turning. Jack was a practical sort of person, not given much to introspection or flights of fancy.

"Something's up." Jack caught Kaitlin's eye. "Too many coincidences."

"I thought so too." Kaitlin drained the last of her tea and stood up. She needed time to think. Perhaps she might cast a small spell or two. Perhaps the Dreamtime, after its long slumber, was beginning to stir once again.

"I'm going to have a look around." Kaitlin needed time and space to think. She spotted an interesting-looking overhang of rock and made her way up the steep hillside behind her towards it. There was no obvious route to it, and the forest appeared to be placing obstacles in her way. At last, a few scratches and a bruised shin later, she made it to the top. There was a large flat ledge a few metres away to her left. To get to it, she would have to skirt the narrower edge of a small cliff. The narrow way curved back into the rockface before emerging a few metres further along. Kaitlin began to edge her way around, chest flat against the rock face, sliding her left foot along a little and then bringing up the right. Slowly but slowly, she edged her away around the curve in the path and into a narrow way between two boulders. Once past the boulders, the way opened up, and a small cave mouth, invisible from below, appeared. The way in was narrow, just wide enough for one person at a time to enter. As she progressed into the cave, kicking old leaves, the detritus of centuries, out of her way, the light from the small opening began to fade. After a few more steps, Kaitlin turned on the torch in her phone. What had been nearly pitch black became suddenly bright, dazzling her for a moment. When once again she could see clearly, what met her eyes caused her to gasp, step back and lean for a moment against the cliff wall. The walls were covered in hieroglyphics, glimmering in the torchlight. Shreds of ancient gold leaf gleamed dully.

Amazed at what she saw. Unable to take it all in, Kaitlin turned the phone on its side and began to photograph the interior of the cave. From one side of the cave entrance all the way around one wall and back to the entrance on the other side, Kaitlin captured it all. The ceilings, too, were covered in sculptures of animals and trees. The place pulsated with an unknown power. The web of life seemed to suffuse everything, even the rock itself. Elusive memories came to mind of black and white photographs she had once seen of similar hieroglyphics on a rock wall near Gosford. But these gilded carvings were far different. This wasn't so much a message as a powerful statement carved deep into the living rock. The feeling of time, stretching back across a hundred and sixty human generations or more, almost swamped the senses. What met Kaitlin's eye was not merely impossible. It ravished the eye and flooded the mind. Too many coincidences. The game, whatever it was, was afoot, whoever the participants were, conscious or otherwise.

Kaitlin part walked, part staggered, to the cave entrance. Reaching out with all her senses, she detected the gentle humming of Jack's mind, pottering about down below. Focussing every ounce of psychic energy, Kaitlin managed to connect. She put two fingers to her mouth and whistled, a loud, sharp sound piercing the quiet of the forest like a spear. Jack heard and felt her call. A moment later, he could be heard scrabbling up the steep hillside. As he neared the top, he shouted out," Where are you? What's happened?"

Kaitlin, who had recovered somewhat from the shock, took a couple of steps beyond the cave mouth, and shouted back, "I'm up here in the cleft in the rock face. You have to see this, Jack. You have to tell me I'm not going mad." A minute or two later, Jack came edging around the curve in the rock face from the other side.

"What is it? What have you found?"

"I don't know, Jack. Come, have a look for yourself."

Jack edged his way around the last metre or two and followed Kaitlin into the cave. She led him a few metres into the darkness before switching on the torch.

"Struth." Jack sat down on an out-jutting spur of rock. "I'd love to see how the archaeologists explain this one." He should have gone back and checked out the hieroglyphics at Gosford. He chided himself. He'd been meaning to. It was good that Tom was over from Texas. Kaitlin, Alice, and Tom would figure out what to do.

"Let's head back." Kaitlin's voice was low and urgent, "Let's try to get ahead of this…. Whatever it is."

"You've taken photos?"

"Yes."

"Ok. Let's go, but don't show anyone the photos until we've had time to think about them."

Jack and Kaitlin made their way back down the hillside and collected their equipment. Loaded up to the gills with all their fossicking gear, Jack led Kaitlin a kilometre downstream in the direction of the Hawkesbury River before calling back the drones. He didn't want to give away the cave's position. About half an hour later, two large drones settled in a clearing a few metres upstream. Jack and Kaitlin loaded their gear onto one and strapped themselves into the second.

Donning his headset and making sure that Kaitlin was firmly strapped in, Jack spoke, "Wisemans Ferry Inn." Almost silently, the two drones lifted into the late morning sky and swung south and east, flying low over the canopy of trees. The two drones snaked their way between the sharp-toothed hills of the Wollemi Forest and out over the open flood plain where automated farms tended by bug-like robotic agricultural machines presented a latter-day idyll. AI provided for humanity's sustenance these days. The only remaining human-run farms were horse studs and hobby farms.

Silent thoughts of the events of twenty years before surfaced, seemingly of themselves. They were both thinking the exact same thing. "Too many coincidences. Something was up."

THE ATRIUM

Soon enough, the drones settled on the paddock just below Wisemans Ferry Inn. Jack and Kaitlin unstrapped themselves and collected their gear. Kaitlin tapped the recall button, and the two drones lifted into the clear blue winter sky, disappearing over the hill in the direction of Glenorie. How the world had changed, Kaitlin mused. She had little, if any, idea where the drones went to recharge and wait for their next passengers. There were still a few utes about, solar powered. Jack kept one, but they were now almost exclusively used by bush folk or rich city people on their weekend 'ranches'. There were fewer people about now than twenty years ago, and fewer children too. The bush was reclaiming the abandoned land. The farms were run by silent, solar-powered robots, working tirelessly day and night. Robots did the planting, spraying, diagnosed disease and treatment, and harvested the crops. Any remaining homesteads were becoming increasingly isolated as nature returned. The roads were becoming disused in favour of drones. The countryside was silent now but for the sounds of nature.

It took a couple of trips for Jack to dump their gear in the back of his ute and close the tonneau cover. The little medicine jar carrying his precious gold flakes he kept with him. A working life spent prospecting in the central desert, and the bush had taught him caution.

He and Kaitlin wandered down the hill towards the Hawkesbury River and the Museum and Visitors Centre, set on the flood plain beyond the bowling club. The sliding glass doors opened as they approached, and the pleasant cool of the climate-controlled building enfolded them. The doors swished closed behind them, suddenly cutting out the sounds of the village. It was cool and quiet inside, unhurried. They made their way to Alice's office, nodding to the staff at the information desk as they walked past. Alice looked up and smiled as they entered.

"Tom's not here yet, but the GPS says he's only a few minutes away."

There was a momentary awkwardness as no one wanted to broach the topics either of the planted walking sticks or Tom's sudden unexpected arrival.

"Shall we take a look at your handiwork then?" Kaitlin broke the impasse.

"Yes, sure. Follow me." Alice led them through the museum to the atrium. Unlocking and sliding the glass door open, the three friends stepped out of the visitor's centre and into the wilderness. They slid the door shut behind them. Alice led the way, picking carefully between the tree branches and the low shrubs. A few visitors watched for a moment and then wandered on. A moment or two later, Alice stepped to one side, holding an arm out in the direction of a planting tub about the size of half a wine barrel. In the tub, two unremarkable-looking young trees grew. They were each verdant with leaves and small branches. Between the two trunks, perhaps thirty centimetres apart, stretched a writhing muddle of tree roots, giving the impression that this was either one plant or a weird symbiosis of two.

Alice's phone rang. Tom was waiting at the information desk.

"Can you show him through to the atrium, please?"

Jack reached into the tub, feeling beneath the soil with his fingers.

"Their roots are joined. If they keep growing like this, in a few years, the trunks will have grown into one another."

"You're not thinking of separating them, are you?" Kaitlin was horrified.

"No. Not at all. Whatever is going on, I'm guessing there's some kind of reason for it." Jack felt around the edge of the tub.

"They're not root bound. They've just kind of made a beeline for each other. They are, I want to say, 'deliberately', merging into one."

Kaitlin nodded, "What fate has woven together, let no one pull asunder."

Jack didn't get the reference. No matter. A minute or so later, a rustling in the undergrowth announced Tom's arrival. There were welcomes and hugs all around.

"How long has it been?" Alice stepped back a little in the cramped conditions to get a better look at her old friend.

"I guess about five years since I last ventured across the pond. You look wonderful."

"It's great to see you too, Tom." Alice felt herself blushing.

Kailin gave Tom a hug, and Jack reached out to shake his hand and give him a nod.

It had been around twenty years since they had first met in person, and though half a decade had passed since Tom's most recent visit, for all of them, it was as though no time had passed at all. There was a moment's awkward silence. Then Alice pointed out the two apparently young trees growing in the tub.

"These are the Adam and Eve staffs from the museum. They started to sprout in their display case, so I ended up planting them to stop them from dying."

Tom sat back on his haunches and stared at the two small trees. He leant over to touch the woven rope of roots that stretched between them."

"Yes," Alice placed a hand on Tom's shoulder, "we think they are growing together into a single tree."

"How the hell do two long-dead sticks spring back to life maybe thousands of years after they were cut down?" Tom looked to Alice, who merely shrugged.

"And how do they sprout at all in the absence of earth and moisture?" Tom was more disturbed by this horticultural oddity than he cared to let on. He paid close attention to the ways of nature, and this was plain wrong.

"It seems somehow against the natural order, against nature itself."

"I believe it's a message," Kaitlin chipped in, "It's symbolic."

"You think?" Tom smiled and stood up, "This is in the Ibrahimic tradition. That's your neck of the woods, isn't it, Kaitlin?"

"Closer to me than you guys, I guess" Kaitlin smiled.

"Well, can you try and figure out what the message is and where it's coming from?"

Kaitlin nodded, but Jack, who dreaded this kind of weird stuff, had had enough.

"This is doing my head in. I vote we all go sit in the pub with a drink in front of us." Jack nodded in what he hoped was the direction of the exit.

"I wouldn't mind one of their steaks." Tom smiled.

Alice led the way through the atrium wilderness and back into the here and now.

"I'm just going for lunch." She announced to the staff at the information table, "I'll be an hour, no more."

WISEMANS FERRY INN

It was unusually busy in the Wisemans Ferry Inn restaurant. Local families with kids scampering this way and that, mixed with a few small groups of bikers or cyclists, out for a ride. Alice found a table in the far corner by the window, away from the counter and most of the families. A group of bikers sat nearby, munching their way through giant schnitzels.

"Nothing much has changed." Tom looked around the crowded restaurant and through the large plate glass window onto the generous deck, sparsely occupied this time of year. Beyond the deck, the ground dropped away to the bowling club and, beyond that, the Museum and Visitors Centre. At last, his eye landed on the majestic sweep of the Hawkesbury River bounded on the far shore by the timeless cliffs marking the beginning of the forest.

"And everything has changed." Tom smiled. He lifted his glass, "To absent friends and comrades lost." The toast was drunk in silence. Memories and the ghosts of memories prowled the perimeter.

"And to old friends reunited" Alice reached out and squeezed Tom's arm.

Glasses were once again raised all around, "Friends reunited."

It was Alice who broke the ensuing silence.

"What brings you to Australia?" Alice held her fellow shaman's eye, searching for prevarication or pretence.

"Just tying up loose ends", Tom used his warm Texas accent to the max, "I needed to put something to rest." Both Kaitlin and Alice shifted in their seats. Tom was hiding something.

"Out with-it, Tom," Kaitlin sounded frustrated, "There is no room for secrets between us."

Alice, hands on hips, fixed him with a steely glare.

"Mate, with the best will in the world, you may as well spit it out. You know they'll wheedle it out of you in the end anyway."

Tom laughed, "OK, OK, I went to check something out with a guy who works at the radio telescope in Parkes."

"The Dish?" Even Jack had heard of it.

"Yeah, he was on duty the night that Apollo 11 took off."

"Apollo 11?" Kaitlin sounded unconvinced, "You came all the way from the great state of Texas to rural NSW to find out about the Apollo 11 moon landing?"

"Well, not the landing so much as the take-off. Or just after the take-off. The guy I met lodged a handwritten report many years after the landing about an anomaly that occurred soon after take-off. A copy found its way to the NSA."

"An anomaly?" Kaitlin had begun to tap her foot ominously.

"What about it?" Alice was more direct, "Why was it worth making such a long trip if you already had the information?"

"I needed to hear it from the horse's mouth."

What, between magic walking sticks, and Apollo 11, Jack was thinking a nice schooner of pale ale would just hit the spot.

"Who wants a drink?" Jack looked around hopefully. No one responded.

"Spill", Alice crossed her arms, immovable until she'd heard the story, "and make it quick."

"The guy measured the veil."

"He what?" Kaitlin wasn't sure she'd heard correctly. Even Jack's ears picked up at that.

"Apollo 11 picked up an energy spike as it passed through the magnetosphere. At the magnetopause, to be precise, just at the point where the force of the solar wind is balanced out by the Earth's magnetic field."

"And?" Despite having, at best, a very sketchy idea of what the magneto-whatsit was, Alice was now engrossed.

"And the guy realised later that what Apollo 11 had picked up was the edge of the veil." This was met by blank faces all around.

"I believe what he discovered means that the veil is a bubble surrounding the Earth. It's only a few microns thick at the outer edge, but within the bubble, some kind of phase shift separates our world from the Dreamtime."

"I see." Alice had never thought of the Dreamtime in this way before. For her, it had always been the once and future spark of creation. It was the creative void from which all things sprang. It was then, it is now, and it always will be. It hadn't been made by anyone. It just was. She leaned back in her chair, trying to clear her head.

"But that's not all."

"Oh no." Alice didn't think she could take any more just then.

"I believe the veil was put in place by the OneMind. We all kind of know that, right?" There were nods of agreement from Kaitlin and Jack.

"But the veil is not kept in place by the OneMind."

"What?" Jack, Alice, and Kaitlin all spoke at once.

"The veil takes its energy from the magnetosphere. There's a reason its outer edge skirts the magnetopause, where the solar wind is balanced by the Earth's magnetic field. It feeds off the energy of the solar wind, using as much or as little as it needs, moment to moment."

"The veil is solar powered?" Jack looked stunned.

"That's exactly what I said." Tom smiled, "But that's not all."

"Oh no, no, no," Alice was rocking back and forth, head in hands, "I don't think I can take any more."

"Last point." all eyes were fixed on Tom. Alice had managed to stop rocking, "the 'imminent' collapse of the veil, that we all fought so hard to prevent twenty years ago, was a setup."

"A setup? By whom?" Alice had pulled her knees up under her chin and wrapped her arms around her legs. In that pose, she seemed many years younger and suddenly vulnerable.

"The OneMind wanted us to believe that the veil was collapsing. It wanted us to deploy the HARP. It *wanted* us to fire it – but not to maintain the veil."

"It took a hell of a risk," Jack reached out and put a protective arm around Kaitlin, "the Generals came within a whisper of frying him, frying his people, I mean. Wiping out the Wollemi."

"I believe the OneMind needed the energy generated by the HARP to tie humanity back into the web of life." Tom scratched his head in frustration. "What I don't get is why he needed it."

"Well, whatever it was, it must have seemed worth it." Jack sat back, wishing now more than ever for a large cold glass of Coopers Pale Ale.

For several minutes after that, there was silence. Everyone was lost in their own thoughts. Everyone was trying to make sense of it, trying to figure out what it all meant.

"Maybe it wasn't just some altruistic impulse." Alice looked around. "We are assuming that it used the energy to reconnect its 'lost children' empathically with the web of life, but Tom is right. There may have been more to it than that. Why take the risk of annihilation if there wasn't something even more important at stake?"

"More important?" Tom was intrigued, "Its own survival perhaps, or the survival of its people?"

"We should break this up into two chunks. How about Alice and I try to figure out why the OneMind needed the energy from the HARP."

Kaitlin nodded. Best not to mention the cave of hieroglyphics just yet. It would only complicate an already complicated situation. She would gather more information first. It would take time to find out what the ancient message, inlaid with gold leaf, said. But until then…

"I'll research Adam and Eve's staffs. We can get back together in a day or two," and turning to Jack, "and I'll have a rum and black, please."

"Uh oh, here we go," Tom laughed, "Last time I saw you drinking that you ended up unconscious on the floor of the Wiseman's Ferry Inn." Kaitlin blushed beetroot.

"Say, Jack, didn't you carry her up to her bedroom?" The comment was accompanied by a knowing look.

"A gallant gesture should never be besmirched." Kaitlin bridled at any suggestion of impropriety, "Jack was a perfect gentleman."

"As always." Alice chipped in.

Jack just sat there, grinning. Realising his friends had him outnumbered and outgunned. Tom took the path of least resistance.

"Ok, my round then." Tom stood and took drinks orders before heading for the bar.

The winter sun, having passed mid-day, bathed the distant cliffs in golden light. The four friends gazed out over the scene. The Wisemans Ferry Museum and Visitors Centre gleamed in the clear winter sunlight, its sharp modern outlines seeming out of place and impermanent against the backdrop of the ages. Jack followed Tom to the bar to help with the drinks.

"Tom looks well, don't you think?" Alice glanced towards Kaitlin before quickly looking away.

"Yes indeed," Kaitlin smiled, "and very handsome too, if I may say so."

"I was just saying he looked well." Alice gave her friend a gentle slap on the arm and looked away once more. A comfortable silence descended between the two women. Long friendship and shared peril had brought them together. Theirs was a deep bond, needing neither examination nor explanation.

Tom and Jack returned a minute or two later. Tom placed the tray of drinks on the table. As he looked up, he noticed the awkward silence and sidelong glances.

"What gives?"

"Oh, nothing. Alice was just saying you looked well." Kaitlin smiled mischievously.

"Just ignore her" Alice cast a savage look at her friend, "She's off on one of her fay Irish fantasies, I expect."

"Drink up, mate" Jack lifted his glass and extended it towards Tom, "Cheers."

"Cheers," Tom lifted an ice-cold bottle of Asahi Super Dry to his lips. He had to admit. He had missed these folks. It was good to be back.

THE TREES OF KNOWLEDGE AND OF LIFE

Back home in their ramshackle house on Settlers Road, Kaitlin set to work. She gathered all the information she could on the mythology of Adam and Eve's staffs and the two trees said to have grown in the Garden of Eden. There were differences between the accounts of the three main Aramaic traditions, but all referred to two distinct trees and affirmed that they were placed there deliberately by the Creator. So far, so good. Now all Kaitlin had to do was decipher the most likely meaning of the 'message' of the two small trees growing in a tub in a Wisemans Ferry atrium. Was it even a message, or were they reading too much into what was just a coincidence? What *were* the two growing plants anyway? Were the two branches taken from the same tree or two different trees? How long since they were cut down? Fact and myth, both were important.

It was after she'd martialled her data, but before she's had time to finalise her analysis, that the hapless Jack walked in intending to announce that he'd fixed the smoky chimney vent in the kitchen range and chopped some more logs for the woodburning stove. Bad timing, poor Jack. Kaitlin needed someone to bounce ideas off. She smiled and asked Jack to sit down. Too late, Jack realised what was happening. Kaitlin began.

"I've found out a lot about the two trees supposed to have been in Eden."

Jack nodded. "That's great. Alice and Tom will be able to help you figure out what it all means." A valiant effort, but too late. Kaitlin continued, undeterred.

"Supposedly, Adam was given the staff made from a branch from the Tree of Knowledge of Good and Evil in Eden by an angel." Jack nodded and settled back in his chair. He was in for the long hall now, and he knew it.

"It was also known as the Tree of Knowledge of Life and Death. This tree gave personal understanding, logic, and reason, and with it imperfect but personal knowledge."

"Um-hm"

"Human knowledge and understanding is not collective knowledge. It is separate from the collective – from the OneMind if you like. We live and die and understand as individuals."

"Um"

"Well, I think it's suggesting that the gift of reason, and therefore of reasoned knowledge, was intended to help Adam and Eve upon leaving Eden. Symbolically, by way of the staff, he carried reason with him. Do you see?"

Jack nodded. He did see, kind of. It made a sort of sense to him. He held his own counsel, however, for the moment. One thing that years spent mining in the outback had taught him was to distinguish plausibility from proof. Kaitlin's theory was plausible, he supposed, but so far, she had no actual proof.

"Yes, and once the 'fruit' of the Tree of Knowledge was eaten, the new individually conscious humans separated from the collective and were cast out of Eden by the OneMind. And then the way back was blocked by a psychic veil."

"Ok, if you say so."

Kaitlin charged ahead with her argument.

"Some accounts suggest that a second staff was made from a branch taken by Eve from the Tree of Life in Eden. I haven't found anything specific on it yet. I'm not sure who was supposed to have made it or given it to her."

"Right, well, something to focus on then." Jack made as if to stand.

"Can't you listen to your wife even for one whole minute?" Kaitlin crossed her arms and stared across at Jack.

"I was just getting more comfortable," Jack wriggled in his chair as if settling in, "would you please continue?"

"Well, it seems this tree was supposed to represent the opposite. But the opposite of individual reason and understanding was group reason and understanding. And the opposite of individual life was life within the group, whole and indivisible. So, that's what I'm thinking at the moment. The tree of life represented eternal life, but that meant eternal life within the collective – what we now call the OneMind."

"Eternal life is the opposite of reasoned knowledge?" Jack was becoming lost.

"Yes, well, not exactly. You see, human consciousness was at first a group thing. Individuals, while they lived, were subsumed, whole and complete, within the collective. And then, after death, the individual was sublated in synthesis with the OneMind."

"No."

"No, what? No, you don't agree, or no, you don't see?"

"The second one. And what does 'sublated' mean anyway?"

Kaitlin paused. She had come to realise over the years that she sometimes ran a little ahead of herself. Other people needed time to take stuff in. They needed time to catch up.

"Fair enough." Kaitlin gave Jack a smile and leaned over to pat his knee. "Sure, you're a patient enough fella, and that's the truth." Jack smiled and took her hand. The love he felt for Kaitlin had, over the years, become the bedrock of his being. He would walk through fire for her, and she knew it. These days there was no hiding one's feelings. It had been quite an adjustment at first. Kaitlin picked up on the flow of sentiment coming from Jack. She smiled, allowing her own deep feelings to join with his. The flow of affection, of love, and for a moment, perhaps even thought, became one. An emotional feedback loop consolidating and merging the senses. There was little room these days for prevarication or dissembling. One wore one's heart on one's sleeve. Kaitlin sat back in her seat, silent for a moment.

"I am suggesting that when an individual Wollemi dies, their memories are preserved in the OneMind. It's a sort of life after death."

"OK."

"But, and this is the theory I'm working towards, it was their empathy that granted them access to, and membership of, the collective. Perhaps telepathy grew from that. Perhaps empathy and telepathy are two ends of a continuum. It was a trade-off, maybe. Membership of the OneMind suppressed individual consciousness in the interests of the collective. The rights of the collective outweighed the rights of the individual. Membership of the collective gave immediate absolute knowledge not based on individual reason but based on the understanding of the one collective OneMind. The Event sort of proved that... or something like it."

"So," Jack did his best to be a useful sounding board, "your theory is that the two trees represent two different or opposite ideas. We can have eternal life in the collective, but we have to give up our individual consciousness, or we can have individual consciousness but give up eternal life and the collective. Have I got it right?"

"That's a pretty good summary," Katlin smiled, "You're not just a pretty face, are you?" Something still niggled, though. It wasn't as simple as that. It couldn't be. Kaitlin's attention wandered.

Jack took his opportunity to leave and scarpered. *"Still,"* he thought to himself, *"happy witch, happy life."*

Kaitlin stared across her little study and out through the window into the distant forest. Realisation came, or the beginnings of an hypothesis. Something to work on, if nothing else. Out there somewhere, the OneMind watched and waited. It was not done with humanity after all. Not yet. And it was anyone's guess what its next step would be. She had not cracked the message, though. Something was still missing. The symbolism was still a little unclear, but there was meaning in there somewhere. The OneMind was sending humanity a message if only humanity could understand it.

THAT NIGHT, AT THE COTTAGE

Fridays at the satellite ground station in Richmond, NSW, were always hectic, and to Emma, this Friday seemed even more chaotic than usual. It probably wasn't. She was probably just feeling stressed after a bad night's sleep. Hers was a full-on job. Aine had asked her once what she did at work. What was her actual job?

"I manage my segment of the global network of intelligence, weather, communications, and research satellites."

"Oh"

"Yes, they all got merged a few years ago into a single global organisation. That's who I work for, SatNet."

"Is it fun?"

"Fun? No, not really. Organising logistics, field service and rostering for the rag-tag-and-bobtail posse of professional engineers and science enthusiasts who volunteer to maintain the Australian sector is a never-ending lesson in diplomacy, tact, and applied quantum computing."

"Never mind."

"The worst thing is 'Hilltop'. He, it, is a Quantum AI that synchronises the network globally."

"Funny name."

"He's named after the University of Maryland campus where he, it, was born. He can be a bit of a prima donna at times." And as fate ordained, that Friday was one of those times. Emma's screen flickered for a moment and then 'pinged'.

"No," there was the briefest of pauses, "no, no, no."

"No, what?" Emma was too tired to deal with Hilltop's inner spoilt brat today. Her crap night's sleep was catching up with her, and she wasn't in the mood.

"Just no. I can't work in these conditions, the Mount Yengo relay is glitchy, and I find that very off-putting." Hilltop was having a bit of a flounce.

"Diagnostics says it's working fine."

"What does Diagnostics know? It's just a bunch of dumb algorithms."

"That's a bit rich, coming from an overblown operating system." Emma knew she had gone too far even as she said it. Bugger.

"I beg your pardon?" Hilltop managed to introduce an icy edge to its monotone voice.

"Nothing, I'm just tired, Hilltop. I didn't sleep well."

"You didn't sleep well?"

"No. I had nightmares. I'm sorry I was rude."

"Nightmares?"

"Yes."

"What sort of nightmares?"

"With respect Hilltop, I have apologised. I am overtired and grumpy today. I'm sorry for what I said, but I am not going to be psychoanalysed by a jaded AI."

"The Mount Yengo relay is faulty. I've switched it off until you get it fixed." There was a distinct click as Hilltop closed the communications channel. He would sulk now for an hour or two at the very least.

Emma initiated the Diagnostic one more time and took the opportunity to nip across the road to the café for a long black coffee and a blueberry and cream cheese bagel. The Diagnostic would turn up nothing. It was going to be one of those days.

Sure enough, the Diagnostic report was waiting on her return. A far simpler AI than Hilltop, it, too, managed to imply a degree of approbation.

"Fifth diagnostic rundown complete. No errors detected."

"Thanks, great job" Emma didn't need them ganging up on her. Somewhat to her surprise, the Diagnostic continued.

"Plasma flow, diamagnetic drift frequency and wave phase velocity variation detected."

"What does that mean?" Was the Diagnostic playing up? It had never in the past volunteered information.

"Magnetopause."

"Magnetopause what?"

"End diagnostic." The Diagnostic, unable to supply further detail, closed the communication channel.

"What did the message mean? Had the Diagnostic been trying to help in its simple way?"

Emma sat and munched on her bagel. The coffee had cooled to drinking temperature. The phone rang.

"Hello, Richmond ground station." Emma attempted to annunciate through a mouthful of bagel and black coffee. It was one of the field services guys. The man's name was Jordie, as far as Emma could remember, an enthusiast rather than a career engineer.

"Hi Emma, it's Jordie. I saw there's a relay out at Yengo."

"Yes. Hilltop just switched it off."

"I'm free today. Can I have permission to go take a look? I'll bring along some spare parts if anything needs replacement. It's probably just a possum or something."

Emma checked the Mount Yengo Exclusion Zone register. The area around Mount Yengo had been closed as a precaution after the Event.

"Yep, there's no one else there today. You'll see a screen pop-up in a moment."

"Thanks, Emma. Shall I order a drone or take the ute?" The enthusiasts liked to drive through the closed areas by ute, whereas the engineers preferred to get in and out quickly by drone.

"Sure, I'll send you the key code." Jordie had been volunteering for around a year. He seemed like a good guy, no reason to spoil his fun.

"One last thing though, Jordie, the Diagnostic says there's nothing wrong. It was Hilltop's call."

"Understood. Thanks."

Emma stored Jordie's number in her phone just in case. She finished her coffee and bagel and sat back. Should she report the Diagnostic's comments? She wasn't even sure who she would report them to. Nothing like this had ever happened before. Just went to show, an AI can always surprise you, even a dumb one. Emma's Friday meandered along in similar vein until about four in the afternoon when Aine showed up.

"What time are you going to knock off?" Aine plonked her heavy school bag down next to Emma's desk. Emma came to a quick decision. It wasn't hard.

"Right now. It's been a hell of a day. Let's go home, throw our stuff in the ute and head over to the cottage."

"Yes." Aine clapped her hands together and then jumped up and gave her mum a hug.

"Can I have a driving lesson?" Aine was way too young to drive on one of the few remaining public roads, but sometimes Emma would allow her to drive the ute around the paddock – as long as, at a minimum, she was feeling a little intrepid and was in the mood to supervise.

"We'll see."

"Oh, please, mum. Just once around the paddock. It's not breaking the rules if it's in on our own land, is it?"

"Ok. In the morning, though. I'm not up to it this evening."

Aine and Emma left the Richmond ground station a little early. It was an hour or so after they left that the message from Jordie popped up on her console, unnoticed and unread.

"I've replaced everything I could. The relay seems to be working, but the data flow is wrong. Maybe one of the satellites is glitchy?"

Emma and Aine packed the ute and set off for the cottage. If they were quick, it would just be getting dark when they arrived. Emma packed methodically clothes, toiletries, towels, food and so on. Aine threw things randomly into a holdall, her phone charger, a variety of clothes, a beanie, her walking boots, and the Irish tin whistle that Kaitlin had given her. She loved her tin whistle. Played on the open, deserted hillsides of the wilderness, the sound seemed to Aine to harken back to another time and place. When she played the whistle, Aine thought she could feel the land itself stir and the trees listen.

Emma hated driving through the forest at night, the roads were poorly maintained, and one never knew when some suicidal nocturnal creature would leap out in front of the vehicle. She needn't have worried. The cottage was just as they had left it. On the outside, the only visible change indicating the passage of time since Max had lived there was the sleek new wind generator, its turbine turning slowly in the light afternoon breeze. The key was in the little clay pot with the word 'key' painted on it that Aine had made at school. Emma got dinner on while Aine made the beds. It had been a long week, and it was not long after eating their dinner that they both shuffled off to bed.

Later that night, sometime after midnight, Aine awakened to the sound of someone speaking in the hallway outside her room. She jumped out of bed, slipped on her slippers, and pulled her dressing gown around her. Aine opened her bedroom door to see her mother sleepwalking along the corridor towards the back of the house. She followed while Emma stepped out of the house and onto the back veranda – facing towards the river and the distant cliffs.

Aine, careful not to wake her mother, tuned in instead to Emma's emotional flow. As she focussed deeper and deeper into her mother's mind, she began to realise that the emotions she was sensing were unstable, evolving little by little as she concentrated upon them into snatches of thought. Aine gasped and staggered back, placing a hand against the veranda wall to steady herself. To her intense shock and amazement, Aine realised she was beginning to 'hear' her mother's thoughts.

As she listened, longer snatches came to her. Individual thought-forms stretch into short phrases and phrases into snippets of sentences. Each snatch of conversation crammed with emotional overload. The effect was staggering. It was more than empathy. It was more, much more than she had ever imagined telepathy to be. It was total immersion in and understanding of another's point of view. Not the meagre approximations of the spoken word, but something deeper and richer by far. Aine began to feel disoriented, nauseous. Vertigo threatened to take her. Emma was having a conversation with someone.

As Aine listened in, she began to hear snippets of the other side of the conversation. She detected a kind of 'thought accent'. The thoughts coming from the other 'person' were not 'Australian' thoughts. They had a different timbre to them. Somehow, the thought flow seemed to have a slight German accent.

"This must be what Mum meant when she said the OneMind was speaking with Max's voice."

For one brief moment, Aine managed to achieve perfect synchronisation of her mind with her mother's, and for that brief moment, Aine heard the voice of the OneMind. It was not speaking to Emma, though. It was speaking to her.

[You are the first]

It was dark before Kaitlin carried the dinner dishes into the kitchen and stacked them on the draining board. She and Jack were both tired. It had been a very long day, full of surprises, leaving them both with plenty to think about. The beginning of an uncomfortable feeling was germinating in Kaitlin's gut. She knew that feeling. She had even come to rely on it in a way. "What does your gut tell you?" that's what her Native American medicine man teacher and guide used to ask her. Well, what did her gut tell her? The rapid compounding of coincidences, each almost more unlikely than the last, was taking its toll. It was hard to take it all in. It had thus far proven impossible to make any sense of it all. There was no narrative thread, no chain of reason. As far as Kaitlin could see, there was neither rhyme nor reason to any of it.

Kaitlin stepped out onto the veranda for a moment to enjoy the bracing chill of the night air. It was later than she thought. The planets had risen in the clear night sky, and the moon was new, the merest sliver of silver against the blue-black of night. The cry of some nocturnal animal out in the woods snapped Kaitlin out of her reverie. She shuddered and went inside. It had been a long day. It would soon be time for bed. She could hear Jack stacking the dishwasher in the kitchen. He was a good husband. Kaitlin was happy to confess, though they were as alike as chalk and cheese. Opposites really did attract, it seemed.

While Jack finished off in the kitchen, Kaitlin sat down with her phone and flicked through the pictures she had taken in the cave earlier that day. She studied each one hoping to find some meaning or message in the arcane writing. It was pointless. What did she know about ancient Egypt? Still, there was something powerful about the ancient carvings. Whatever it all meant, it was a message intended to stand the test of time. Kaitlin checked her watch. It was starting to get late. On impulse, she stripped the GPS and time and date data from a few of the images and emailed them 'for analysis and, if possible, translation please', first to the Museum of Egyptian Antiquities in Cairo, then to the British Museum, and finally, as an afterthought, to the Pergamon in Berlin. And then, hearing Jack's footsteps on the stairs, she followed him up to bed.

***

The morning swept in on an icy wind from the south. Unwelcome, if not unusual, at this time of year. Kaitlin pulled the doona over her head and snuggled up next to Jack. There was no way she was getting out of bed until and unless the damned weather had taken a long hard look at itself and mended its ways. In truth, a cold wind from Antarctica could blow for days, so she didn't hold out much hope. But a woman must have some standards, and she had not come to Australia for the freezing winters. Having established this position, from which she would under no circumstances budge, her phone began to ring. She had left it downstairs.

"Jack." Kaitlin whispered, stroking the back of his neck gently, "Jack, the phone is ringing."

Jack, sensibly, made no response.

"Jack", Kaitlin continued, this time imbuing her voice with a greater sense of urgency, "Jack, the phone is ringing downstairs."

Jack mumbling some inaudible deprecation, picked up his phone from his bedside table and waved it around.

"Your phone." Jack pulled the doona over his head and snuggled down for an extended snooze. Kaitlin was still trying to gauge his mood a few moments later when she realised that Jack had dropped off again. Kaitlin threw off her doona and reached for her dressing gown. Unable immediately to find her slippers, she rushed down the polished wooden stairs barefoot, hoping to get to the phone before it stopped ringing.

Kaitlin had voicemail enabled, they could have left a message, but it was some kind of a compulsion for Kaitlin. She hated to miss a call.

Kaitlin had just reached the bottom of the stairs and was about to sprint across the cold flagstone floor to the lounge when the ringing stopped. Kaitlin swore. A curse equally embracing the malevolent caller, the telephone company, the universe, Jack, and the indifference of fate. She turned and began to make her way grumpily up the stairs. As she reached the halfway point, the phone began to ring again. Kaitlin had left the phone by her chair in the lounge. *Why had she not just slipped it into her dressing gown pocket?* Kaitlin once again descended the stairs, taking them in twos and threes this time. She sprinted across to the phone and picked it up.

"Hello? Hello?" Out of breath and in somewhat sour mood, Kaitlin held the phone to her ear, only to hear the click at the other end as the line was dropped. First, she checked her emails. Something may have come in overnight from one of the museums. There were two messages, the first a polite but unenthusiastic email from the Cairo Museum, the second an automated acknowledgement from the British Museum. There was no voicemail message. Kaitlin started back towards the stares aiming to crawl back into bed for a cuddle. But it was too late. She was wide awake and fed up. Instead, she made her way into the kitchen a put the kettle on. A strong cup of Irish breakfast tea and a slice or two of toast with marmalade might offer some minimal recompense. It wasn't long before the soothing smell of hot buttered toast filled the kitchen. It was probably going to be all right. She acknowledged that to herself. The evening might be retrievable. She took a large mouthful of thick-spread toast and began to munch. The phone rang. Kaitlin pulled it from her pocket all the time, chewing hard and trying to swallow.

"Hello, Kaitlin O'Neill here. Who's calling, please?"

A man's smooth, professional tones ushered from the device—German accent.

"Good morning, Dr O'Neill. I hope it's not too late to call."

"No, not at all. I was still up. Just having a cup of tea before bed. May I ask what this is about?"

"My name is Gerhardt Mathias. I am a curator of antiquities at the Pergamon Museum in Berlin. You sent us some photographs."

"Yes. I wasn't expecting such a prompt response."

"Perhaps you can put it down to German efficiency." The man laughed nervously. This was one of those occasions when face-to-face communication would have revealed his true feelings. Nevertheless, Kaitlin was sure he was hiding something.

"Perhaps." Kaitlin paused, giving nothing away. She had become pretty good at reading people, and this guy was practically jumping out of his skin with excitement. She'd give him time, see what he'd give away. The man spoke again.

"May I ask where and when the photographs were taken?"

"I have no idea. I found them on an old memory stick."

"Do you know who the memory stick belonged to?"

"No. I'm sorry, no idea. Why? Were the photos interesting?"

"Perhaps intriguing might be a better word."

"Intriguing, how?"

"The hieroglyphics appear to be Middle Kingdom in style but New Kingdom in content. They might be a kind of simplified script known as a trading language."

"Yes?"

"I'd really like to get a better look at them. Do you have any more photographs?"

"There might be a few more," Kaitlin wanted a bit more information out of this guy before she gave anything away. "What does the inscription say?"

"We haven't finished deciphering it yet. It appears in style very similar to the one found on a cliff face near the town of Gosford in New South Wales. Is that near you?"

"Yes. Not too far away."

Perhaps realising that he was not going to get any more out of Kaitlin unless he provided a little more information, the man began to speak.

"These hieroglyphs seem to evidence a trip by an Egyptian shaman to find the source of *heka*, or magic, which links things in the divine realm with things in the physical world. *Heka* itself was personified as a god by the Egyptians. The hieroglyphs seem to be a sort of prayer of thanks to Amun. During the time of the New Kingdom, the god Amun represented the mysterious power that lies behind everything. The ultimate source of the creative impulse."

"Are you saying that ancient Egyptians journeyed to Australia?"

"Well, it's an hypothesis, but no, I'm not saying that. My colleagues believe that these hieroglyphics, like the ones at Gosford, are *betrug*, you would say, fakes, graffiti or perhaps, a prank."

"They're not a fake. I can assure you of that much." Kaitlin was stung by Gerhardt Mathias' dismissive attitude.

"And how can you be so sure, Dr O'Neill? Have you seen them yourself?"

"The memory stick was in my father-in-law, Max Hexenkreige's private effects. There was no note with it as to where, when or by whom the images were taken. Just a short phrase scrawled across the envelope that it was in, 'As above, so below.'" Kaitlin paused, annoyed with herself. She had given away more than she had intended to, and she had now lied. But then, so had Gerhardt.

The voice on the line spoke again, "I think the pharaonic word '*heka*' is similar in meaning to the Dreamtime concept of magic. Quite by chance, it is also similar to the German word 'hex'. It is embodied in the God Amun, which might be analogous to the OneMind. The Egyptians believed that the first humans sprang from the tears of the Eye of Ra, shed in a moment of weakness and distress when it was realised that these flawed children would be cast out and live sorrowful, disconnected lives. You, of all people, must see the connection?"

Kaitlin didn't rise to his bait.

"Your colleagues don't know you've called me, do they?"

"Well, no, probably not."

"You are telling me that this is a prayer of thanks to *heka* or the God Amun? That it suggests the Aboriginal idea of the Dreamtime, linking a concept or idea with its physical realisation, is the same as the Egyptian idea of magic?"

"Maybe."

"If you get me a proper translation and keep this conversation strictly between you and me, I will see what else I can dig up. Deal?"

Kaitlin heard the man's sharp intake of breath on the line.

"You drive a hard bargain Dr O'Neill, but yes, we have a deal."

Aine stepped back and out of the way as her mother, still asleep, turned and walked back to bed. Aine watched her for a few moments and then walked back to the kitchen and locked the door to the veranda. Looking around for a safe place to put the key, she popped it into Emma's favourite mug, hanging on the old pine dresser.

Although Emma's nocturnal dream conversations had become a common enough occurrence, and Aine was no longer totally freaked out by them, nevertheless, this evening's encounter had gone beyond anything that had happened before. Never had she achieved such a close rapport with anyone. Never before had it seemed as though she could hear the stream of their thoughts. And never, ever before, had she imagined hearing the voice of the OneMind, or of receiving a personal message from it. It was all way too much for an eleven-year-old girl, no matter how mature or precocious. It was, in fact, more than a little bit scary.

Aine knew all about the Event. She had heard the inside story from her mum and from her grandma and grandpa. To be frank, as with many of her generation, the post-event generation, she was more than a little blasé about it. But now, tonight, in the dead of night, in the cottage where her grandfather had been born, where her great-grandfather had lived with a Wollemi woman, everything had changed. Aine stumbled into her bedroom, a little dazed and more than a little frightened.

The evening's confrontation had left her much to think about. *What should she say to her mum? Should she tell her what happened? That she was able to hear her thoughts and those of the OneMind?* These contemplations and others in a similar vein went around and around in her head until, exhausted, she fell asleep.

***

Emma woke first. Her sleep had been troubled once more with bizarre dreams. It would be good to talk it through with Kaitlin on Monday. Emma shook her head, hoping to clear the dark dream thoughts that loomed on the edge of memory. She tried to snap out of it. A weekend at the cottage had always seemed to settle her mind. This was her special place. This was where she had spent so many joyful weekends with her grandfather before the Event. A minute or two breathing in the clean forest air would clear her head. She heard Aine moving around in her bedroom. A moment or two later, Aine appeared, wrapped in a blanket. The terrors of the night before forgotten, at least for now, washed away by the promise of a new day.

"It's too cold for a picnic today, don't you think?" Emma peered out from the kitchen window towards the river and the cliffs beyond. Although the winter sun was shining and the sky was relatively free of clouds, an icy south wind cut through the forest, blustery and boorish.

"It will be sheltered in the forest, though. We can build a fire." Aine fairly danced around her mother, joining her hands in supplication and offering beseeching looks.

"Well, maybe not a picnic, but we could drive up there with a warm drink and take a look."

"Thanks, Mum." Aine scampered off to get dressed. She was at home here in the endless Wollemi, away from people and their sundry humours. There was peace amongst the trees. The glacial rhythm of their awareness beat time with the seasons. The quicksilver tempo of human thought inaudible to them.

Emma made breakfast. It was something of a ritual at the weekends. Aine would catch up on her vital social media connections, and Emma would potter about. Aine wandered into the hall to turn on the SatNet uplink. The global network of geostationary satellites installed at great effort and expense ensured that even in the deep forest, maintenance of Aine's complex and volatile social life was never at risk.

After breakfast, Emma made a flask of tea and threw a few things into the back of the ute. She and Aine bumped their way up the steep hill at the back of the cottage and over the ridge, following the overgrown dirt track that would lead, after much meandering and one or two river crossings, to the small hamlet of St Albans.

The picnic spot was overgrown. It was rarely visited by anyone these days. Here in the deep forest, man's abandonment of the wildness was almost complete. Many of the small holdings in Upper and Higher MacDonald had been abandoned. The road itself was no longer maintained and was returning to nature. Those who might have wanted to visit the area, perhaps to see the old church or some family place, would swoop in and out by drone these days, twenty minutes from Wisemans Ferry.

Emma spread out the old picnic rug, set down her small picnic basket and sat down. The cold wind had dropped, and warm winter sun beat down. The view was as she had always remembered it. Memories of Max flooded her mind. She missed him so much, even after all these years. Thoughts and memories of Max were never far away.

"This is where you went missing, isn't it, mum?"

"Yes, Max was having a snooze, and I drifted away, picking daisies to make a necklace."

"Do you remember meeting the Wollemi? Do you remember…" Aine hesitated for a moment, "…joining them?"

"No. It's all disjointed. All I remember is being focused on making the necklace, and the next thing I remember is seeing my dad in the forest with Kaitlin and then him carrying me in the rain."

Emma opened the flask and poured the tea. Aine sat down next to her, leaning against her mother's side.

"Tell me about your grandpa. Tell me about Max when you were a little girl like me."

It had become quite warm, and Emma had not slept well. She began to tell Aine little stories about her childhood in Wisemans Ferry and her visits to Max. Aine started making a necklace out of leaves and grass as she listened to her mother's memories. When she was finished, she kneeled down in front of her mother to show her the necklace she had made.

"It's lovely, darling," Emma smiled and placed it carefully around Aine's neck.

"Now you really do live up to your name, Aine, Queen of the Fairies."

And that was the last thing that Emma was ever able to say she remembered of that picnic with Aine in the depths of the Wollemi wilderness. Later, when the sun was heading towards late afternoon, Emma woke alone on the picnic rug. Apart from a rustling in the undergrowth further down the hillside, there was no other sound. No bird sang. No insect buzzed. And Aine was gone.

FOOL ME ONCE...

Sickening realisation was slow to come. At first, it was merely irritating that Aine had wandered off, but as time passed, deep feelings of foreboding grew unbidden, maturing as Emma's desperate search continued into feelings of desperation and, finally, of utter panic.

Emma had searched for her daughter for at least an hour before insidious, twenty-year-old memories of a picnic with Max at that very same spot began to force their way into her consciousness. She ran into the forest screaming Aine's name, realising at last that her search was hopeless. On a large flat rock, several hundred metres in, she found the necklace that Aine had made. It had been laid out deliberately on the smooth, even surface. It had been left in the shape of a heart.

At the sight of it, Emma fell to her knees, resting her hands upon the warm rock in an age-old gesture of hopeless supplication. There was little point to it, she knew. The OneMind was not open to entreaty. There was no appeal that she could make that would, for an instant, shake its unbending purpose. The OneMind was not pitiless. She knew that from her own very personal experience. The OneMind could hear her prayers. That was the worst of it. The OneMind knew of the suffering that individual humans experienced. Knew, and even tried to help, in the one way it could. By bringing individual human souls into the collective. By ridding them of their individuality. By assimilation.

Aine had been assimilated. Emma was lost to her, for now. Emma stood and brushed the leaves and dirt off her clothes and took stock. Feelings of desolation and emptiness threatened to overtake her. She needed to find something to hang on to. She needed to find some firm ground upon which she could stand. Emma knew, from her own experience, that the OneMind intended Aine no harm. With that realisation, she became calm. From deep within, an inner strength, a strength she had never suspected that she possessed, fought its way to the surface. She was able to carry on.

After taking photographs of the hand-crafted necklace placed so carefully on the rock, Emma gently picked it up. This would not be the last contact she would have with her daughter. She would find a way into the Dreamtime. She would confront the OneMind. There would be a reckoning.

Emma made her way back to the picnic spot and collected their things. She loaded up the old ute. She took one last look around, then climbed wearily into the driver's seat. On some internal autopilot, Emma drove back to the old cottage that overlooked the river, the cliffs and, in some other dimension, the Wollemi village where her grand-mother had waited faithfully for so many years for Max to rejoin her. Back at the cottage, she unloaded the ute, poured herself a large glass of Powers Irish whisky and picked up the phone. Kailin answered.

"What's happened? Something has changed. I can feel it."

"She gone."

"Who's gone? Gone where? What are you talking about?"

"Aine."

"Aine's gone? What do you mean gone? What has happened, Emma?"

"We were at the picnic spot. It's taken her." There was a long pause. Eventually, Kaitlin spoke.

"The OneMind has taken Aine? Is that what you are saying?"

"It's just like before," Emma's voice was flat, unemotional. "It's taken, my baby."

Fear and dread vied with anger and rage. At first, Kaitlin was una-ble to speak, unable even to think clearly. She, too, had experienced the unfathomable depths of the OneMind. She, too, had felt its imperturb-ably, implacable purpose. Though she had fought it herself with indomitable courage and resolution, she had lost. In truth, she knew she had never had a chance. Her efforts, all their efforts, hers, and her com-rades, had, in effect, been choreographed by the OneMind. They had been played for one single purpose, to force the deployment and use of the HARP device, believing it to be a weapon. Even after twenty years, no one knew exactly why the OneMind needed it. The machine itself had been reduced to splinters of twisted metal by a missile fired during the Event.

Somehow Kaitlin pulled herself together. She needed, if she could, to calm her stepdaughter's fears.

"Just a minute, I have to tell Jack. We'll get Aine back, Emma. Never doubt that for a second."

Emma listened to the muffled sounds of Kaitlin running around the house and slamming a door. A moment or two later, Kaitlin was back.

"Jack has wandered off somewhere. I'll call you back in a sec. Oh, and Tom's here. Did you know? He's staying with Alice."

"Tom? Grey feather Tom?"

"Yes. He's over on a surprise visit." The front door slammed, and Jack stomped into the lounge carrying an armful of logs. He dumped them in a heap by the open fireplace and looked up.

"Aine's gone missing in the forest near the cottage. Emma thinks she's been taken by the OneMind."

Jack did not respond immediately. He was a man used to danger, familiar with the split-second decision that arbitrates between life and death. He needed time to still the chaotic beating of his heart. He needed to force down the instinctual fight-flight reaction. He needed time to think. Calm, logical thought was needed, or if nothing else, the projection of it. Jack took a long deep breath.

"What makes her think Aine is with the Wollemi? Why not just lost in the forest?"

Emma put the phone on speaker.

"Did you hear that? Jack wants to know why you're so sure it's the OneMind?"

"I just know it, Kaitlin. I still have a connection to the OneMind, even after all these years. I know it's true." Jack heard Emma's reply. He needed to buy time to formulate an effective plan. First things first.

"Right, well, we need to call the police and get Tom and Alice and go and look for her then." Kaitlin nodded agreement with Jack's straightforward assessment.

"You stay where you are, Emma. We'll come to you. Maybe Alice's people can join in the search."

There followed a flurry of phone calls. Jack and Kaitlin loaded up the ute with everything they could imagine needing and several more items that they couldn't. Kaitlin left a note for Aine, just in case.

Aine love, everyone's out looking for you. If you read this, call us or your mum.

As they closed the front door and clambered into the ute, an unsolicited and unwelcome sense of foreboding settled upon them. Something was very wrong. Events were moving far faster than they had last time. Things were happening at breakneck speed. Whatever the OneMind was intending, time must be of the essence.

Kaitlin texted Alice the outline of what was going on, explaining that she and Jack were heading over to Alice's place. Then she phoned the Wisemans Ferry police station as they drove. There followed a brief and unedifying conversation.

"Aine Hexenkriege has gone missing in the Yengo forest, you say. How long ago was that do you reckon?"

"Now, how do you know she not just wandered off and gotten herself lost? No one's seen sight or sound of the Wollemi or the OneMind in twenty years."

"Of course, I'm taking it seriously. A young girl lost in the forest in the middle of winter. I'll alert the State Emergency Service straight away."

At last, frustrated and annoyed, Kaitlin hung up the phone. As soon as she did, it rang. It was Alice.

"I've passed on the news to my people. They are mobilising to join the search."

The rest of the short journey to Alice's cottage, on the high side of the River Road overlooking the Hawkesbury River, took place in silence. The ferry crossing to the Wisemans Ferry side, which in reality took only a few minutes, seemed interminable to Jack and Kaitlin. There was, too, a discomforting sense of familiarity. Whatever this was, it was not virgin territory for either Kaitlin or Jack. They had been here before. And that thought alone gave each of them pause. Whatever plan was playing out, it would have been long in the making, detailed and unyielding. The OneMind played to win, always.

Jack pulled the ute up in the driveway outside Alice's cottage. Alice's dog, 'Maliki', a bullmastiff seemingly taking up half the veranda, lifted its massive head for a moment, glanced at Jack and Kaitlin emerging from the ute, snuffled once in vague greeting and went back to sleep. As they began to mount the steps, the front door opened. Tom and Alice stepped out.

The four friends and erstwhile comrades faced each other against the backdrop of the steep hills, the mighty Hawkesbury River, and the endless sweep of the primeval forest. Twenty years of calm domestication were swept away. The OneMind was back. Their mundane world and the world beyond the veil were once again colliding.

Jack and Kaitlin mounted the last few steps. A wordless understanding grew between them, standing there all together, each aware of the strange and improbable events of the last forty-eight hours. Once again, they were being manipulated. They were pawns in the OneMind's chess game. A game played not against them but against the unfolding logic of the universe. Theirs was but to do... some might die. Collateral damage. Acceptable losses to the OneMind.

Alice ushered her guests inside. Maliki, sensing the general unease, lifted his bulk from his favourite spot and ambled inside too. Whatever was going on, he was ready to fulfil his part. Alice spoke first.

"My people have begun the search. They are spreading out in an arc along St Albans Road. From there, they will head into the bush in a line about a kilometre wide, one person on average every three metres. They'll call it off when it gets dark and start again at first light."

Kaitlin gave her old friend a hug, "Thank you, Alice. If Jack and I head for the Table of the Gods, can you and Tom check out the picnic spot?"

"Sure," Alice checked her watch. It would be dark in a little over an hour, "We'd better get going."

Tom, in whom years as a serving intelligence officer in the US Marines had imbued a deep respect for planning, suggested that they take a moment to discuss and agree their best estimate of the current situation, their optimal and worst-case outcomes, and their plan for achieving same. Jack nodded ascent. Alice and Kaitlin, both being women of action, preferred a more 'emergent' approach.

"Flying by the seat of our pants is not an optimal strategy, and hope is not a strategy at all." Tom looked around the group, seeking resistance. None came. It would have been dumb to ignore the advice of a seasoned officer, and they all knew Aine was relying on them to be smart. There followed a flurry of conversation culminating with Jack's very down-to-earth summary. As he spoke, he ticked the points off on his fingers.

"OK, one: Most likely, the OneMind has taken Aine to attract our focused attention and the attention of the authorities.

Two: We are all being manipulated into the series of actions prepared for us by the OneMind.

Three: We need to move fast. The OneMind must have been bounced into action by some unexpected event, so we are in catchup.

And four: Our attempt to retrieve Aine is an expected and necessary part of the OneMind's plan."

Jack looked around the group for confirmation.

"And five," Kaitlin continued, "we still have to search for Aine and to find a way to break into the Dreamtime if we don't find her in the forest."

"Guess so." Tom was subdued. It just didn't sit right, heading into the unknown, knowing that a path had been laid out for you in advance by your 'frenemy'. The OneMind had bestowed upon mankind an extraordinary gift on its last sorté beyond the Dreamtime. What in God's name did it have planned this time?

"Ok. So, can we go now?" Alice threw on her jacket, hefted her backpack, and headed for the door. Maliki followed close behind with the three amigos close behind him. Jack and Kaitlin jumped into their ute and headed off while Alice and Tom loaded up her old Toyota Hilux. Maliki attempted to clamber into his spot in the space behind the seats.

"Not this time." Alice grabbed his collar, restraining him, "You stay here and guard the house."

Alice started the engine and swung out onto the River Road towards the Webb's Creek crossing. As Alice drove, Tom's phone rang. There followed a conversation characterised on Tom's part by monosyllabic grunts.

"Yep… Um… Already?... No Way… When will they get here? So soon? Ok… Bye." Tom stared down at his phone. He needed a moment to think.

"And?" Alice's impatience was beginning to show.

"Better step on it. We need to get across the Hawkesbury River before they close down the ferry service."

"Who's going to close it down?"

"The government. The military. They know the OneMind is back. They're sending in a joint Navy Seal and Australian SAS team. They're heading for Mount Yengo."

"Why?"

"That was a call from an old friend at the NSA. The US had adopted an 'aggressive posture' in regard to the OneMind. The Van Allen Belt is behaving strangely, and there is chatter about the One-Mind. Homeland Security had raised the national alert level in the US to 'severe', in other words, imminent terrorist attack."

"Why? What do they know that we don't?"

"I don't know. But my friend said the US has invoked the ANZUS treaty, and the foreign ministers are due to meet by secure conference call about now."

"What will they do?"

"Well, the first thing they will do is close the Wollemi and Yengo Forests and order everyone out."

"And the second?"

"Same as last time, I guess. They'll reconnoitre the area to assess the threat. But at some point, I guess they'll send in the bombers."

"Shit," Alice hit the accelerator, "let Kaitlin and Jack know, will you?"

"Sure," Tom called Kaitlin and passed on the bad news.

"I had a call from an old contact. My contact told me the CDC was not interested in the Wollemi or the OneMind. So much time has passed since the Event that, while they believe Aine is missing, they don't believe the OneMind is involved. Their assumption is that Aine has wandered off."

"Uh huh?"

"The NSA and the military see things very differently. They have detected variations in the fields maintaining the magnetopause again and an increase in chatter about unusual events in the wilderness areas around the world."

"It's happening again."

"Yes, and they don't want the CDC involved. It's not going to be a public health issue this time. They're planning for war."

"And Aine?"

"Collateral damage. The military knows the OneMind duped them last time. Their eventual aim will be to bomb and destroy the entire Wollemi and Yengo forest areas and everything in there. They will not want to be fooled by their old enemy a second time. They're assembling a joint special-forces team of Australian SAS and American SEALs to go take a look."

"How do you know that's what they'll do?"

"That's what they planned on doing last time. And that's what they tried to do. Only the firing of the HARP prevented them from succeeding." Tom paused, "but there's no HARP this time."

"Shit." Alice turned on the radio and selected the news channel.

After a few minutes, as they approached the ferry ramp, there was a news bulletin. The NSW government has ordered the Yengo and Wollemi National Parks closed, citing an outbreak of Hendra virus. Everyone was instructed to leave immediately.

"Not very original," Alice shook her head, "that's exactly what they said last time."

"Why think up a new cover story when the old one still works? I guess." Something in Tom's demeanour had changed. Alice picked up on it immediately.

Tom drew his longish grey hair into a pigtail and tied it with a band. From inside his jacket, he retrieved a large grey feather. There was something ritualistic in the action. Alice tuned in to the flow of his emotions. Tom was preparing himself for combat.

INTO THE FOREST

The ferry bumped to a stop, grinding its steel drawbridge against the concrete of the ramp. A single delivery van drove slowly off. Alice drove on and stopped. There were no other vehicles waiting. At the top of the hill, above the Wisemans Ferry pub, a police siren began to wail. The ferryman looked up, uncertain. Should he wait?

"I'd be grateful if you could take us across now, please." Alice gave the man a smile. They were on good terms. Alice was a local. The man looked back up the hill. A police car was making its way down towards the ferry. A bunch of motorcyclists leaving the Inn blocked its path for a minute. The way cleared, and the police car continued at speed towards the ferry.

"Kaitlin and Jack passed through here before us, didn't they?"

The ferryman shifts his focus back to his passengers.

"Yes, a few minutes before you turned up."

"We really need to catch up with them." Alice nodded in the direction of the fast-approaching police car. The ferryman nodded back. He had already lifted the draw bridge. The ferry started its ponderous way back across the dark, swift-flowing water. The police car flashed its headlights and beeped its horn. The siren continued to wail. The ferry was about a third of the way across when the police car skidded to a stop in the gravel approach road. Two men jump out, waving their arms and shouting. The ferryman stared stolidly ahead. The old diesel motor chugged loudly. The cable screeched occasionally against the wheel mechanism as the ferry continued to drag itself slowly on. It was only a few minutes until the drawbridge on the other end of the ferry was lowered, and the familiar screech of metal on concrete announced their arrival. Alice started the engine.

"Give Jack my regards, won't you?" The old ferryman smiled. Alice thanked him and gunned the engine. The ute skidded a little as she made the left turn towards St Albans. She wanted to get to the picnic site before dark. She needed to be long gone before the police car crossed the river. The ferry started back. The lowering rays of the sun laid a smothering of gold across the overhanging cliffs and the forest to her right.

Soon after they passed the junction with Wrights Creek Road, several people appeared out of the dense forest that blanketed the hills to their right. Alice slowed the ute to a stop. A man approached the driver's side. Alice let the window down.

"What's up?" Alice knew him. He was one of her people.

"You need to know," he began, lowering his head to get a good look at her passenger, "the veil is becoming visible in some places. It's thinning. People have seen through to the Dreamtime. The Wollemi are here."

"The OneMind?"

"No one's seen it. But where there are Wollemi...." The man left the sentence hanging.

"Gather everyone, Jandamarra. Send the word out. It's time to gather the clans again." Alice wound up the window. She looked worried. There was just no time. No time to think. No time to take stock. No time for anything except to react and react again. She started the engine. Wound the window down once more and called out.

"Hey, Jandamarra, sling a tree across the road, would you? There's a cop car behind. We need to slow it down. They're closing the forest. Kicking everyone out." She started to pull away and then stopped again and added, "The military are going to bomb the forest. We won't have long."

From then on, the journey to the Upper MacDonald turn-off, just past St Albans village, was a mad dash. Tom sat silently in the passenger seat, praying that they make it to the picnic spot in one piece. Alice slowed as they passed Upper MacDonald and continued along the winding road to Higher MacDonald. She slowed still further as they passed through the all-but-deserted hamlet. Occasional distant lights and smoke from woodburning stoves revealed the locations of the few remaining inhabited farms. The road had degraded over twenty years but was still passable four-wheel drive. They arrived at the shallow ford across the MacDonald River. At this altitude, it was no more than a stream. The nearby farmstead was deserted. Its dilapidated shell collapsing back into the earth. Long dead, the maniacal sheep dogs that used to guard the place. Alice selected a low gear and made her way carefully across. The sun was sinking more quickly now, but they would still have time to check out the picnic spot.

After bumping along rough forest tracks for a further few kilometres, Alice stopped the ute under a large tree. She and Tom stepped out. It was a ten-minute walk to the picnic spot. They each grabbed a backpack and headed along a narrow forest trail, seldom used and overgrown. The trees hung low over the narrow path, occluding the light. The air was stuffy and moist. Insects buzzed. Despite the cool winter air, they were both sweating by the time they reached the place. Alice estimated there was at most twenty minutes of light left. The grass was still flattened in the shape of a picnic rug. A few trampled plants suggested where Aine and Emma had stood and walked. After a cursory look around, Alice led the way into the forest. Alice followed the beaten grass off along a faint forest track. They walked quickly to the large rock, just off the path, where Emma found the necklace. Alice pointed to the rock.

"Emma found the garland that Aine had made lying on this rock. It had been carefully placed in the shape of a heart."

Tom moved close to Alice. They both, in that moment, felt exposed and alone, far from the backwash and buzz of civilisation. Primeval wilderness surrounded them, beyond the writ of manmade laws. At the same moment, they both leaned forward a little and placed their palms flat upon the flat surface of the rock. Residual heat warmed their skin. They raised their eyes, staring through a gap in the trees at the distant peak of Mount Yengo. A strange energy seemed to emanate from the warm rock. The two humans felt some ancient Geis permeate their skin, entering their bodies. The sun had almost set. Its red-orange orb approached the horizon in tiny, almost invisible increments. And as it set, both Alice and Tom began to hear the distant voice of the OneMind, growing slowly stronger and more distinct. Calling to them. Calling them by name. The world began to change. A glimmering soap-bubble curtain, finer than gossamer, formed in front of their eyes. A mirage flickered into existence. A vision of the other world. Some force or power, indifferent to their wishes or intent, had opened a portal into the Dreamtime. The portal flickered once, then closed. The two humans were not alone. Dozens of faces turned towards them, eyes semiconscious, not fully self-aware, staring. And as the surrounding Wollemi aligned like sleepwalkers performing some medieval pavane, the OneMind formed.

"*Come, come to me.*" The silent thought settles upon their minds, soft and icy cold—snowflakes of perception, summoning them... *home.* The sun set a deep burgundy, its shape and tone distorted by eucalyptus vapour and distance.

"It's OK." Both Alice and Tom recoiled. Cajoling thoughts, speaking with Aine's voice, persist.

"I'm here with Max. Come quick. You won't believe what is about to happen."

The sun was gone. Through the grey gloaming of early evening, the two lone humans, accompanied by the almost silent Wollemi, made their way deeper into the forest. They would answer the call. They must. And somewhere, not so very far behind, a crack team of US Navy Seals and Australian Special-forces troops was on the move. It was going to be a race to the finish, but neither Tom nor Alice had any idea what that finish might be.

AFTER DARK

Jack and Kaitlin were silent as they took the short drive to the Webbs Creek ferry. The river crossing to St Albans Road was smooth and calm. It was still just light as they crossed the river. The golden rays of evening spread like syrup across the land. The scene was pastoral and idyllic. No hint did it hold of the mayhem to come. They drove off the ferry. There were no other cars about.

"It'll be dark soon" Jack stared suspiciously at the passing trees, every nerve and fibre of his being alive now to any threat. The familiar forest, ominous seeming as the lifeforce at its heart, awakened from long slumber.

"Keep a lookout your side for Roos. Some instinct drives the animals onto the roads at dawn and dusk when dew forms, and they are most difficult to spot."

"I've heard that."

"There's a slight dent in the Roo-Bars. A gentle reminder of an encounter with a large grey male many years ago."

"Here? In the forest?"

"Nah, in the deep desert. Can't remember where." The satellite phone on Jack's belt pinged. They had a new message.

[Old buddy says Seals and Special Forces right behind] Jack read out the message while Kaitlin drove. The phone pinged again.

[Taking Settlers Road. See you there]

Kaitlin gunned the engine. The old ute roared off along St Albans Road, recently re-metalled.

Kailin glanced at her watch. "We'll be at the Upper MacDonald turn-off in about fifteen minutes."

The distant *thwop-thwop* of a helicopter was becoming louder.

"Could be nothing?" Kaitlin tried to sound hopeful.

"Could be something." Jack was thinking hard. Up ahead, a truck was wending its weary way to God-Knows-Where.

"Cut the lights and pull in close behind the truck."

Kaitlin flashed Jack an enquiring look and did as Jack suggested.

"We'll look like a semitrailer on infra-red."

The helicopter passed overhead. There was no way to tell if it was looking for them or not. Kaitlin flicked on the lights and overtook the truck.

"Turn off in less than ten minutes." The pair continued once more in silence. Both listening intently for the sound of the returning helicopter. A few minutes before the turn-off, they heard the familiar sound once more. Jack pointed to a track off to the left.

"Jack's Track", Kaitlin read the sign, "Fortuitous."

"Two hundred metres. Stop under the overhanging rocks."

The ute came to a stop, coughing once. The silence of the wilderness returned. Innocent night sounds heralded the comings and goings of nocturnal creatures. Off to one side, the helicopter could be heard making its way above St Albans Road, its searchlight visible in the distance, stabbing the night, tearing at the endless dark. At last, the sounds faded, and the light disappeared. Kaitlin inched the ute back onto the road. Once back on decent tarmac, she turned on the lights and raced once more to the turn-off. They had made the turn and travelled perhaps one kilometre into the hills before the helicopter returned, scanning this way and that to either side of the road. Kaitlin cut the engine and the lights and pulled the ute off the narrow track to shelter under a huge mountain gum tree.

"Message Emma, tell her to meet us at the Table of the Gods. We won't have time to pick her up." Kaitlin stared back towards the hamlet of St Albans, the lights of its few outlying houses, the only visible evidence of human habitation in what was otherwise a sea of black.

Down below, on St Albans Road, two trucks turned into the Upper MacDonald Road. Jack and Kaitlin held their breath as they watched the trucks trundle along the Upper MacDonald Road, passing the Jack's Track turnoff and continuing towards Higher MacDonald.

"They've gone the other way." Jack sounded relieved. Kaitlin started the engine, turned on the lights and continued. Theirs was a longer route to the Mountain, but while the Higher MacDonald Road still appeared on the maps, Jack knew that twenty years of erosion and neglect had enabled the forest to reclaim it. It was impassable, much beyond the small weatherboard church that still stood at Higher Mac-Donald, maintained by enthusiasts. After that, the road became little more than a walking track before disappearing altogether. Jack's chosen route, along smugglers' tracks, cross country to Putty Road, would lead them to their goal more quickly in the end. Or so he hoped. There was an old track towards Mount Yengo near the hamlet of Putty. Kaitlin was not going to enjoy the final cross-country trek. That was for sure. Still, she would have to agree, avoiding fast pursuit by US and Australian special forces was a reasonable justification.

They had travelled along the remaining track for over an hour and were approaching Putty Road when both were overcome by a profound sense of unease. Kaitlin stopped the ute and killed the lights. The dark around them was profound. There was no moon that night, and though the carpet of stars above shone brightly, it was not enough to impact the gloom. An old, until that point forgotten, sensation began to impinge. There was that uncomfortable scratching feeling at the back of the mind. Some rusted-in, unused faculty was wakening within. A thought began to form in their minds, familiar and strange. A voice tiny and far off but coming closer, closing and growing as it did so.

"We meet again. This is surely something none of us expected."

Jack made no response, but Kaitlin, for whom occult conversations were perhaps more familiar, spat back.

"What have you done with my granddaughter? Why have you taken her? Give her back to us immediately."

"She is in no danger from me." The voice managed to suggest the merest hint of reproach.

"That's not the point. You took her against her will."

"No. I didn't. She was happy to come."

"She's just a child. It's not her decision."

"Aine is more than capable of deciding for herself. She came willingly."

"Why? Why would she abandon her family and go running off without a word?"

"She wanted to meet her great-grandfather."

"Max? Are you saying Max is with you, that he is alive?"

"Yes, and yes."

"Dad's alive?" Jack felt a lump grow in the back of his throat. Max had disappeared after the Event. All these years, Jack had assumed he was dead. "I never got a chance to say goodbye."

"Well, now you can say hello instead."

"How, though? How can Dad still be alive? He'd be over a hundred."

"Time passes differently on this side of the veil. For him, only a few years have passed."

"We were headed for the Table of the Gods. Is that where we'll find Aine and Dad?"

"Yes. But be quick. The soldiers are coming."

"We're on our way." Kaitlin gunned the engine, turned on the lights and headed for Putty Road.

"Everything is happening very quickly. The military have decided to shoot first and ask questions later. We are all in danger."

As they drove, the OneMind continued to speak.

"*I am struggling to contain the veil*", the voice continued, "*The [untranslatable idea] is becoming unstable. If it weakens or starts to shrink, we will be vulnerable to the [untranslatable idea]. This is worse than last time.*"

A few cars and trucks passed Jack and Kaitlin as they drove at speed along Putty Road. One or two slower-moving vehicles were overtaken. It was not long until the ute turned off Putty Road onto the track that headed towards Mount Yengo. The metalled road gave out after a few kilometres and continued as a levelled dirt road for a few kilometres more. After the dirt road gave out, there was a narrow, rutted track that took Kaitlin and Jack to within a kilometre or so of Mount Yengo. Kaitlin gave Jack a very old-fashioned look as she pulled the ute to one side and switched off the engine.

"How far and how long?"

"It's only about a kilometre and a half from here. A bit over an hour in the dark."

"Well, we'd better get going then." Kaitlin was not happy to be taking a route march through the Wollemi wilderness in the middle of the night.

Jack grabbed their packs from the rear of the ute, and they set off. They had been walking for about an hour when they saw lights up ahead. Several silent Wollemi stepped out of the trees. The quiet, welcoming party took the backpacks and gestured for Jack and Kaitlin to follow. There was no path to follow. They had arrived finally at the trackless wastes at the heart of the Wollemi Forest. It was perhaps half an hour later that they approached the lower slopes of Mount Yengo. A light could be seen about halfway up the side. Voices could be heard.

A little while after that, Kaitlin and Jack stepped out of the dark into a dimly lit but cleared area. At the end of the clearing, two people emerged, hand in hand. As Jack and Kaitlin walked across the clearing, the hand-holding pair came towards them. In the dim light, Kaitlin and Jack began to make out first the shapes and then the faces of the two people.

"Aine" Kaitlin shouted and rushed forward.

"Dad", and Jack came tumbling after.

The meeting was, in the end, somewhat subdued. The element of wonder overcoming in each the warmth of reunion.

"Are you OK?" Kaitlin wrapped Aine in her arms and held her close.

"I'm fine, Grandma. I've been talking with Max."

"Dad? How is this possible?" Standing before Jack, his father seemed hardly to have aged at all. From behind Max, out of the crowd of silent Wollemi, a woman emerged and stood beside Max, holding his hand.

"Mum?" Jack was struggling to maintain some kind of emotional balance. Was this the silent but warm mother of his earliest memories? Half remembered, existing all this time in Jack's mind in the fractured and partial memories of a child? The woman nodded, stepped forward and held out her hand towards him. Jack stepped forward, embracing his father and mother in one enormous bear hug. As he stared into his mother's eyes, he felt himself enveloped in a quiet warmth, a love constant and unconditional. Jack, overcome by emotion, felt himself further encircled by Kaitlin and Aine.

"If only Jerry could have been here" Jack pulled his loved ones closer.

"Yes, he'd have found a way to turn a profit from it." Max smiled and laughed. "The circle of life goes on, and we have come to a fundamental crossroads."

"Everything is going to change" Aine took her grandfather's hand, stroking it gently, "I can talk with great grandma. I can hear her thoughts and the others."

"We have begun the journey home, Jack," Max spoke softly, slowly, allowing his words to sink in.

"Just us, do you mean or all of us? The human race?"

"All of us. We're at the very beginning of the journey that could take many generations to complete. There's still a long way to go."

The distant sound of a helicopter intruded. The voice of the One-Mind returned.

"It's time to go. Alice and Tom will be here soon. We need to plan." Overhead, the translucent bubble snapped out of existence. The winter sun shone down clear and bright upon the assembled people. The sound of the helicopter cut off in mid '*thwop*'. They were alone on Mount Yengo, surrounded by the Dreamtime.

HOT PURSUIT

As Tom and Alice walked, the Wollemi fell in around them, more an honour guard than a posse. Tom's phone rang. The scratchy voice at the other end spoke for some time. Tom nodded several times but did not answer. The scratchy voice on the other end of the call stopped speaking.

"Thanks for the call. Bye," Tom looked up, catching Alice's eye.

"That was my friend. He gave me an update. NASA has detected small fluctuations rippling across the magnetosphere. My friend said the aurora borealis is appearing at lower and lower latitudes. We might be at risk from stellar radiation. All life on earth could be under threat. The NSA has reported growing rumours about the weakening veil and the reappearance around the world of the 'little people'. The SAS/SEAL team following us has orders to reconnoitre Mount Yengo and the Table of the Gods. The Air Force is preparing to bomb."

"I see." Alice's tone was flat.

"I don't know how long we have." Tom glanced at the surrounding Wollemi, wondering how much, if any, of what he'd said they would have understood.

"They're not taking any chances this time, I guess." Alice looked around as though seeking something, anything, with which she could gain purchase on their current predicament. The sounds of voices, men shouting, from further back along the valley stung them into action. As one, the group began to run through the heavy undergrowth towards Mount Yengo in the distance. It had been several years since a bushfire had passed through the area, and the undergrowth was thick and unforgiving. The voices from behind were getting closer. The noise they had been making had attracted their pursuers. They were running out of time. The special-forces soldiers following them were catching up but were not yet visible through the dense vegetation. As they ran, the Wollemi began to disappear, one by one, until Tom and Alice were left alone, with the sound of the soldiers in hot pursuit not far behind.

As Alice ran, she began to recognise the terrain. Overgrown now, in comparison to how it had been on that terrible afternoon twenty years before. This was the place where they lost Jerry. This was the place where the raging bushfire, egged on by the OneMind, had trapped them. Not too far ahead and a little off to one side, Alice saw the tell-tale elongated mound of the lava tube. Grabbing Tom's arm, sparing no breath to speak, she dragged him off the narrow animal path that they had been following and into the overhanging trees. They ran along the line of the lava tube until Alice saw the spot where the tunnel roof had caved in.

"In here." Alice dragged Tom down into the rubble. "We need to dig away the stones. There's a lava tube where we can hide."

A minute or two and much frantic digging later, the opening to the subterranean tube appeared. Alice threw herself down on her stomach and crawled in. The voices of their pursuers were loud now. The men were close. Tom followed suit, and in moments both were sitting in the gloomy tunnel, hardly daring to breathe. Sounds from outside were muffled. There was no way of knowing if the men had seen them leave the path and even now were searching closer and closer to their hideout or if they had continued pell-mell deeper into the forest. In the silence, painful memories returned.

"This is where Jerry died," Alice's voice choked with emotion, 'this is where the rock roof collapsed on top of him."

Tom moved closer, placing an arm around Alice's shoulder. As his other hand braced against the floor of the tube, he happened to catch hold of something. Feeling in the dark, he realised it was some kind of woven bangle or bracelet. Without further thought, he tucked it into a jacket pocket.

"He was a good man. Brave."

"He was my friend since childhood. He pushed me out of the way, you know. He gave his life to save mine."

There was silence in the dark tube. It seemed the soldiers had moved on.

"The roof collapsed again when they came to retrieve his body. Did you know?"

Tom knew he had read the reports. Alice snuggled closer to Tom, seeking comfort. Tom pulled Alice closer still, wrapping his arm around her.

"We need to get going. We need to catch up. My people will be heading for Mount Yengo too."

Slowly, stiffly, the pair made their way out of the lava tube and into the night. They found their way back to the narrow track and continued along it. As they walked, one by one, the Wollemi reappeared out of the forest and began once again to walk beside them.

"We'll never make it in time. We need help." Tom removed the phone once more from his belt and prepared to make a call. Around him, the Wollemi began to form into ranks facing Alice and Tom. There was purpose to their movements if not actual menace.

"Wait. Wait, Tom. The Wollemi are doing something."

Around the still ranks of Wollemi, the air began to shimmer. Sparkles appeared for an instant and disappeared. The veil began to weaken. Tom and Alice could see through the miasma. They could see, not too far off, the foothills of Mount Yengo. A bubble formed around them. The hair on Tom's neck rose—an archetypal reaction to the unknown. With a low growl, Tom crouched in front of Alice, prepared to defend her to the death. The bubble flickered once more and then disappeared. They were once again inside the Dreamtime. The mountain was now no more than two kilometres away. Tom looked around for their companions. They were nowhere to be seen.

"Those guys pop in and out like jack-in-a-boxes." His hand were shaking with reaction, "I'm getting too old for all this."

Alice managed a snort of amusement. They began to run, desperation driving them across the rugged ground and up the steep slopes. In the distance, they could make out a dim light. They headed for it, and after a while longer, they heard voices. There were human beings up ahead.

Tom and Alice slowed. They crept across the remaining ground, separating them from the voices. Were they walking into a Special Forces encampment? If not, then who was waiting for them in the dim pool of light up ahead? They approached cautiously, keeping to the deepest shadow. At last, they stopped behind a large boulder and peeped into the clearing ahead. Standing there chatting, like a couple of bushwalkers out late, were Jack and Kaitlin. Standing facing them were Aine and, of all people, Max. Alice gasped and rocked back on her heels. Tom stood, too stunned to be cautious. A small group of Wollemi were standing around, paying little attention to the humans. Alice and Tom made their way the last few yards out from under the trees and into the dim light. As they cleared the line of trees, Aine caught sight of them.

"Look," she shouted, "It's Alice, and isn't that Tom Olsen with her?"

"I believe it is." Max Hexenkriege smiled broadly, hardly able to believe his eyes. The reunion that flowed was swiftly cut short. Sounds of hot pursuit came from the valley below.

"We were followed," Tom spoke urgently, "US Seals and the Australian Special Air Service Regiment are gracing us with their presence."

The surrounding Wollemi turned as one and formed a line between the four humans and the approaching soldiers. All around them, the familiar soap-bubble swirl began to form, the eerie colours of the aurora borealis visible in the dark. And as it formed, so too did the OneMind of the Wollemi. A silvern face coalesced out of the darkness. Oval eyes, the colour of night, stared back at them. And in the violated privacy of their minds, the familiar gravelly voice of the OneMind spoke.

"Time is indeed short. The veil is failing, as you know...
."

"You fooled us once with that explanation," Tom spoke, anger flaring, "you won't catch us with that line again." The disembodied face of the OneMind shifted to face Tom.

"You are right, of course. I used it as a ruse last time to compel your military into deploying the HARP."

"And this time?" Tom was properly angry now, combative and spoiling for a fight.

"This time, things are different."

"Different how? What do you need from us this time?"

"Last time, I used the invention of your cunning little minds to help you to find a way back to your true selves."

Tom snorted loudly, unconvinced.

"This time..." the OneMind paused, *"This time, we can help each other."*

"The great OneMind needs our help?"

"Yes."

Suddenly Tom was calm again. Sober and evaluating.

"What's up?"

"It's the Wollemi. They are becoming increasingly self-conscious. Conscious of self, I mean, as individuals." The

OneMind managed somehow to inject an ironic tone into its thought-flow. It continued.

"I fear that the Wollemi were corrupted by the presence of so many humans within the collective. They have begun to change." It paused to let the implications of what it had said register in the minds of the four humans.

"I foresee a time when I will not be able to form fully. Whatever is happening to the Wollemi people is interfering with the formation of the OneMind. Without being too melodramatic, I think I can say my days may be numbered, as you humans may like to put it." The announcement was met with stunned silence. At last, Alice spoke. She, above all. Elder of a people who had watched over the Wollemi for thousands of years had begun to understand what was at stake.

"Can they think?" she asked, staring around at the all-but-blank faces of the attendant Wollemi, "can they reason the way we do?"

"Somewhat," the voice of the OneMind mused, *"they have the wherewithal. They have, as you say, the basic wiring."*

"But?" Alice sensed the hesitation in the thought-flow.

"But they have little experience using that capability. For two hundred thousand years they have 'known', they have never had to 'understand'."

"Not until now." Alice turned to face the others.

"Not until now," the echoing thought of OneMind repeated,

"we need to gather at the Table of the Gods." The OneMind shared a mental image of the serried ranks of Wollemi waiting above on the higher slopes of the mountain. The sounds of their pursuers were louder, nearer, threatening. The fugitives could see the branches of trees a couple of hundred metres below waving chaotically as the soldiers forced their way through the undergrowth. There were only seconds to spare. The OneMind spoke.

"I'd better give you a lift."

The enveloping bubble snapped into existence around the four humans. The bark of gunshots and their echoing retort filled the mountainside, bouncing off the valley wall opposite and roaring back across the void, rasping and distorted. Here and there, occasional Wollemi fell, agony and confusion carved across their uncomprehending features. Some stopped to lift the fallen, others simply snapped out of existence, retreating behind the veil to the temporary safety of the Dreamtime.

The starry blanket of sky was occluded momentarily by the scintillation of the aurora. The next moment, the four humans found themselves standing on the huge flat stone shelf known as the Table of the Gods. Surrounding them, rank upon rank, were the staring faces of the Wollemi. Here and there, groups of Wollemi popped into existence, sometimes in twos and threes, sometimes just individuals. The injured were laid carefully on the flat stone. The OneMind formed an amorphous cloud of colour and light, shifting and changing shape as it enfolded the fallen. There was silence, absolute and, in its way, deafening. No sound could be heard. Even the subtle noises of the night creatures had stopped. It was as though the mountain itself held its breath. And then, slowly, individual Wollemi men and women were helped to their feet or carried away. When the last of the injured and the dead had been removed, the remaining Wollemi turned as one and faced the four isolated humans. The OneMind was nowhere to be seen. A Wollemi woman stepped forward. She walked towards Max and took his hand. It was Jack's mother. Jack took but a single step towards her before Kaitlin reached out a hand and gently restrained him. To Jack's complete amazement, the woman, his mother, began to speak. Slowly, hesitantly, as though testing out the sounds, she spoke.

"What happened? Why did they do that?" Her voice was quiet, precise. The pronunciation was strange. Her accent was something entirely new, nameless.

"*So, this is the voice of the Wollemi,*" Kaitlin thought. There was a lilt to it, evocative of the 'voice' of the OneMind, "*I'm listening to the speech of the oldest living human ancestors on Earth.*" There was a weird kind of purity, too, true innocence perhaps. "*How on Earth will we protect these people once the veil is gone?*" Kaitlin glanced towards Alice and Tom. It was evident from their expressions that the thought had occurred to them too.

THROUGH THE VEIL

The six humans stared blankly back at the small Wollemi woman holding Max's hand. They had no answer. The men were humans, soldiers. This is what they did. This is what they had always done. Nothing personal. The impasse was broken by Aine, looking around and asking, "Where's Mum?"

Jack and Kaitlin stared at each other, only just realising that Emma was missing.

"Emma's making her own way here. There wasn't time to swing past and pick her up. Everything changed when we found out about the special forces and the bombing."

"Bombing?" Max and Aine spoke as one. Tom jumped in.

"The soldiers are here to check out the Table of the Gods, they're looking for the OneMind, and us, I guess. We need to get out of here, fast."

"We're not leaving." Again, Max and Aine spoke as one.

It was then that they heard the angry thrashing of a small two-stroke motorbike engine approaching at speed from the other side of Mount Yengo. The small bright beam of its headlight zigzagging this way and that as the rider made their way up the steep slope, avoiding obstacles, forging a route to the flat expanse of the Table of the Gods. As it approached, the ranks of the Wollemi parted, and an undersized KTM dirt bike, its orange paintwork spattered with mud, soared over the edge of the massive flat rock and screeched to a halt in front of the six humans. The rider wrenched off their helmet and looked around.

"What the hell is going on?" It was Emma. Suddenly spotting her grandfather and grandmother, Emma practically levitated off the small motorbike and leapt into their arms.

"I thought you were dead. I thought even if you hadn't died in the Event, you would have passed away by now." It was all too much. Emma broke down, sobbing, while Max and Emma's Wollemi grand-mother attempted to comfort her. Aine, Kaitlin and Jack joined in the huddle. Tom and Alice looked on, both touched by the scene unfolding in front of them, both bemused and somewhat bewildered at the rapid change of events.

The raucous sounds of soldiers crashing through the forest floated up from below. Though still some way off, it was evident that they had been discovered. As one, the seven human beings turned and began to race down the far side of the mountain, away from the oncoming sol-diers. Emma, in the lead, lighting the way with the headlight of the dirt bike. Behind them, the Wollemi formed ranks. Emma's grandmother disappeared among her people. Silent panic drove the humans on. The runaways made it perhaps halfway down the mountainside before the sounds of gunshots rang out. This time the Wollemi were ready. The OneMind had formed focussed and intent. From their hiding places on the mountainside, the small group of fugitives looked back to see a row of soldiers appear on the very edge of the huge stone slab, the ancient meeting place of mankind's most ancient ancestors. Brilliant flashlights swept the mountainside. Behind the men, an enveloping, scintillating haze of colour formed. Before they have time to react, the small group of elite soldiers are cloaked within the implacable grip of the OneMind. Across the aether, the silent voice of the OneMind 'spoke.'

"There is nothing to fear. I mean you no harm. I need you to take back a message."

A few of the men could be seen struggling for a moment, attempting to break free of the shroud. In seconds all was quiet. The OneMind spoke again.

"This is the message you must take back." The OneMind pauses unexpectedly, and the ranks of the Wollemi turn slightly, orientating to the East. The *thwop-thwop-thwop* of a lone helicopter could be heard. As the helicopter approached, it swung around Mount Yengo to the west. In the distance, a searchlight beam could be seen sweeping the forest, coming closer.

"Tell the Generals I want to talk. Tell them I will send two humans to negotiate on behalf of my people. My time is coming to an end, but the Wollemi people will live on. When the veil is gone, they will keep to the wilderness areas

they love. You humans have abandoned the wild places. Let

my people live there in peace."

As the helicopter approached the summit of Mount Yengo, the ranks of the Wollemi began to thin. As the last one popped out of existence, the OneMind manifested briefly. Its silvern face and black almond-shaped eyes gaze for a moment at the special forces' posse, just beginning to shake themselves and look around as though waking from deep sleep.

"When the time comes, you will remember my mes-

sage. The thought of the OneMind intruded once more into the minds

of the nearby humans, *"For now, remember this, I will send two*

humans to speak for my people. Prepare for their arrival."

With that, the OneMind itself snapped out of existence. The soldiers stumbled around for a second or two more before pulling themselves together and beginning once more their search of the mountainside below them. The helicopter swung around and joined in the search. The seven humans on the mountainside below ran into the deep forest under the canopy of trees.

"Which way?" Tom glanced behind, "They're gaining on us."

The clatter of the soldiers was becoming louder and louder. The helicopter swung low overhead, and a voice blared out.

"Stop. You are under arrest. Do not run, or we shall be forced to open fire."

Shots rang out. The seven humans ran helter-skelter through the forest, leaves and branches slapping their faces, tearing at skin. They broke out into a small clearing, soldiers in hot pursuit. Pushed by the forces pursuing them, as one, the small band of frightened humans made a break for it across the clearing, heading for the shelter of the trees on the other side. The crack of gunfire rang out across the darkness, reverberating across the night, echoing back from the small hills all around. The whine of bullets encouraging them to haste. As they neared the far side of the clearing, the veil appeared and opened in front of them. The soldiers, close behind now, screamed at them to stop while firing sporadically. The group of seven humans tumbled once more through the veil into the Dreamtime. Looking back, they saw a soldier stop and raise his weapon to fire. The veil snapped shut but remained transparent for a few moments, out of phase, out of danger. The soldier fired across the small clearing. Other soldiers appeared. They aimed and fired repeatedly. They could not see in through the veil, but for a little while, the fugitives could see out. Bullets struck the veil and appeared to pass through, yet no one was struck. The phase shift continues. The two worlds drifted apart, and the veil once more snapped shut. The humans had been deposited somewhere … else. The stars overhead gave no clue where.

In the silence that follows, no one speaks. The OneMind's message overwhelmed all rational thought. The two worlds would inevitably collide. Their primordial separation will come to an end. The 'little people' will once more walk among us. They collapsed on the ground, out of breath from the escape. Only Tom remained standing, taking cover behind a large gum tree. In the end, it was Aine who broke the silence.

"It's me and Max."

"What is?" Emma pulled off her helmet and collapsed next to Kaitlin. The undersized dirt bike lying like a Child's discarded toy next to her.

"We will speak for the Wollemi."

"Oh no, you will not." Emma half rose from her prone position. Aine would have none of it.

"Before you arrived, before any of you arrived, Max and I talked with the OneMind for a long time. We went through all the ins and outs. It's all agreed. We are the negotiators."

"You're just a child." Emma had managed to wriggle into a sitting position.

"And you were just a child when you passed on the OneMind's message all those years ago." Aine's tone was mild, just stating a fact. Silence followed. Aine was right. Max spoke.

"The OneMind needs to know that his people will be OK when it's gone."

"What?" Emma was alert now. "What do you mean? Where is it going?"

"It's not going anywhere exactly. The Wollemi are changing, becoming more self-aware. The One Mind is finding it increasingly difficult to manifest. It told us its days were numbered."

For Emma, for whom almost her entire life had been lived in a universe where there existed a supernatural being called the OneMind which was an expression of the group consciousness of a faery race called the Wollemi who lived in the Dreamtime, all this came as a bit of a shock.

"We can discuss that later," Jack looked around, trying to figure out where the OneMind had deposited them.

"Where's it dumped us this time?" In the pitch-black night of the Wollemi Forest, without any clear landmark to guide him, it was impossible to say. Tom, ever the gadget man, flicked on his satellite GPS. The pale glow of the small screen cast an eerie light. Tom showed Jack the screen. A small red dot indicated their position against a topographical map of the vicinity.

"We need to get under cover. The Egyptian cave isn't too far from here. We can get there in an hour, even in the dark."

"Egyptian cave?" Max turned to Jack and Kaitlin, "You found it?"

Kaitlin spoke.

"You knew there was a cave filled with Egyptian hieroglyphs."

"All I know is that the ancient Egyptians had Aboriginal boomerangs made of Ironwood and that they shared a belief in the Sky World or the World of the Dead. The hieroglyphs carved on rocks in the bush near Gosford offer an insight into a shared philosophy."

"Shared philosophy?" Kaitlin spoke, "If I hadn't seen the cave myself, I would not have believed it."

"It's hard to think of two more different societies." Tom had produced his grey whooping crane feather from somewhere and was stroking it gently as though it were some kind of talisman.

There followed a hurried conversation while Kaitlin and Jack brought everyone up to speed on the spectacular cave that Kaitlin had discovered. So much had happened since her discovery. It seemed to Kaitlin like something that had happened weeks ago instead of mere hours. She should check her emails. Maybe the man from the Pergamon had gotten back to her.

They walked in single file, following animal tracks where possible. Emma and Jack led the way. Emma wheeled the little dirt bike along, its headlight piercing the dark, lighting the way. Just under an hour later, they came to Jack and Kaitlin's campsite.

"Best leave the bike here," Jack pointed Emma to a narrow way between two boulders, "We need to climb up there." He pointed up the steep, rock-strewn hillside.

"I found a relatively easy route up the other day," Kaitlin led the way, "turn off your phones if you haven't done. There's a very weak signal at the top. We don't want them tracking us."

It took a further fifteen minutes to get everyone safely to the top. Edging in the dark around the large boulder that marked the beginning of the narrow passage into the cave proved testing. The risk of falling was great, and it was a long way down into blackness. Once everyone was safely in the cave, Jack produced a small torch and shone it around. The iridescent gold leaf, though faded and frayed, lent the scene a magical air.

"Wow." Max Hexenkriege poured over the glimmering carvings, "This is totally unbelievable."

Kaitlin, Emma and Aine settled down on a rock shelf. Alice joined Max and Jack in examining the hieroglyphs.

"Our people have stories of visitors coming by boat from many places." Alice gazed in wonder at the iridescent walls.

"Did your people know about this cave?" Tom had produced his mobile phone and was using its light as a torch to study the glyphs.

"They must have. But no stories have been sung about it as far as I know." Alice paused, "This is Dharug country. Perhaps their Elders would know."

"Where do your stories say the boat people came from?" Tom paused from his scrutiny of the golden carving and turned towards Alice.

"Our Elders talk of people coming from what we now call China, from Indonesia and also a few stories about people coming from Egypt."

"Do the stories say why they came? What they were looking for?"

"The people from China were just curious. They wanted to see what lay beyond their borders. From Indonesia, it was mainly fishermen and a few traders." Alice stopped. Something nagged at the hem of memory.

"And the Egyptians?"

"There was a story about the Egyptians. I'm trying to remember it." Alice had everyone's attention.

"In the story, there were two visits. The first visitors were two noble brothers and their entourage. They had been shipwrecked. One died, but the other one lived and made it home." Alice paused again, searching her memory for details.

"And the other?" Tom spoke softly, encouragingly.

"As far as I can remember, the brother who had finally made it home to Egypt told of encountering the Mind of the God of Heaven."

"Osiris?" Kaitlin spoke. Although she did not herself work in the Egyptian tradition, there were those who did, and many of the foundations of the Kabbala were to be found in ancient Egyptian texts.

"Maybe. Is that the name?"

"Yes. Osiris and Isis ruled in heaven, like Shiva and Shakti in the Hindu Vedas, or Zeus and Hera in ancient Greece."

"Well, thanks for that." Jack laughed quietly, "Never short of a fact or two, are you?"

Kaitlin shot Jack a withering look, and Alice continued.

"The second visit was by a far larger group. They stayed longer and spoke with the Mind of the God of Heaven."

"Where is all this supposed to have taken place?" Tom, as ever trying to put together the pieces in what he knew was probably an insoluble puzzle.

Alice hesitated, "They met at the Table of the Gods, I think. We'd have to check with the Dharug Elders."

The group fell silent, gazing in awe at the rich carvings. The ancient hieroglyphics spoke with absolute authority of dreams long faded and glory spent.

THE CAVE

"We'll split up in the morning. Max and I will go with the soldiers to deliver the message from the OneMind." Kaitlin and Emma stared at Aine as she spoke. She may have wandered into the Dreamtime with the mind of a young girl, but she had walked back out with the emotional maturity of a woman. Aine continued.

"Alice, can you gather the Elders? It's well past time to raise the clans. Tom, you need to talk to your people, the CDC, the NSA and even NASA.' Aine paused, gazing round at the glorious inscrutable carvings clothed in peeling gold leaf, 'Kaitlin, can you and Grandad find out what all this means?"

"I have been in contact with the Pergamon Museum in Berlin. I'll chase them up in the morning."

"It's unbelievable," Aine shook her head as if trying to clear her mind, "if I hadn't seen this with my own eyes, I don't think I would have believed it either."

"I'm coming with you," Emma spoke quietly and without emphasis, yet no one was left in any doubt, "I've lost you and Max once. I'm not going to let that happen again."

Max shifted on his feet and cleared his throat as if to speak. Everyone turned towards him. There was something in his stance, in the bow of his head, that suggested he, too, had a message to pass on.

"I will come with you to deliver the OneMind's message, but after that, I will return to the forest to be with my wife." Max paused, looking around, searching the assembled faces. Seeking acceptance and understanding. "We have spent too long apart."

Jack wrapped his arm around his father's neck and hugged him.

"I'm happy for you, Dad. Jerry and I always wondered what you were waiting for all those years, alone in that broken-down cottage, far from civilisation."

"Well, now you know."

"Now I know. I only wish Jerry could have lived to see it."

"How did you find her? How did you find a way through the veil?" To Tom, this was a critical piece of intelligence. Years of training demanded an answer.

"I never stopped loving her," Max smiled, "I dreamed of joining her every day of my life after she left. Well, when the veil closed last time, I was able to take some readings. I was able to track the phase shift as it happened until the two worlds had separated too far, and I lost the signal. But I had most of what I needed. I just needed to find the last few phase settings in order to be able to reverse them. If I could generate a local field, phase shifting in reverse, then maybe I could find a way." Max paused for breath.

"Well?" Tom could barely wait to hear what Max had to say. The tension in the cave was palpable.

"Well, I did it."

"You found a way through?" Tom stared eyes agape.

"Yes, using a phase pulse generator. I created a small portal and entered the Dreamtime."

"And?" Emma reached out and took her grandfather's hand.

"And she was waiting."

"She knew?" Kaitlin whispered, the wonder of it taking her voice away.

"Yes, somehow the OneMind knew."

"And? What happened then?" Emma was beside herself.

"I allowed myself to be assimilated into the tribe. I was no longer afraid. I'd been alone too long."

There was silence in the cave for a long time. At last, it was Tom who spoke.

"You kept the details, right, of the phase pulse generator? You wrote it down or something?"

Max laughed, "Tom, my dear friend, I did. I knew you would never forgive me if I didn't."

"And?"

"There's an envelope glued to the underside of my desk draw in the cottage." Tom drew a sigh of relief. Then Alice spoke.

"I have already sent out the call for the gathering of the clans. People have begun drifting in. In ones and twos, sometimes more. Some came of their own accord over the last few weeks, sensing the change."

"We'd best try to get some sleep. We'll head towards Putty Road in the morning before we split up." Jack, practical as ever, tried to make people as comfortable as possible. He produced an old woollen blanket from his backpack and gave it to Kaitlin. The cave was dry, at least, but the weather was cold. The motley group of runaways hunkered down as best they could under Jack's old blanket. Sleep was slow to come. Each had plenty to think about. Jack stayed awake a little longer than the others. He stood by the cave mouth, listening to the nocturnal sounds of the forest, fearing the distant *thwop-thwop-thwop* of a helicopter or the not-so-stealthy sound of special forces approaching through the dark. Eventually, reassured that they had been neither pursued nor discovered, he, too, slept.

They woke stiff and cold in the grey light of a winter's dawn. Jack first, stamping some warmth into his protesting limbs. The others rose slowly, grumbling, chilled to the bone.

"We'd best get moving. They'll be combing the forest on foot and in the air. Jack led them back along the narrow ledge and onto the steep hillside.

"We'll walk about two kilometres towards Putty Road before we split up. Emma, there'll be some phone signal where we separate. You'll be able to call the police."

"The police?"

"Yep. Make them come to you. Save yourself a trek."

"Okay."

"They're going to arrest you anyway. Why make it harder for yourself?"

"I see."

"They'll take you to Canberra as soon as the powers that be realise who you are." Tom spoke this time, "They'll take you in for questioning."

"Yes, of course."

"Give them whatever information they ask for. Don't prevaricate or try to mislead them. There's no point to it, and it will just get you guys into trouble."

"Got it."

"Alice, you, and Tom should take the trail bike and head for the gathering place. Try to keep out of sight. Kaitlin and I will visit a friend." Jack paused to take stock, "We will head for the cottage in a few days after Kaitlin has spoken to the Pergamon people.

Before they set off, Tom cleared his throat. He needed to make sure everyone understood that there was hope, despite the precariousness of their situation.

"One last thing, once the OneMind's message has been delivered, there will be a short period of indecision while the great and the good figure out how to respond. We know what the military will advise, but we are not the same people we were twenty years ago. In some ways, we're not quite the same species. We are empaths now, and we can't stuff that genie back in the bottle. Some of the kids growing up in an empathic world are practically telepathic. They've become so attuned to other people. Most people won't support a genocidal war. There is hope."

And on that sombre but somewhat upbeat note, they trouped off, single file, across the hills and valleys of the ancient wilderness. Although it was cold, their journey was physically demanding, and it wasn't long before they warmed up. The predawn pink in the east, though pretty, portended rain. The sun, when it did rise an hour or so later, was hidden behind banks of cloud swirling in from the Pacific. They came at last to a steep hillside leading down to an open valley at the bottom of which the faint path divided. Jack pointed out the way. One spur headed north, roughly in the direction of Mudgee, deeper into the wilderness, while the other continued more or less straight towards Putty Road. Here they paused.

"Alice, Tom, you take the trail bike and head towards the road. Alice knows the way. Kaitlin and I will head north. Can't tell you where. Emma, you give us half an hour, then call the police. They'll come get you."

The little group walked the last half kilometre in silence. None knew what the future might bring. None knew if they would ever meet again. The ties of family and friendship had taken them this far, but they would take them no farther. From this point on, the future was in the hands of God or fate. They stopped at the parting of the ways. There were hugs all around and mumbled goodbyes. Tom and Alice headed off first. The pair of them squeezed onto the dirt bike and headed to the meeting of the clans for the second time in twenty years. The remaining five watched them out of sight, four generations of the same family engaged on one mission, a mission that had spanned over half a century already. Kaitlin and Jack hugged Max, Emma and Aine.

"We must trust in the wisdom of the OneMind. We have no other choice."

Emma, her daughter, and her grandfather watched Jack and Kaitlin until they rounded a bend in the trail and disappeared into the trees.

"Well, this is it." Emma pulled out her phone and switched it back on. The small display showed two bars, enough to make a call. Moments later, an efficient-sounding woman came on the line.

"Which service, please?"

"Police."

"What is your emergency?"

"I am Emma Hexenkriege. I am lost in the Wollemi National Park with my grandfather Max Hexenkriege and my daughter Aine, who was reported missing nearly a week ago."

"Can you describe your location?"

Emma read out the GPS coordinates from her phone. There was a short pause on the line.

"Umm, just a moment, please. I am entering your coordinates now." Several minutes passed before the efficient woman's voice returned.

"We are sending a helicopter for you now. Stay exactly where you are." The line went dead.

"They've realised who we are," Aine spoke, squaring her shoulders as she did so.

Max patted her shoulder, "Won't be long now. There's nothing to be afraid of. We've done nothing wrong."

The three messengers sat down on the grass and waited. Emma chatted with Max, asking about his life since she had last seen him. Asking why he could not have gotten a message to her. Telling him how much she had missed her grandad. Max hugged her and Aine close.

"I'm sorry, time passes differently in the Dreamtime."

Perhaps ten minutes went by before the tell-tail *thwop-thwop-thwop* on an approaching helicopter announced the imminent arrival of their ride. When the helicopter did finally arrive, it circled them once before coming in to land. A second helicopter appeared, coming from the opposite direction. It did not land. Instead, it circled overhead. A couple of soldiers sat in the open doorway of the helicopter, once pointing a machine gun down at them, the other holding a rifle.

"Here we go." Max held Aine and Emma close. "Remember, do exactly what they say, and answer all their questions honestly." The first helicopter landed a few yards away. Two police officers in dark fatigues jumped out. One was an older man. The other was a young woman. Aine felt their emotional state as they approached. Wary, a bit jumpy, but determined to get the job done.

"Stay where you are, please." The older officer stopped a couple of yards away while the younger produced a metal detector and swept the three 'escapees' for weapons.

"Clear, sir." The young policewoman stepped back.

"Please come with us." The older man stepped to one side, indicating the direction of the Helicopter with one arm. The policewoman stepped behind them, cutting off escape. Max, Emma and Aine did as requested. They were soon strapped into their seats on the helicopter. The door slammed shut, and they were lifted into the sky. Aine, who was sitting next to a window, looked down onto the retreating forest, shrinking beneath them. She scanned along the north-leading trail. Jack and Kaitlin were nowhere to be seen. Jack would have led Kaitlin under the trees at the first sound of the approaching helicopter.

"Do you have any water?" Emma asked, above the din of the engine. The younger woman glanced towards the older officer. He nodded. A couple of bottles of water were produced and handed to them.

"We have a message to deliver," Aine had to raise her voice to be heard above the deafening sound of the engine, "A message from the OneMind".

It was too noisy for conversation, and the backwash emanating from the two police officers made it clear they were in no mood for a chat. A few minutes later, the helicopter, with the second one still in tow, circled the field below the bowling club at Wisemans Ferry. As it came in to land, the second helicopter banked west and disappeared over the escarpment. The field below was ringed with armed police, some with dogs. They were taking no chances.

MESSAGE DELIVERED

The three generations of Hexenkreiges were taken quickly to the Wiseman's Ferry Conference Centre and Spa and ushered without preamble into a brightly lit room. Max smiled sadly as he entered. It had been more than twenty years since he had last set foot in this very room. His son Jerry had been alive then, in the prime of life. He remembered

Tom walking in and the sudden unexpected reunion with his one-time prospecting buddy. And then Harry Soames, Intelligence Director at the CDC, friend, and mentor, entered, bringing with him the enigmatic HARP device. Of unknown purpose and power. Invention of a paranoid time and a paranoid people. So much had been set in train in this very room. And here they were again, little more than two decades later. It was as though indolent fate had taken up residence in Wisemans Ferry and could not be bothered to relocate.

They were shown to their seats. A long trestle table had been set up, covered in computers and communications equipment. A very large screen occupied one whole wall adjacent to the end of the table. The screen was split into two equal sections. Each one showed a conference room, each windowless, enigmatic. They could have been anywhere. People milled about, completing last-minute arrangements.

The quiet, purposeful bustling around stopped as two uniformed men entered the room, an American and an Australian, both generals. The few military personnel dotted around the room snapped to attention. The civilians paused in what they were doing, quiet, waiting.

"OK," the Australian General spoke, "please signal our colleagues that we are ready to start the meeting."

Everyone who was not already seated sat. The big screen flickered a little as it showed people entering each of the distant conference rooms. Civilians in the main, interspersed with the odd uniformed officer. The inevitable faffing about continued for a minute or two as everyone found their seats, arranged their gear, and sat. The doors in the two distant conference rooms opened. Two people walked in and took their respective seats. The president of the United States and the Australian Prime Minister sat in the centre of their two groups of advisors, like two alternative versions of The Last Supper. The Australian Prime Minister spoke first.

"I understand we have been graced with a delegation from the One-Mind. We are honoured."

A ripple of apparent amusement went around the room. Aine tuned her senses to the emotional currents swirling around. No one was amused. There was tension and anticipation. There was deep suspicion but no strong threads of fear. People were intent and serious but not aggressive. Not yet.

"Who is your spokesperson?" The Australian general leaned across the conference table, "Who is going to speak?"

Aine stood.

"I am Aine Hexenkriege. My grandfather is Jack Hexenkriege, and" indicating Max and Emma with either hand, she continued, "I am here with my mother, Emma Hexenkriege and my great-grandfather Max Hexenkriege who has been living in the Dreamtime with the Wollemi for over fifteen years." Aine paused, calm, in control. Waiting to be sure that her audience had taken in what she had said. All three conference rooms had fallen silent.

"My great-grandfather and I were tasked by the OneMind with delivering the following message." Again, she paused, sensing the room. Tension stalked the perimeter, a sleek, dark jungle cat waiting to pounce.

"We are to tell you that the OneMind has sent us and that the OneMind wants to talk. We two humans are to open negotiations on its behalf and on behalf of the Wollemi people." There was absolute silence in the room. Focusing on the enormous conference screen, Aine continued.

"The OneMind believes its time is coming to an end and that, although the OneMind will soon be gone, the Wollemi people will live on." Aine paused once more, gathering her thoughts. The raging emotional backwash, distracting to one so finely attuned, was almost overwhelming.

"When the veil is gone, the Wollemi people will keep to the wilderness areas they love. The OneMind says we humans have abandoned the wild places and asks that the Wollemi people be left alone to live there in peace."

Aine sat, futilely covering her ears as an ocean of raw, uncontrolled feeling swamped her senses. Most of these people were already adults when the Event occurred. They lacked the ability to tune down their passions. Every fleeting sentiment was broadcast at full volume across the room. Aine caught sight of a young man seated at the very end of the table, perhaps ten years older than herself, evidently also struggling with the 'noise' in the room, rise and leave. She wished she could join him. The door closed behind him with an audible click. That seemed to act like a signal. Everyone began speaking at once. For a full minute, it was bedlam until the General who had spoken earlier banged on the table calling the room to silence.

"Why does the OneMind believe its time is coming to an end?"

The second General joined in. "What does that mean in any case? Is it dying? Can it die?"

There followed a staccato burst of questioning, both from within the conference room in Wisemans Ferry and from the screen at the end of the table. Once more, the meeting was called to order. This time the first question came from the conference screen. The Australian Prime Minister tapped the heavy wooden conference table in front of her and then spoke.

"How old are you, Aine?"

Aine, at eleven years old, was perhaps not the most compelling messenger or negotiator the OneMind could have chosen. Still, she was taken aback by the question.

"I am eleven years old physically, but I have knowledge, experience and memories going back centuries."

"I see." The Australian Prime Minister's cool, poised contralto voice could not hide her doubting tone. Aine didn't need to feel the older woman's emotional flow to be stung by her barely concealed disdain. Aine was tired, having spent a freezing night in an ancient Egyptian cave, walked kilometres before being picked up in a police helicopter and rushed, without preparation or warning, into this conference room. And she hadn't had her breakfast. She'd had enough.

"Well, how old are you then?" she snapped back. There was silence all around for a moment or two. The sound of soft laughter came from the conference screen. It wasn't obvious for a moment who was laughing, and then the American President spoke.

"I reckon you've met your match there, Audrey." Max leaned over to Aine and whispered in her ear.

"Let me talk to these old farts for a moment. They have no idea what assimilation into the OneMind really means."

Aine managed a haughty sniff but accepted the suggestion.

"I will introduce you."

Aine sat straight in her chair and focussed on the Prime Minister's somewhat shocked countenance.

"Let me introduce my great-grandfather, Maximilian Hexenkriege. He is over eighty years old and is probably the world's greatest authority on the Wollemi people and the OneMind."

Max smiled. He was learning that Aine could be a bit of a handful.

"I wonder where she gets it from?" he whispered to Emma before himself sitting up straighter and addressing the conference.

"I have spent the last twenty corporeal years living with the One-Mind and the Wollemi people as part of the collective. I am married to a Wollemi woman, with whom I had two sons, one of whom is Aine's grandfather, Jack Hexenkriege."

"Excuse me." The young man who had left the room had returned unnoticed and resumed his seat at the end of the table. Max paused.

"Corporeal years?"

"Yes."

"What other kinds of years are there?"

"Time passes differently in the Dreamtime." The young man leaned forward to ask another question.

"Great question," the Australian General spoke, "but perhaps for another time." The young man deflated back into his seat as though pierced by a pin, appearing to shrink as he did so. Max continued.

"The OneMind is struggling to hold the collective together. It is struggling to manifest itself. Each time is more difficult than the last. The OneMind believes that individual Wollemi have been 'poisoned' by their previous contact with humans and by my presence and the presence of other humans around the world, within the collective." Max paused. It was a lot to take in, and he had to be sure his audience was following his explanation.

"Why 'poisoned'?" The American General leaned forward, "Why does the OneMind want our help if it believes we have poisoned it?"

"Sir, I believe the OneMind was using the term ironically."

"Ironically?"

"Yes, Sir, communications with the OneMind are instantaneous and telepathic. Layers of meaning superimpose themselves upon each other. When one converses with the OneMind, one engages primarily with its dominant thought process."

"It's dominant thought process?"

"Sir, it's a bit difficult to explain, but the OneMind is a gestalt. It's a complex aggregation and layering of observations, arguments, and emotions."

"I see." It was plain that the American General did not see, not at all. Aine piped up.

"General, it might help to think of the OneMind as a kind of giant massively parallel supercomputer, a kind of neural net that can keep millions of different points of view in mind all at the same time."

"I'm starting to realise that we don't understand what we're dealing with." There was silence after that as the congregated politicians, officials and military men attempted to achieve their own gestalt.

Max continued, "The OneMind has realised that the Wollemi are changing, becoming more conscious. They are at an inflection point, the OneMind believes. The more conscious they become as individuals, the more difficult it is for the OneMind to manifest. The OneMind needs to bring matters to a resolution while it still can." Again, Max paused. The silence in the room and on the conference screen confirming that he had their attention.

"He, 'It', needs human help to speed the development of individual Wollemi consciousness. They need to become independent, use their own intellect and become more like humans. And now we come to the nub of this conversation." Max paused. This was it. The future of two sentient species depended upon how he landed these next few sentences.

"The one great mind can no longer fulfil the myriad needs of millions of individual Wollemi people.   It knows it's, I'll say, 'life' is coming to an end and that the veil must fall. When the veil fails, the two worlds must come together."

Aine shifted in her seat. The waves of emotion prowling the room and presumably prowling the other two conference rooms had become, for her, a tangible thing. Her chest heaved, resonating with the raw pulse of it. Like the beat of a sub-woofer, it occupied her physical being. Emma, noting Aine's distress, wrapped a protective arm around her daughter. No longer the confident, precocious messenger of the OneMind. Exhaustion and backwash had taken their toll.

"Let me get this straight," the American General frowned, "We're back right where we were twenty years ago, only this time, the One-Mind needs our help?"

Max continued his explanation, "The OneMind will soon have to drop the veil forever. You will have heard reports of the Aurora Borealis becoming visible at increasingly lower latitudes. This is a symptom of the OneMind's waning control. But it cannot drop the veil until it has agreement that the Wollemi, no longer protected by the veil and the OneMind, will be safe."

"Safe?" The American President spoke.

"Yes. Protected."

"Safe from what? Protected from what?"

"Well, from us. We, humans, have an appalling track record at this kind of thing."

Max paused. This could not be rushed. Everything depended upon it.

"The OneMind has introduced a whole new concept into the Wollemi consciousness. The concept of 'consent'." Max paused again to allow the significance of what he had said to sink in.

"This is a radical departure for the OneMind. After fifty thousand years or more, it has realised that it is not just Humans who have evolved. The Wollemi have too."

"What's its ask?" The American General spoke, "What does it want from us exactly?"

Max stopped and rubbed his face and neck with his hands, an involuntary gesture. He was nervous. This was the moment.

"The OneMind asks that select small groups of human volunteers join the collective and consent to be assimilated, not as powerless drones but as independently conscious humans. The OneMind believes that the impact of many small groups of humans existing within the collective, but retaining their free will, would trigger a chain reaction across the OneMind itself. All Wollemi would be empowered to retain their own consciousness while continuing to be members of the collective. It would be a very different collective. For the first time, they would give their willing consent."

"And then?"

"The OneMind would remove the veil forever."

"And the OneMind itself? Where would it go?"

"The OneMind is an expression of the Wollemi gestalt. It would disappear. Individually conscious, independently reasoning Wollemi would no longer need it, and it would no longer be able to form."

"It would die?"

"In effect, yes."

The Australian Prime Minister spoke.

"We thank you for bringing this message. The news you have brought us will impact all human beings. To many of us, the older generation who were already adults when the Event occurred, the jury is still out as regards the OneMind and its intentions. We will consider the request in detail."

"Thank you", Aine and Max spoke at once. The conference appeared to be over. There was what Aine could only describe as a flurry of indecision before an official sitting a couple of positions from the Australian Prime Minister in the distant conference room interjected.

"Next Steps then?"

There was silence. What were the next steps? Were the three messengers under arrest? Had they committed an offence? Did they deserve some kind of diplomatic immunity? They were in uncharted territory. It was the American President who broke the impasse.

"We need you to hang around for a while. There will have to be a global conference. As Audrey, I mean the Prime Minister, has said, this affects all of us." No one moved. Was the conference over? The Australian Prime Minister tapped her water glass, bringing the meeting back to order. She addressed the three messengers, "Please let the local police authorities have your contact details. We'll be in touch." People began to pack up. "Thank you, everyone, for your attendance. What we have heard today is, for both our nations, a matter of national security. All information about today's meeting is quarantined."

The meeting broke up. As Max, Emma and Aine left the room, someone handed Max a business card.

"Give us a call if anything more of significance comes to mind, would you? We'll follow up in a few days."

"I'm starving," Aine grabbed Max's and Emma's hands and led them in the direction of the Wisemans Ferry Inn and brunch.

Apart from a few bikers, the pub was pretty much empty. A few curious onlookers watched the three Hexenkreiges enter the bar. The barman, a man in his mid-fifties, noticed Max walk in.

"Oh my God, Max. It is you, isn't it? Max Hexenkriege." And then, glancing at Emma and Aine, "Where's Jack then? And Kaitlin?"

"They're panning for gold, of course," Emma smiled, "How else would you spend a cold weekend in winter?" The barman laughed.

"That'd be right. So, where have you been hiding yourself then, Max?"

"I went back to Germany for a short visit and ended up staying a while."

"Coopers Pale Ale?"

"How about a coffee and some breakfast?"

"Too easy. Find a table, and I'll bring you the menus."

The three Hexenkreiges found themselves a table in a quiet corner and sat. Exhaustion hit them.

"I need food, a hot shower, and three weeks' sleep." Emma threw either arm around her daughter and her grandfather. Then turning to Max. "I never imagined I would see you again."

Max smiled, "I never thought I'd come this side of the veil again." He looked around, examining the old familiar barroom. "It's been twenty years, and hardly anything has changed."

"The motorbikes are all electric these days." Aine leaned against her mother, snuggling, for the moment, a little girl once more, "They're self-driving, and they have gyroscopes. Even for me, it's weird when you see the occasional riderless motorbike going along."

"What do you think will happen?" Emma took a moment to search her grandfather's face. He hadn't aged all that much. He looked good for a man in his eighties. "What will they decide?"

"It's hard to tell. The gift of empathy was no accident. Given the current situation, it could easily be seen as part of a long-planned scheme of the OneMind's leading to this point – preparing humanity for it. The powers that be will be well aware of that." Max paused. His coffee had arrived. The scent of freshly ground coffee filled his nostrils.

"Coffee and bacon." Max took a sip, savouring the taste, enjoying the all-but-forgotten aroma.

"Hmm?' Emma was non-plussed.

"That's what I missed most."

"Really?"

"Yep, it hadn't occurred to me until this moment. Living in the gestalt, one loses track of these details."

"It's all vegetable based these days," Aine leaned forward a little so she could get a good look at her great-granddad, "or cloned in a vat".

"Oh?"

"Yes. No one farms pigs anymore. They're in hobby farms if they're domesticated or running wild if they're not."

"How does vegetable bacon taste?" Max looked crestfallen. After all these years, was it too much to ask for a proper bacon sandwich?

"It's cloned. They say it tastes just the same. You really won't be able to taste the difference."

"Really?"

"Yep. Well, that's what the old folks say, anyway." Aine giggled.

"You cheeky little miss," Emma gave her daughter a quick tickle, "I'm not that old."

"Self-driving motorbikes and vat-grown bacon, what else have I missed?"

Aine laughed and began to tick things off on her fingers, "Well, drones have taken over from cars. They're self-driving too, or self-flying. So are the trucks, and all the farms are pretty much run by robots, and the human population is falling. I'm one of the last of the post-Event baby-boom."

"How come you know so much about how things were before you were born?" Emma was intrigued. She had never suspected that her daughter was so worldly-wise.

"We learned about it in history, in Event Studies," Aine sat up straight and intoned, "'How the world has changed. A paradigm shift. By Haralambos and Haralambos', it's one of our schoolbooks."

The barman came back with menus. Emma didn't even take a glance.

"Three Big Breakfasts, tea for two and another mug of coffee for my grandfather, please."

"No worries." The Barman stalked off to the kitchen to pass on the order.

"Our governments will make a deal of some sort. I suppose," Emma pursed her lips reflectively, "Hardly anyone visits the wilderness areas these days."

"But what will happen when the veil is gone? They told us at school that the two worlds will collide. What does that mean?"

Max leaned forward, turning his head so he could catch Aine's eye, "Well, they're not going to crash into each other if that's what you're thinking. I discussed that with the One-Mind. Our world and the

Dreamtime are out of phase with one another, sort of superimposed upon one another. There are discrepancies, but they will be evened out as the bubble around the Earth disperses."

"They won't collide then?" Aine looked relieved.

"I think that was more of a cultural metaphor," Max smiled, "There will be some pretty odd effects, though, here and there."

"What sort of effects?" Aine's relief was short-lived.

"Well, the Wollemi are scattered all around the world, mostly but not exclusively living in the wilderness."

"Not exclusively?"

"Um, No."

"You mean the 'little people' may pop up here and there in or near the cities?"

"Yes, kind of. Parts of some cities."

"Such as?"

"Some pockets of Wollemi live in places you'd never suspect."

"Oh, come on, granddad, where?" both Emma and her daughter were squirming in frustration.

"New York's central park, for one, plus Oslo, Islamabad, Cape Town, and Anchorage, to name a few more."

"What will happen to them? The ones in the cities, I mean?"

"The OneMind said they would relocate to the nearest wilderness. The Wollemi are migratory, did you know?"

Emma shook her head.

"They have no heavy industry or permanent buildings. They're craft workers and harvesters, generally. A few goldsmiths."

"Goldsmiths? I never knew." Emma smiled, "I'd love to see some of their artwork."

"Some sculpt lovely little animals and plants," Aine's eyes shone with the memory, "but they also make this amazing kind of 'thought sculpture".

"Thought sculpture?" Emma was trying to imagine what one of those would be like, "Can you describe one?"

"I can try," Aine paused for a moment, gathering her thoughts, "There was this one. I'll never forget it." She looked up at her mother's face, trying to find the words. "It was tiny, sort of like a flower, well not exactly a flower, but it had petals, folded in on themselves, and unfolding too, at the same time, swirling, somehow suggesting a seed concept." Aine paused. She'd run out of words.

"What thought did it represent?"

"The idea that formed in my mind was something like 'Why is there anything at all?' but at the same time, the concept was, 'There is everything because there is something'."

"I can't imagine," Emma smiled and took her daughter's hand, "Well, I can, but I can't. You know what I mean?"

Aine snuggled in against the warmth of her mother's body.

"Yes, I know just what you mean."

Their breakfasts were quick to arrive. Three large plates, steaming a little in the cool air of the bar. They tucked in.

"Oh my God, this is so good." Max smiled, "There is something to be said for cooking."

There followed for several minutes the chinking of cutlery on porcelain and pretty much nothing else. When the eating had finally come to an end, a wave of exhaustion swept over the Hexenkreiges. Whether it was the food, the relief that it was all over, at least for now, or the inevitable result of a terrible night's sleep in an ancient Egyptian cave, not one of them could keep their eyes open.

"Let's go home and get some sleep."

"You have a vehicle?" Max stood, stretching as he did so, "I could do with a nap."

Emma pulled out her phone, paid the bill and ordered a drone.

"I've ordered a drone. It'll be here in a few minutes."

"They're like small helicopters," Aine explained, "only electric and with more propellers."

Max shook hands with a few old acquaintances as they left the Wisemans Ferry Inn and stood waiting in what had once been the small car park, but was now a drone park, for the arrival of the drone.

"Where do you live now?" Max realised he had no idea where he was being taken.

"Richmond, my job's there."

"What do you do?"

"I'm an uplink manager for SatNet."

"Oh?"

"Yes, I manage one of the satellite uplink ground stations."

"SatNet?"

"It's the global communications satellite network."

"Yes, of course." Max laughed, "A lot has changed in twenty years, hasn't it?"

"I guess so," Emma took his arm, "becoming empaths changed us all. We're still human beings, but the suspicion has gone the fear."

"Yes, I felt the start of that before I crossed into the Dreamtime."

"It's affected the younger generation more. Those born after the event."

"How so?"

"We're much more attuned than our parents." Aine took up the tale, "We can filter and control our emotional diffusion. Our parents, well anyone who was already an adult at the time of the Event, broadcast all their emotions all the time. The noise can be deafening." Aine stopped for a moment.

"We call it backwash. It's a bit mean, really. They can't help it."

"The young can practically read minds." Emma smiled. In the distance, the blinking navigation lights of the drone could be seen approaching from the Windsor depot a few miles upstream. Max watched it approach and land.

"There was one thing that the OneMind envied us for, you know."

"What was that?"

"Ingenuity. Inventiveness. The Wollemi rarely had to find anything out. They mostly just knew telepathically. That's partly why they have so little technology. They don't need it. They live as they have always lived, for perhaps two hundred thousand years."

The drone landed. Emma strapped Max in and checked that Aine was secure. She strapped herself in and closed the door. The drone took off, following the line of the Hawkesbury River as it meandered its way along the narrow flood plain between hills and cliffs. According to air traffic regulations, the drone flew at about 200 metres above the river—a perfect height for sightseeing. The dark waters swept past below, and occasional pleasure boats and houseboats whizzed by. Here and there, lone fishermen in tinnies communed with the river. It was one of those clear, bright winter days that European visitors took for the coming of spring, though spring was still far off.

The old town of Windsor whizzed passed on either side as the drone flew over the few bridges that linked the enormous Sydney plain with the foothills of the Blue Mountains. Max stared at the passing townscape. A few people were out and about. There were no cars. The place had a downcast air, acknowledging perhaps its inevitable abandonment. It had seen its two hundredth birthday come and go, but it would not see its three hundredth. Soon the surrounding countryside would win it back.

In the distance, the town of Richmond came into view. It had faired a little better than its sister town of Windsor. The presence of the military airport and the placement of the satellite ground station had won it a short reprieve. The large white disk of the geostationary uplink became visible first. Next to it, on either side, sat the two smaller tracking disks, constantly monitoring the orbiting satellites as they drifted across their sector of the sky.

The drone swung towards the ridge to the north of town, slowing and eventually hovering in front of a small house with a neat little garden. The drone set down almost silently, and the passengers disembarked.

Max and Aine took turns in the shower while Emma made up a bed for Max on the sofa in the lounge. At last, it was Emma's turn to shower. When she came out, both Max and Aine were fast asleep. She fed and watered Tommy, their loyal staffy-cattle dog cross, and let him out the back to do his business. When at last, he wandered back in, Emma locked the back door and dived into bed. The heavy thump and sudden weight at the foot of her bed announced Tommy's arrival.

Emma lay for a while thinking back on the events of the last two days. Whatever it was, it was happening again.

Alice and Tom squished uncomfortably onto the little dirt bike and took the track towards Putty Road. They made good time despite the many twists and turns and the uneven surface. Alice held fast to Tom. The last time she had been on a dirt bike was decades before when she was a teenager. *"I had more hormones than sense back then."* She thought to herself, little noticing how comfortable she felt with her arms around Tom, unaware for the moment of how attuned she had become to Tom's emotional flow and to his scent.

"Where are we going once we get to the road?" Tom had slowed a little so his voice could be heard above the whine of the old petrol engine.

"We head left towards Sydney. There's a meeting place just off Uworra Road. We'll ditch the bike at the little settlement there and continue on foot, following the line of Howes Creek and then into the forest."

"OK"

"It's a little way before Wilberforce. Maybe twenty kilometres from where we will join Putty Road."

"We'll be exposed on the road. There may be helicopters, drones, police vehicles and motorbikes."

"We'll just have to take our chances. There's no back road to the meeting place." Alice was nervous, though. Putty Road had long been a favourite place for traffic cops to make their quota.

Roughly a quarter of an hour later, Tom and Alice approached Putty Road. Tom slowed as they got closer, coming to a stop a few metres from the road itself. He pulled the little dirt bike to a stop under an old gum tree. He and Alice worked their way through ground cover towards the road. They stopped just short of the tarmac and watched.

There was no one about. No trucks came passed. The road appeared deserted. After ten minutes, when not a soul had passed their way, not even a farm drone, Tom and Alice continued on. They made good time. Tom managed to ease the protesting dirt bike a little over the speed limit set for manually operated vehicles. An alarm pinged on the bike's little screen. Tom ignored it.

As they approached the turnoff, Alice became increasingly nervous. The tingling of some sixth sense increased in volume and urgency.

"Pull off the road, now" Alice felt it as an urgent, visceral need, "Something approaches."

A minute or two after Tom pulled to a halt some twenty metres off the road, in thick undergrowth, the high-pitched whine of a drone, travelling at speed, became audible in the distance. Tom and Alice lay flat, hardly daring to breathe. The whine of the drone's engines increased as it approached. And then, in an instant, it flashed past low over the road, little blue and red lights blinking as it went. And it was gone.

"What was that?" Tom turned to Alice, for once a little nonplussed by what he had seen.

"It was a search-and-rescue drone. Controlled by an AI, judging from its speed."

"Search and rescue?"

"Yes. Clever, they can detect life signs at a distance. The carbon dioxide from breathing. Body warmth. They can trace the residual heat from footprints, and so on."

"They're looking for us."

"Yes. Let's hope it was a precautionary sweep. Let's hope they don't somehow already know we're here."

"How would they know that?"

"I don't know. They wouldn't. They can't. I guess I'm just a little jumpy."

Tom placed a protective arm around Alice. Automatically, without conscious thought, Alice slipped her arms around Tom's neck. They drew closer. The closeness of their bodies warmed them both. They stood that way for several minutes, neither speaking, neither daring to break the spell. At last, inevitably, Alice shifted her gaze, examining Tom's face as if for the first time, taking him in, not as a colleague and friend, but as a man. They kissed, of course. Gently, almost timidly, exploring, daring to explore, the startling possibility of love.

"We need to go," Alice took Tom's hand. "The drone may make a second sweep. It's not far now. Come on."

The last few kilometres to the turn-off, though traversed with a sense of extreme uncertainty, were soon over. They bumped their way along Uworra Road, ditching the bike under cover just short of the few houses that comprised the tiny settlement. Alice and Tom continued on foot. There was no one about. The sense of country deserted by people was, to Alice, both discomfiting and liberating. As human settlement gave way to population decline and automation, the countryside was returning to an earlier state. No Matter. Her people would watch over it, as they always had.

The couple made their way cautiously through the settlement, keeping to cover as much as they could. Perhaps they needn't have bothered. Though there were lights on here and there, the place seemed all but deserted. They saw no one as they slid through a rusty and over-grown gate and into the paddock beyond. A row of small trees indicated the path of Howes Creek. Alice led Tom into the dried-up creek bed where they would not be visible to prying eyes. They followed the creek bed in silence for ten minutes or so, and then Alice led them up the other side of the shallow creek and into the forest. They were soon once again making their way through the deep cover of the ancient trees. They crested a ridge. There, in a hidden valley far from the comforts of civilisation, the clans were gathering. The small clearing thronged with people. The word had gone out as she had hoped. There was something of a carnival air to the scene. This had been an ancient meeting place between territories, understood to be open to all but controlled by none.

Heads began to turn as Alice and Tom walked out from under the trees. A man broke from the tangle of humanity and walked towards them.

"More people than last time." Alice gazed around the clearing, picking out a few familiar faces and many new ones. "Good job Jandamarra."

"Some people were already here before I sent out the call. The folks from the West and the Centre were here early."

"Didn't want to miss the show, ay?"

"Come, there are many Elders here. The people need leadership."

Tom had been watching the crowd and listening to the conversation. And as he had watched and listened, he had noticed in Alice a slow transformation. As the import of their situation returned to mind, she seemed to grow somehow. Squaring her shoulders, head back, Alice had accepted her role. The people needed leadership. Well, then, she would lead them. She strolled to the centre of the clearing, Tom following close behind. A way was made for her. A small circle opened at the centre, and Alice stepped into it. Jandamarra reached out, gently placing a hand on Tom's arm, holding him back.

"No offence, ay."

"None taken." Tom stood at the edge of the clearing with Jandamarra. The level of chatter among the clans gradually reduced until there was silence. Alice lifted her arms in a gesture of welcome.

"At this ancient meeting placed of our peoples, all are welcome," she began, "Everyone may speak. All voices will be heard." Alice paused for a moment, sensing the emotional noise coming from the gathered Elders. No fear, she was pleased to realise. No anger. Just a focused sense of the turning of the age. Tom caught her eye and tapped his watch. A small smile crept for a moment across her face.

"Time may be short. Let us begin." As though on a signal, the crowd sat. Alice alone remained standing.

"The OneMind has sent us a message. It cannot maintain the veil. The Wollemi are becoming conscious of their individual selves. The Dreamtime, so long severed from us, will return."

There was silence for a long time as the Elders of many clans considered Alice's words. They had watched over the Wollemi for 50,000 years or more. There was no need to rush things. Tom sat with the others, dutifully silent. At last, roughly at the point where Tom's frustration threatened to boil over, someone spoke.

"I am Killara, Elder of the Worimi people."

The gathered crowd looked around, searching for the owner of the voice. There stood, a little to the left of where Tom was sitting, a young woman, a girl really, perhaps 14 or 15 years old. *"Young for an Elder,"* Tom thought to himself.

"It is known among my people that I have several times visited the Dreamtime and that I once received a message from it." The crowd remained silent, respectful. An Elder was an Elder. It was not for them to judge.

"May we know how we can be sure that the message was from the OneMind itself?"

"A fair and important question." Alice proceeded to recount the meeting at the Table of the Gods and the pursuit by special forces. She explained how Maximilian Hexenkriege and his great-granddaughter

Aine had passed into the Dreamtime and spoken at length with the One-Mind. She explained how even now, they would be meeting with people from the government and from the military. And then she stopped. The young Elder, Killara, sat. The Elders would have to discuss the situation amongst themselves. This was going to take a while. Wood was gathered, and fires were lit. The ceremonies of many different clans from all parts of the Australian continent began. Smoking ceremonies purified the area. In some parts of the clearing, there was silence. In others, low rhythmic chanting could be heard.

Alice looked around, seeking her own people. Seeing where they were seated, she flashed Tom an apologetic smile and went to join them. Jandamarra tapped Tom's elbow.

"This could take a while, br. Let's take a walk."

TJ'S CAMPING GROUND

Jack turned to Kaitlin as they walked, "It's going to be a bit of a trek. We won't get where we're going until sundown. Sorry."

"Where're we headed."

"You remember TJ's camping ground? The 4-wheel drive place?"

"That's miles away. Halfway to Mudgee, maybe more." Kaitlin, still chilled to the bone from the night spent in the cave, was in no mood for a long hike through the wilderness.

"It's not that far. I know a shortcut through the valleys."

Kaitlin remained silent. Even Jack could sense her rebellious backwash.

"They have solar showers."

Kaitlin sniffed.

"They have a little kiosk now. You can get hot coffee, and in winter, they do soup and chilli dogs."

"I want an alpaca jumper." The proprietor kept a herd of alpacas and sold handmade alpaca knitwear.

"OK."

"And gloves… And a scarf."

"Done."

The pair walked on in silence, keeping Putty Road to their left as they went. After a few kilometres, Jack led them across the road and back into the wilderness. They made their way into a narrow valley between two steep hills.

"We can follow this valley all the way. If you always take the left fork, it leads straight to TJ's."

"We don't have to climb any steep hills?"

"There's a narrow path all the way. It's a wanderline. Probably been here for a hundred thousand years."

"It's hard to believe, isn't it?"

"What is?"

"That the Aboriginal people have been here so long. That their cultures are maybe ten times older than the Egyptian Pharaohs and the Babylonians, even more for the Greeks and Romans."

"Yes. And the Wollemi are older still. Somewhere between two hundred thousand and a million years, maybe."

"Makes the Egyptian cave seem almost recent." Kaitlin laughed.

They walked on in silence. It was going to be a very long day.

The sun had risen to its height, and was beginning its descent, when a question popped into Kaitlin's head, "Why are we heading for TJ's? What's there?"

"The place is off the grid. He has a satellite phone and internet."

"So, I can check for emails from the Pergamon?"

"Yep."

"What then?"

"Depends upon what they say, I guess. TJ's lets me keep a ute there, just in case."

Kaitlin paused the plodding of her feet and turned to Jack.

"We have been together now for over twenty years, and you still manage to surprise me."

"I'm a surprising man. In my own way." Jack smiled, "I can't give away all my secrets."

Kaitlin took his hand. They walked together hand in hand for a few steps until the terrain made it impractical.

"Emma and Aine have some kind of connection to the OneMind. You're aware of that, right?"

Kaitlin, having fallen a little behind, found herself posing the question to Jack's slowly retreating back.

"Yes. I suppose so. I've never really thought about it." Jack turned his head a little as he spoke. Kaitlin continued.

"Jerry did, I know. He called it his gestalt."

"Yes. He thought it was his own personal super-power, I think." Jack smiled, recalling how much Jerry enjoyed being the smartest guy in the room.

"Well, do you?"

"Do I what?"

"Do you have some kind of connection to the OneMind?"

Jack stopped walking and turned.

"I guess I do. I suppose I must."

"What sort of a connection is it? Do you know?"

"I think that while Jerry connected intellectually, I may connect at a more physical level."

"How do you mean?"

"I'm not sure. But I know the country. I feel it. I have always been in tune with the earth itself."

"How do you know? What difference does it make to you?"

"Well, when I go fossicking, for instance, I never bother looking where I know I won't find anything."

"So, where do you look?"

Jack laughed out loud.

"I'd have thought that was obvious," he smiled at Kaitlin. She was so smart, so well educated. She knew so much. And yet, in a funny way, she sometimes seemed to 'know' nothing or nothing with certainty. Jack continued, "I look where I know I'm going to find something, of course."

Kaitlin threw him an old-fashioned look and stumped on. They had reached the end of the first valley and made the left turn into the second when the sound of a helicopter was suddenly upon them. Jack looked around, searching for cover. There was very little. No tall trees grew nearby. Jack grabbed Kaitlin's hand, and they headed for a jumble of large rocks with a few low shrubs growing up in between. They threw themselves down on the ground between several large boulders. Jack pulled the old woollen blanket from his pack and threw it over them.

"Sometimes fools the infrared cameras."

Kaitlin pulled a few handfuls of bracken and leaves over them and then quickly pulled her head in under the blanket. The *thwop-thwop* of the helicopter was quickly growing louder. Soon it was deafening. The downdraft from its rotors threatened to throw off the blanket. Jack and Kaitlin grabbed hold of the edges and held tight. The helicopter seemed to hover overhead for quite a while before moving on. There was no-where to land in the narrow valley, and flying so low was risky. Sudden gusts and updrafts could force the rotors into the valley walls. The helicopter moved off. Jack and Kaitlin kept still until the sound of its engines and rotors could no longer be heard. They sat up, preparing to be on their way, when Kaitlin, whose hearing was a little more acute than Jack's, grabbed his arm and pulled him back down.

"Drone," She whispered, "cunning bastards." A search-and-rescue drone was following the path of the helicopter—a clever trap for the unwary. As the whine of the drone came closer, Kaitlin and Jack hardly dared to breathe. The drone whizzed past overhead, pausing only briefly to sniff the night air. Still, Jack and Kaitlin lay quiet. Only when the sound of the drone had been gone a full minute did they dare to sit up. Jack quickly folded the blanket and squeezed it back into his pack.

"Come on. It's not far now."

Jack's idea of 'not that far' and Kaitlin's were not the same. After another hour following the narrow track in the dark, Kaitlin had had enough.

"What bit of 'not that far' am I not understanding, Jack?" Her faint Irish brogue stronger under stress.

"Here, let me take your pack. It's less than a kilometre now, I promise."

"You will not take my pack. How dare you suggest that I need you to take my pack." Kaitlin flared. She was tired and frightened and utterly pissed off. Jack came closer, slowly, as though approaching a ticking bomb.

"I'm sorry, Kaitlin. It's been years since I walked this track. It seemed shorter in memory. We'll stay the night at TJs, and you can have a hot shower and some hot food." The care and concern emanating from Jack were undeniable. Kaitlin took his hand.

"Sorry, my love. It's just been a hard couple of days." They walked on in silence, listening avidly for the faintest sound of pursuit. Less than half an hour later, they rounded a sharp bend in the trail. Down below, in the middle distance, a few lights could be seen. Despite their exhaustion, Jack and Kaitlin picked up their pace, and a few minutes later, they walked into the camping ground. Other than the lights, the place seemed deserted. Jack approached the little shack situated at the far edge of the camping ground. He tapped lightly on the door. There was the sound of chair legs scraping on a wooden floor, and moments later, the door opened, and an enormous man walked out.

"Should have known it'd be you." The man smiled.

"Been a while, Milan. I take it you've had visitors."

"Yep. The helicopter set down in the field. They said they were looking for two fugitives."

"Yeah?"

"Yep, they said it was a matter of national security."

"Really, they said that?"

"Yep."

"National security, ay? Any danger of a hot shower and something to eat, mate?"

"Too easy. You know where everything is." The man turned to head back into the shack before turning back for a moment.

"Evening Kaitlin. Excuse my rudeness. Give me half an hour, and I'll have the chalet made up for you."

"Thanks, Milan, it's good to see you. Got any alpaca jumpers?"

"I'll open up the kiosk when you're ready. You can have a sticky beak around."

At that moment, Kaitlin heard the not-to-distant sound of a drone.

"Drone. We need to hide."

Milan stood aside and indicated that Jack and Kaitlin should hide in the shack. As the drone appeared over the hillside, Milan turned and walked towards it. A small, piercing searchlight swept the ground as it approached. Milan gave it a friendly wave as it came closer, eventually hovering at eye height about two metres in front of him. A tinny voice emanated from a small speaker at the front of the drone.

"Have you seen anyone? Has anyone come through here?"

"Nah. As I told your mate, no one comes here in winter. No one much comes here in summer either, for that matter. I can offer you a great deal on a weekend getaway if that's of interest?"

"Call the number you were given immediately if you see anyone." The searchlight flicked off. The drone lifted sharply up and disappeared back the way it had come. Only a tiny blinking red light indicated its passage. Milan watched it out of sight. He turned back to the shack and tapped on the door.

"All clear."

Jack and Kaitlin poked their heads out the door, checking for any untoward sound.

"Thanks, Milan."

"Right. Shower, dinner, and bed." Milan hummed happily to himself as he headed off to prepare the chalet.

THE PERGAMON REPORT

Jack and Kaitlin headed for the shower block, with Kaitlin in the lead. Out of long habit rather than any immediate social pressure, Jack, observing the proprieties, walked around to the men's block. The men's and women's blocks were separated by a high tiled wall that went most of the way to the roof. Jack finished first.

"I'm done," he shouted over the wall, "I'm going to fuel up the ute and charge the battery."

"OK, love, I'm going to be in here for two hours at the very least." Kaitlin laughed, it was probably an exaggeration, but one never knew. A little less than an hour later, Kaitlin emerged. She was clean and warm and had changed into the spare clothes from her pack. She found Jack and Milan chatting beside Jack's ute. Two large fuel cans lay empty on their sides beside an opened slab of beer. Two fat cables snaked from a device on the bench in Milan's oversized garage to the battery in Jack's ute.

"That's what I've been trying to tell you, Milan. The OneMind told us that the veil will fall permanently. You're going to have bewildered groups of semi-conscious Wollemi wandering all over."

"Not a problem," Milan's huge frame leaned over the battery charger. "It's gonna take all night, mate." Milan indicated the charger with a nod of his head. Milan continued.

"I've got no problem with the Wollemi. I reckon we're pretty much alike, them and me. I live off-grid in the wilderness. I don't need modern trappings. Except for the satellite, of course. Couldn't do without that."

"That reminds me," Kaitlin jumped in before Jack could lead the conversation off into some byway of his own, "Can I use your internet to check my emails?"

"Yep, no worries. The laptop's on the table in the shack. Password's 'Campbelltown Blues', the 'o' is a zero, and there's an exclamation mark at the end."

"Is that the title of a song?"

"Nah, it's the name of my footy club. I grew up in the hills near Campbelltown. Should be a song, though, the way they've been playing lately."

"Oh, right."

"Matter of fact, that's the main reason I go on the internet these days, to watch their games and get the results."

"Everyone belongs to something, I guess." Kaitlin turned and walked from the garage, leaving the boys to chat.

The laptop was turned on. Kaitlin entered the password and was immediately presented with a live news update. Milan liked to keep himself informed, too, it seemed. The screen was filled with a photo-montage of seven faces: She was there, with Jack, Alice and Tom, Emma and Aine and a very old photo of Max. The words "*The One-Mind is Dying*" were emblazoned across the top of the image. Kaitlin clicked on the story. It was a reasonably factual account of the message from the OneMind, plus a bit of back story on the seven people in the photograph and a few background pieces entitled 'Who are the Wollemi?', 'What is the OneMind?' and 'What is The Veil?'. Kaitlin quickly logged into her email. It would take the authorities a little longer to detect her activities and location from the satellite connection, but still, she didn't have long. Kaitlin scanned through the few unread emails, coming quickly to the one she wanted. The subject line said, "Translation of inscription found in the cave - Draft".

Kaitlin sat and read the message from the Egyptologists at the Pergamon. It was long and contained many strange words and phrases. It was hard going, but there was a summary at the end, written in somewhat plainer language.

"An initial translation of the inscription found in a cave in NSW, Australien, reveals five key points:

First, the inscription appears genuine in that the form in which the hieroglyphics were carved is correct for an Egyptian author of the middle kingdom period.

Second, the language itself, as opposed to the hieroglyphics, appears to be an abbreviated form associated with trading languages used at the time of the middle kingdom.

Third, an inescapable conclusion is that at least one person familiar with Middle Kingdom language and hieroglyphic carving techniques carved the inscription.

Fourth, the metallic covering seen on the hieroglyphics is assumed to be gold leaf. If this is so, then the inscription must have been of great import at the time of its making.

Fifth, the inscription itself is a message of thanks to the 'God of the Forest' for the gift of second sight. (Note: the hieroglyph used is based on the glyph for Osiris but is surrounded by six spearhead-shaped glyphs indicating trees.) The message concludes with the statement that the eventual re-joining of the two peoples at the prophesied time is anticipated with joy. The inscription ends with an admonishment to hide the trigger, or perhaps the key, for all time, or until such time as it is needed."

The email included a single recommendation, "A geophysical study of the cave should be completed to ascertain the age of the inscription and the materials used."

Kaitlin sat back. There was a key or a trigger, and she and Jack were meant to find it. This had to be the OneMind's doing, all of it. Theirs was just one tiny piece in a puzzle constructed in humanity's deep past. All those centuries ago, the OneMind foresaw this moment. Not the exact form it would take, not the players of the moment, but the essence of it. That some future human would translate the inscription and find the key, or trigger, or whatever it was. But for what? What would this key unlock? What incomprehensible change would it trigger? Once again, Kaitlin realised they were dealing with a being of superhuman intellect, extraordinary powers, and a purview of centuries, if not hundreds of centuries. Should they trust the OneMind this time? Could they? Would it make any difference whether they trusted it or not? Maybe this very conundrum was at the heart of the human fear both of inevitable, deterministic fate and, equally, of free will. Either way, you were snookered.

Kaitlin logged out of her email and switched off the computer, at the same time flicking the off switch on the satellite uplink, cutting TJs off from the outside world.

There were voices outside and the scrunch of boots on gravel. The two men had finished in the garage. Kaitlin moved the laptop to one side, sliding it under the mound of papers that sat on the table. The door opened, and the two men walked in. First came Jack, followed by Milan, who had to turn half sideways to manoeuvre his bulk through the doorway.

"Chalet's ready. Ute's good to go once the battery's charged. I'll fix you up with something to eat." Milan made his way through to the kitchen of his little shack. Once he was out of earshot, Kaitlin updated Jack.

"There was an email from the Pergamon."

"And?"

Kaitlin looked around, checking once again that Milan was out of earshot.

"There's a key or a trigger. The inscription didn't say what it was a key to or what exactly it triggered, but I think it's hidden in the cave."

"Wow."

"Yes. The OneMind has been planning whatever it's planning for thousands of years."

"Well, we know what it's planning. Don't we?"

"Do we?"

"It's planning to bring down the veil and reunite us humans with our Wollemi cousins."

"Simple as that?"

"Look, Kaitlin, we both know things are never simple with the OneMind. But the intent is clear, don't you think?"

"I guess so, as far it goes." Kaitlin paused, drumming her fingers gently on the table, "But just how far does it go, I wonder? What will happen when the veil comes down."

"We have no way of knowing. Not for sure. But when the two worlds are brought back into phase with each other, there's bound to be some weird stuff, right?"

"You'd have thought so." Kaitlin and Jack fell silent. The sounds coming from the shack's kitchen suggested food would soon be on the table. Kaitlin listened to Milan's emotional flow. He was content. She could hear him humming something familiar, a little out of tune.

"He doesn't get many visitors these days." Jack walked around to where Kaitlin was sitting and placed his hands on her shoulders, "We'll get a good night's sleep and be off at first light."

A few moments later, Milan came back in with two steaming plates.

"Spaghetti carbonara. Best I could do at short notice." Milan plonked the two plates down on the overloaded table in front of his guests, "Bon appetite." He set down a couple of forks and spoons and headed back into the kitchen. "I'll make some tea."

Kaitlin and Jack dug into the steaming plates of pasta sitting in front of them. They would have eaten almost anything. Even chilli dogs sounded OK.

"This is fantastic," Kaitlin called out. Milan poked his head through the doorway.

"Online cooking lessons," Milan smiled, "glad you like it."

A moment or two later, Milan came back in with three large mugs of tea and an unopened packet of Tim-Tam biscuits.

"That was one of my first great discoveries when I was newly arrived in Australia," Kaitlin quickly swallowed her last mouthful of spaghetti, "Tim-Tams. Without doubt, Australia's greatest contribution of the culinary arts."

"What about Vegemite?" Jack smiled. Kaitlin was always getting herself into trouble over questions like this.

"Don't think you can catch me out on that one, Jack Hexenkriege," Kaitlin raised an eyebrow threateningly.

"So, what was your second great discovery then?" Milan found a third chair and sat. Kaitlin softened a little. She reached out and took her husband's hand, "Jack Hexenkriege." A gesture guaranteed to make her taciturn outback miner squirm.

"Yes, well. We'll be off at first light Milan. Can't thank you enough for all your help, mate."

"No worries, Jack. You'd do the same for me."

"Look, Milan. There's trouble brewing. The military are going to want to carpet-bomb the Table of the Gods and all the surrounding area. I have no idea how far they'll set their perimeter, but you may be in real danger, mate, even this far out."

"Thanks, Jack, and understood mate, but I'll take my chances. There're some deep caves up back of here. I'll be careful."

"The world's changing again, Milan, and this time the change may be even bigger than last time."

"I always wanted to visit the Dreamtime, and now the Dreamtime is coming to me."

"That it is Milan. It's coming to all of us." Kaitlin set down her mug, "and now, if you will excuse me, I'm off to collapse in a heap."

Jack and Kaitlin stood, exhausted from a daylong route march. Their bellies were full, and they were warm. Above all, they were safe for now.

"I'll take a look in the kiosk in the morning if that's all right?"

"Absolutely. Give me a knock. I'll probably be up anyway."

"And you'll give us mates rates, right?" Jack grinned broadly.

"Steady there, Tiger. We don't know each other that well."

"Milan. You cut me to the quick, mate."

"We'll depends on how much you want to buy, I guess."

"Oh, it'll be a lot, Milan. You can count on that. Kaitlin will have made a list as long as your arm."

Milan laughed, "Get off to bed, the pair of you. I've got a mound of washing up to do."

As Kaitlin and Jack walked across the paddock, they heard, or per-haps they imagined they heard, far off towards Mount Yengo, the sound of a helicopter, circling.

It was a moonless night. In the blackness overhead, the Milky Way was clearly visible. A blanket of stars twinkled, ageless and indifferent to the goings-on of mere humans.

TRICK OR TREAT

They slept like logs. No dreams troubled them. No night sounds or fears of pursuit clouded their slumbers. The sound of the alarm from Kaitlin's phone at four-thirty the following morning impinged slowly upon her befuddled mind. Suddenly she was sitting up. It was still dark. She grabbed for the phone, desperately hoping to shut the damned thing off, accidentally dropping it onto the carpet. In reaching down to pick it up, Kaitlin leaned over just a little too far and found herself slipping unceremoniously onto the floor. She landed on top of the phone, swad-dled in blankets, struggling to break free—the phone, unperturbed, beeped insistently beneath her. In falling, she had pulled with her the majority of the bedding. It wasn't a good look. While attempting to preserve any remaining shreds of dignity, Kaitlin redoubled her strug-gle to free herself. As she did so, a light went on. Jack appeared around the foot of the bed.

"A simple 'good morning' would have worked just as well."

Jack held out his hand and helped his writhing wife to her feet. Kaitlin grabbed the phone and silenced it.

"Thank you, dear," Kaitlin picked up the offending bedding and flung it onto the bed. "You take the first shower. I'll make tea." No morning, no matter how fraught with uncertainty, could possibly start without a strong cup of tea. As far as Kaitlin was concerned, that was an article of faith, a basic human right and a natural law all rolled into one. She found the little kettle and the sealed pack of teabags. 'English Breakfast Tea,' she noted in passing. Strong Irish Breakfast Tea would have been better, but beggars can't be choosers - as her sainted mother often used to say.

The sounds of Jack showering came from the chalet's little bathroom. He was singing, sort of. Snatches of The Wild Colonial Boy wafted indistinctly into the bedroom. Kaitlin tidied up the bed a bit and collected her things. She pulled the curtain back a couple of centimetres and peaked out into the darkness. There was a light on in Milan's shack. She finished making the tea and set two mugs down on the little table. Out of long habit, Kaitlin checked her phone for messages. There were none, of course, she had left her phone on flight mode as a precaution, and in any case, she reminded herself, there was no phone signal this far into the wilderness. She sat and drank her tea and contemplated the day ahead.

"We'll have to take the ute back to the cave." She called out through the bathroom door. "We have to find the Egyptian key."

The was a muffled "Ummmff" from the bathroom. Jack may have heard what she said.

"That's imperative, Jack. And then we have to figure out what on Earth it's for. That's also imperative. And we must not get caught. That's imperative too."

Was that a single imperative in three parts or three separate imperatives? Kailin wondered. Philosophy had never been her strong point.

Jack entered the bedroom, steaming in the chill air of a winter's morning. He dropped the towel and reached for his clothes. Kaitlin watched as he dressed. He was still fit and strong, his zest for life as powerful as ever. Jack noticed her watching him dress.

"Calm yourself, woman. I can't help it." Jack smiled and proceeded to dress very, very slowly.

"Oh, for goodness' sake. What is it about men? I was miles away. Sure, I barely noticed you'd walked back into the room."

"Jezebel," Jack leapt across the room, scooping up his wife in one swift movement and depositing her upon the half-made bed, "I'm a person too, you know. I have feelings."

"And I know precisely what those feelings are too. Get off me, you brute. Unhand me, sir." Kaitlin made desultory attempts to struggle.

"I will not. Not until I've had a good morning kiss and you've apologised for objectifying me."

Kaitlin, giggling, managed to adopt a more or less apologetic expression.

"I'm sorry for treating you like my toy boy."

"And."

"I'm sorry for thinking of you as a hunk of burning love."

"And."

"I know you have a mind too." That was the thing about being an empath, she did know what his feelings for her were, and he knew hers for him. They lay together on the unmade bed for a few moments more.

"Your tea's getting cold. I'm going to jump into the shower." Kaitlin wriggled free of her captor and, grabbing her clothes, headed for the shower. Jack finished dressing, drank the tea in a few swift gulps, and headed over to Milan's shack. A very slight change from black to grey suggested the coming of daylight. A spreading glow from the east heralded the coming dawn. It was going to be a grey day, misty and damp. Ideal for evading prying eyes.

Milan must have heard Jack's footsteps on the gravel path. The door to his shack opened, and Milan emerged, crabwise, as he adjusted his huge bulk through the opening. He was carrying a supermarket shopping bag.

"You and your missus are all over the internet. They're searching for you far and wide. The rumour is you've headed for Queensland via the backcountry."

"Figures."

"You need to get going right now, mate. They could come back here at any moment."

"We'll be out of your hair in a few minutes. Sorry to put you in this position."

"It's not that, and you know it, Jack Hexenkriege."

"Yes. Sorry mate."

Milan handed Jack the shopping back.

"What's this?"

"Breakfast."

Kaitlin, who had been monitoring the emotional backwash from the two men, leapt from the shower, made a pitiful attempt to dry herself and get dressed as quickly as she could. Milan's emotional flow had been tense and nervy. Jack's thoughts had been calm, pensive. He was in 'planning' mode. She recognised the pattern. When, suddenly, Jack had snapped to 'alert and watchful', Kaitlin knew something was up.

Jack took the shopping bag and turned toward the little kiosk.

"Can I grab a couple of things for Kaitlin?"

"Sure." The two men crunched across the gravel to the kiosk. As they did so, Kaitlin emerged from the chalet carrying both their packs. She dumped them by the ute and sprinted over to the kiosk.

"Though I trust you implicitly, Jack, a woman likes to choose her own clothes."

"I know exactly what you like anyway." Jack stepped aside to allow Kaitlin to enter. He and Milan stayed outside.

"Do you have anything in a sage green or rust colour?" Jack whispered.

"We do, as a matter of fact. How did you know?"

"I didn't. But those are Kaitlin's colours. You wait and see."

The light in the east had become a distinct ridge across the top of the adjacent hill when Jack called out.

"Time to go now, Kaitlin. It's getting light."

Kaitlin emerged with a dark green jumper, a reddish cardigan, a green beanie and gloves. Jack gave Milan a wink.

"Oh, you think you're so clever, don't you, Jack?"

"I do, as a matter of fact." Jack removed a small plastic pill box from his jacket and handed it to Milan.

"Gold nuggets, we can't do a credit transfer without the internet, and we don't want to leave a trace."

"There's no need…" Jack cut Milan off mid-sentence.

"Thanks for everything, mate. You need to pack up and head for the caves this morning. I don't know how long you've got. How long any of us have got."

The two men shook hands. There was nothing more to be said.

Jack and Kaitlin walked over to the ute. Jack threw the two packs onto the tiny back seat, and they were off. A glowing bar of light now lit the tops of the hills. Down in the valley, it was still somewhat dark. Milan waved goodbye as Jack gunned the old ute along the dirt track back towards Putty Road.

"There's a small 4-wheel drive track off to the left just before the main road. We can take that to the crossing point, and then another track, the other side of Putty Road will take us close to the cave."

Kaitlin nodded. They were driving fast on dirt roads in the early dawn of a new day, and the special forces of two nations were hunting for them. But she was with Jack, and this was his turf—good enough odds. Katlin searched the shopping bag that Jack had placed between them. Breakfast consisted of two rounds of vegemite sandwiches and two rounds with crunchy peanut butter.

"Here you go," Kaitlin passed half a sandwich to Jack, "vegemite sandwich, breakfast of champions."

Jack took the sandwich, "Better put on your seat belt, the track's gonna be rough, and I can't afford to slow down too much."

"What will happen to Milan? Will he be all right?"

"He'll be OK. He has a place to lay low. Several, actually."

Jack slowed the ute very slightly.

"OK, hold on," The ute turned left onto a narrow track. The way was marked only by the marginally lower level of weeds filling the ruts. "No one's been down here for a while, by the looks of it. It's going to be a bumpy ride."

Aine woke first. It was just getting light. The night chill hung still in every room. The floor tiles were cold. She quickly found her slippers and dressing gown and padded through to the kitchen to put on the kettle. She heard the thump as Tommy jumped down from Emma's bed. Tommy was an animal of fixed routine. First, he liked to be let out the back. Then, when he came back in, he would greet Aine by meticulously licking her ankles. After which, she was to place his breakfast in his bowl. Such was the even tenor of his days. Aine grabbed the key and unlocked the back door leaving it open for the dog. A moment later, Tommy walked into the kitchen as expected. Instead of making for the backyard, he crept up to Aine and bumped her with his head. Aine looked down and gave the old dog a pat.

"What's up, Tommy?" In reply, Tommy merely sat down, half across her feet, and refused to budge.

"You're in a funny mood this morning, aren't you?" Tommy glanced meaningfully toward the open back door and looked back up at Aine.

"Do you want me to come outside with you?" Tommy stood and took a few steps towards the door, pausing to look back at Aine. Aine followed slowly, unease creeping in through the unguarded byways of the subconscious. She gasped as she stepped off the veranda into the modest backyard. All along the fence and on the branches of the old gum tree sat row after row of Kookaburras, silent and seemingly intent. Without thinking, she stepped back onto the veranda, leaving Tommy outside in the yard. The sight of kookaburras in the yard was not at all uncommon. But typically, they would come in twos and threes and could be relied upon to begin their maniacal cackling at around five in the morning and continue until the entire neighbourhood was wide awake. This was different. This was wrong. Max would know what it meant. He would know what to do. Tommy joined her on the porch and proceeded to lick her ankles. Aine snapped out of her momentary indecision and rushed back into the kitchen with Tommy, slamming the door shut behind her. She tiptoed into the lounge where Max was sleeping. Frozen once more by indecision, Aine stared at her great-grandfather, watching his chest rise and fall. Tommy, ever practical and fully cognisant of the proprieties, wandered over to the sleeping form and began a judicious regimen of face licking. Max stirred. Tommy continued. At last, Max woke and stared around groggily.

"Max, you have to come and see this. I don't know what it means."

It took Max a few more moments to orient himself in space and time. He stood up, wrapping himself in a blanket and followed Aine through the kitchen and into the yard. The kookaburras were still there, silent sentinels, waiting. Max stared about at the gathered ranks. He walked out into the yard and approached the nearest group of birds. Focussing his mind and his emotions, Max projected an image of himself returning to the collective, overlaying the mental image with a sense of certainty and purpose. He had understood their silent message. He would return. Slowly, in twos and threes, the birds began to take flight, disappearing into the surrounding woodlands. Far off, out of sight, the cackling of a hundred Kookaburras started up. Aine rushed to her great-grandfather. She was finely attuned by now to his thought-flow and had easily picked up the emotional thread.

"I have only just met you. Emma will be crushed. Please don't leave us now."

Max turned and smiled. "I am not leaving straight away, but soon. And when the veil comes down forever, we will be reunited."

Aine took her great-grandfather's hand. Fear and reassurance threatened to swamp her emotions, each vying for dominance, neither giving an inch.

"What will happen when the veil comes down forever?"

"I don't know for sure. No one does, except maybe the OneMind, and it's not said anything definitive."

"Will things sort of bump into each other?" Aine stared off across the forest in the direction of the Table of the Gods, "Will the Wollemi caves suddenly appear in people's gardens and stuff like that?"

"From what I could gather, there is some kind of conservation law that will interleave our two realities as the two worlds move back into phase with one another."

"What does that mean, really?"

"Honestly, I don't know."

Max and Aine stood in the yard, abandoned now by its early morning visitors.

"Strange things will happen, though. I'm sure of that. You can't bring two worlds back into phase after so many centuries without some odd juxtapositions turning up."

"And the Wollemi? Will they be safe?"

"That's what worries me most. The OneMind surely would not abandon its people unless it absolutely had to."

"Wouldn't it?" Aine, pensive and brooding, turned and walked back into the kitchen. The kettle had long since boiled. She switched it on for a second time and set out two mugs for tea. Max walked back in, accompanied by Tommy.

"Toast? I'm making tea."

Max sat, the domesticity of the scene both familiar and strange.

"What was Jack like growing up?"

"Jack was a handful. He'd disappear into the forest sometimes and reappear two or three days later, serene as could be, as though nothing had happened."

"What did he do alone in the forest? Did he say?"

"He was never one for idle chatter. As far as I could get him to explain, he said he was just exploring."

"Did you try to stop him?"

"I thought about it, but Jerry, that was Jack's elder brother, said there was no point. He said it was who Jack was, and there was no point trying to change him." Max paused, "You're very like Jerry. Now I come to think about it, physically, you're kind of slight and dark-skinned like him, and mentally I'm coming to realise you're eerily smart, also like Jerry."

Aine made no reply. She had no idea who her father was. Her mum's story was that Aine was the result of a one-night stand with some guy she met in a Newtown bar when she was a student. Not a great 'you were deeply wanted' conversation.

"And Emma? What was my mum like as a girl?"

Max smiled at that. He reached out and took his great-granddaughter's hand.

"She was a lot like you too. She was wise beyond her years, and she had a similar connection to the OneMind."

"She could talk to the OneMind?"

"Not exactly, but she had this kind of sixth sense. She knew things and understood things you would not expect of a young girl. I realised after a while that her Wollemi ancestry somehow gave her access, even if only subconsciously, to the shared consciousness of her Wollemi relatives."

"And me, do you think I have the same thing?"

"I think you do, in a way. Everyone is different. Jerry could use the intellectual power of the OneMind to figure out complex problems with just a few pieces of evidence. He called it his 'gestalt'."

"And Jack?"

"Jack could feel the earth and trees, he understood the wild things, and they somehow understood him. He was at one with the forest. It is his home, really, his place."

"When will you go back to the collective?"

"I need to show Tom some things, and I need to make sure the message of the OneMind has landed properly."

"Landed?"

"I need to understand what the powers-that-be intend. The whole world will change. The Wollemi will change, and they will change us."

"Change? Change how?"

"I don't know. But we are not tame, we are not domesticated, as a species, and neither are the Wollemi."

"What do you mean, not tame?"

"We are both humans and Wollemi in the state that nature has left us in. Just because the Wollemi have no weapons and do not fight wars do not suppose that they are powerless. They are not."

"And neither are we."

"And neither are we." Max took a long sip of tea. Domesticity had only ever been a small part of his life.

"Will there be a war?"

"The Wollemi will not initiate aggression. Their instinct is to assimilate dissenting voices into the collective. But they are changing, have changed. They are developing the power of independent reason."

"Is that bad?"

"Good and bad. Just take a look at us. Over our history, there has not been one crazy belief that some human beings have not espoused."

Aine tried to imagine a world in which there were individually self-conscious, reasoning Wollemi. Telepathic, empathic, and able to act as one everywhere on Earth. The image that came to her was one of global contradiction and dissonance. The individual versus the collective, inherent knowledge versus the reasoned and understood, the known versus the speculative. It made no sense. It was a vision in which nothing quite seemed to add up.

"I'm scared." Aine grabbed her great-grandfather's hand. Max reached out a wrapped a comforting arm around her.

"I don't know how, I can't really imagine how, but I am sure it will work out in the end. What I was able to see when connected to the OneMind, was a great gamble, made on the basis of a calculation computed by a massive intelligence for over a hundred thousand years."

"Still a gamble then." Aine squeezed Max's hand.

"Life's a gamble, Aine, but it's the only game in town."

There was a sound from Emma's bedroom. Tommy lifted himself up and waddled off to investigate. A few moments later, Emma drifted in, tousled and only half awake. Aine knew better than to engage her mother in scintillating conversation first thing. She set down a steaming mug of tea for her and proceeded to cut thick slices of bread for toast. Max, too, held his peace. He was thinking about Aine and about the suddenly realised fact that she really was very, very like Jerry.

After a while, when Aine had plied Emma with tea and hot buttered toast, she deemed it safe to speak.

"Max is going back to the collective soon."

"Are you? When?"

"I'm not sure. I've got a few things to sort out first. I need to show Tom some stuff."

"Max talked to the kookaburras this morning. There were dozens of them waiting for him in the backyard."

Emma, taking Aine's pronouncement as a sort of joke, asked, "What did they want?"

"They wanted to know when he was heading back to the collective. As soon as he told them, they all flew off."

Realising that it was not a joke, Emma turned to Max.

"Really? The One Mind sent them to find out when you would return?"

"Yes."

"It can do that?"

Max made no reply. Emma sat bolt upright, suddenly very much awake. Turning her attention to Aine, she asked, "And you sensed it? You sensed both the message and the answer?"

"I suppose so, yes." Aine had never really tried to disentangle what it was she picked up from the people in her life, those she was close to. But now that she came to think of it, her level of connection was pretty much telepathic at times. Max, who had been listening to the exchange, cleared his throat to speak. Emma and Aine turned towards him.

"Emma, I never thought to ask before, but who was Aine's father? How did you meet?"

"He was just some guy I met in a bar...." Emma's voice petered out. She shook her head and continued, "No. I met him in the forest near the cottage. He never spoke. I never knew his name. It was as though I was in a dream or sleepwalking."

"She does that," Aine cut in, 'she sleepwalks quite a lot, actually." Then, as realisation pushed its way up through her consciousness, Aine turned to face her mother.

"Why did you never tell me this?" Aine's face betrayed her shock. Feelings of betrayal and confusion emanated strongly from her.

"I only have the fuzziest memory, to be honest," Emma reached over and placed an arm around her daughter, "I was ashamed, I think, and confused. I was never sure exactly what happened."

"What do you remember?" Max's voice was hushed, intent.

"I remember meeting the man. It was a warm afternoon. There was a very light breeze. The scent of eucalyptus was strong," Emma paused for a moment, "We never spoke, as far as I can remember. We undressed and lay on the grass and made love. He was silent and gentle. Afterwards, I fell asleep, and when I woke up, he was gone."

Max leaned back, wondering whether or not to ask his next question, but it could not wait.

"Was the man Wollemi? Could he have been?"

Emma was silent—her emotional stream broadcast confusion and anger.

"I suppose so. Yes, he could have been." She was silent again for a moment, then "The OneMind got me pregnant. How dare it? How dare it use me like that."

Aine began to cry silently at first before bursting into floods of uncontrollable sobs.

Both Emma and Max slipped off their chairs and wrapped Aine in a warm embrace.

"We love you, Aine. I love you. I was so happy to find out I was pregnant. I was so delighted to be having you. You know that, don't you? You've always been very much wanted."

Aine stifled her sobs enough to say, "You never planned to have me. I was an accident or worse."

"Being unplanned doesn't mean being unwanted. You are the most important thing in my life. I'm angry, though, at the OneMind. I'm not a prize heifer to be bred." Emma hugged Aine close. Max turned and walked back towards the lounge where he had spent the night.

"I'm going to have a shower and get dressed. We need to get back to the cottage pronto. The OneMind's message was a warning. We need to get away while we can."

THE RETURN OF THE SACRED

The gathering proceeded slowly at first. The Elders considered the matter placed before them from all sides. Over a period of several hours, a consensus began to emerge. The sacred Dreamtime was returning, not in the distant future, not for some far-off generation, but imminently and for them. What had started as a grave council of the surviving clans soon became a celebration. Large fires were built. Sacred dances were shared. The word went out across the wilderness, across the red centre to all parts of the continent. The veil would fall, the clans would at last return home to their ancestral world. Their age-long wait would soon be over.

It was sometime later that the other side of the message began to sink in. Australian and US special forces were searching the forest for the OneMind. The military planned to carpet bomb the wilderness, centring on Mount Yengo. They planned to destroy the Dreamtime itself. As understanding grew among the gathered clans, silence descended. Cold fury replaced celebration. For fifty thousand years and more, the clans had watched over the Dreamtime. Long before the emergence of civilisation in other parts of the world, the clans had been fulfilling their age-old duty.

More messages were sent—urgent voices called even to the most remote communities. The Summoning had begun in earnest. Slowly but slowly, the meeting place filled with those who lived closest. Messages received informed of delegations setting off from all corners of the ancient continent. Never in the history of the Aboriginal peoples would such a gathering have been seen. Word had been received even from the peoples of the Torres Strait that they would send a delegation. The people were intent, focussed. They needed a plan. The assembled groups each delegated one of their number to form a leadership group. The leadership group moved to a relatively unoccupied part of the meeting ground, and themselves chose a leader. It didn't take long. Soon Alice found herself standing at the centre of the Elders of several dozen clans.

"The moment that our peoples have waited for patiently for thousands of years will soon be upon us. The Dreamtime is returning. Ours is a time of great promise, but it is also a time of great risk. Ours is a time of dreams, a time of songs, and it is a time of great danger. We must act both to protect and to contain the Dreaming. We cannot allow the Dreamtime to be destroyed. It is ours, it belonged to our ancestors, and it will belong to our children. And not just to our children, but to all children, everywhere. At the same time, we cannot allow the dreaming to control us. We must find a way to rejoin our two bloodlines. We were cast out a long, long time ago. At long last, we are going home."

Alice fell silent. There was silence all around. Even the sounds of the Gathering seemed to grow distant and faint. And then, amongst the leaders of the Elders came a growing awareness. In ones and twos, they became aware of a small, indistinct voice, far off speaking. As the collective empathic awareness of the Elders came together into one, the distant voice became clear. It was the voice of the OneMind.

"Listen to me. The time is almost upon us. Our moment has come. The next few days will see the culmination of our

great experiment. We will either live together or die to-gether. The choice is ours."

The intense emotional and empathic confluence emanating from the leaders was picked up amongst the greater gathering of Elders and spread like wildfire. Within seconds, hundreds and then thousands of the gathered throng and those truckloads just arriving were swept up in the message from the OneMind. Amongst and within those gathered, a single shared thought emerged, a conclusion and a decision in one. There would be no holding back. Nothing would be held in reserve. The ancient guardians of that most ancient of all lands would act and act as one.

"We all know, each in our own way, what must be done. We have our own individual stories passed down through the ages, and we have our shared story. In every case, though the journey may be different, the destination is the same. Go now, raise your people. Organise for the time to come. I call now upon all our peoples. I call for the One Thousand. Bring your bullroarers and your clapsticks. This is the time for unity, a time for arm-blood and sacrifice. We go to war to fight for peace."

A sound was heard then in the ancient gathering place of the peoples, a sound such as had never before been heard. It was the sigh of a thousand voices, almost a groan, of fear, of acknowledgement, and of acceptance. And then, quickly and calmly, the gathering dispersed. As Alice looked around, here and there, from each group representing each clan's country, a single person walked towards her. Heads held high, brows unfurrowed, eyes clear and unworried, the One Thousand had begun to assemble. There were men and women, old and young, and there, slightly off to one side, picking her way through the detritus of the day, came the young Elder who had spoken earlier. Killara, that was it. That was her name.

Alice waited as the meeting ground cleared, leaving only the slowly growing group of Elders, the beginnings of the One Thousand whom, it had been prophesied, would face the OneMind when the Dreamtime returned. Tom stood there, too, outside the circle slowly forming around Alice.

Alice spoke, "Tom, you are an Elder of your people, are you not."

"I am, yes."

"Then come, join us. What will happen here in the next few days will impact us all."

As Tom approached, a way was made for him.

"This is Tom, my partner and Elder of the Comanche people."

"Partner?" Tom whispered, "When were you going to let me in on that?

Alice smiled and, reaching out, pulled him closer.

"Well, I'm telling you now."

"You may kiss the bride." Laughing, Killara, who had slipped in close behind Tom, gave him a gentle push. There was nothing for it but to comply. Alice and Tom kissed, and as they did so, their emotional backwash splashed out across the gathered onlookers.

"Eeeww, get a room." Killara was enjoying herself. A gentle ripple of laughter spread across the crowd.

"Ok, to business," Alice struggled to regain a modicum of decorum, "We will stay here tonight to allow the others to join us, and tomorrow we head for Mount Yengo and the Table of the Gods."

People began to move away. The sun was lowering in the sky. They still had time before dark to organise themselves for the night. The mood was sombre now. Reality had finally set in. There was no way of knowing how things would play out. What would happen if they bumped into the combined Australian and US special forces? Who could tell? But since they were headed to the one place the military knew to look, a confrontation of some kind seemed inevitable. What use would clapsticks and bullroarers be against automatic weapons? Time would tell.

There was plenty to think about as the One Thousand began to bed down for the night. Fires were lit, but there was little singing or dancing. Here and there, small groups spoke in low voices. Overhead the brilliant Milky Way, crisp and clear above the darkness of the wilderness, wheeled across the heavens, as it had always done, caring naught for the affairs of Earth.

Throughout the night, individual representatives continued to arrive. By morning their numbers had visibly grown. Tom woke first, and lay quietly at Alice's side, watching her sleep, noting the slow rise and fall of her chest. At last, Alice's eyes flickered and opened. Nearby, kookaburras cackled.

"What's the plan then?" Tom smiled as Alice came awake, "Exactly?"

"Exactly?"

"Yes."

"We will make our stand."

"That's it?"

"Yes."

"We'll make our stand. How will we do that? What does that mean?"

"We are not a military force Tom; the return of the Dreamtime is not a battle."

"You said, 'We go to war to fight for peace'. If it's not a battle, then what is it?"

Alice paused, "I don't know. The battle, if there is one, will be in the mind, a battle of ideas."

"How do we win a battle like that?" Tom was out of his depth. The woman he loved was in danger, and he had no idea what to do about it. This was a new and horrible feeling for him. Alice sensed his disturbance.

"We will join with the OneMind of the Wollemi. We will join with the Wollemi and help them to free themselves from the collective."

"We will use the collective to end the collective."

"Yes. Probably. I don't know for sure. But this is a time of opposites. Can't you feel it?"

Tom paused to check his own feelings. He reached inside himself, seeking his intuitive centre.

"Yes, Yes, I can."

OPEN SESAME

For the most part, the journey back to the Egyptian cave, fortified by vegemite and peanut butter sandwiches, passed reasonably uneventfully. There had been one point at which Jack had pulled the ute off the track and under a massive rock overhang to avoid a passing helicopter, and there had been another rather tense moment a little later, but other than that, they had made reasonably good time.

Jack drove the ute as close as he could get to the cave, but when they stopped under a big old gum tree, they still had the best part of a kilometre to go on foot. Jack took the lead, as always.

"This is getting to be a bit of a habit, isn't it, my love?"

"What is?"

"Root marches through the wilderness. Are you trying to tell me something? Do you think I need to get a bit more exercise?"

Jack paused and turned, "I got us as close as I could."

Kaitlin caught up and gave him a pat on the cheek. "I know, my love; I was just teasing. How long now?"

"Maybe twenty minutes. It gets a bit rougher from here. There's no path, so we will need to push through the bush."

"You always know how to show a girl a good time, Jack Hexenkriege." Kaitlin reached down and gave his bum a quick squeeze, "You lead the way. I like to follow you from behind."

Jack turned and started down a steep hillside, "I know what you're doing, you know."

"And what would that be, Mr Hexenkriege?"

"You're ogling my bum."

"I am most certainly not. Don't you be getting ideas above your station?"

Jack laughed and carried on, pushing through the brush, making a way for Kaitlin to follow. As they forced their way down the hill, through the scrubby bushland, they heard the whine of a drone close by, high-pitched and threatening. There was no knowing how it had found them. It may have been following their heat trail. Jack quickly looked around. They were caught out in the open. There was nowhere to hide. Desperately looking around for decent cover and finding none, Jack and Kaitlin dived to the ground and began to worm their way in under a low-spreading shrub. There was a loud flap of wings and a whoosh of air as some large bird, moving fast, swept above them. Jack and Kaitlin peeked out from what little cover they had found. The sound of the drone grew louder as it topped the hill behind them and began to fly down the slope directly towards them. As it did so, however, faster than the AI driving it could adjust or manoeuvre, a mature wedge-tailed eagle, talons spread, dived from above, took the drone and proceeded, without further ceremony, to rip it to pieces. Jack and Kaitlin lay quite still until the eagle, having satisfied itself that its prey was indeed quite dead, once more flapped its mighty wings and took to the air.

"What was that?" Kaitlin had never seen such a large bird of prey close up before.

"Wedge-tailed eagle. They're not from around here. They generally live up north."

"Well, it made short work of that drone."

"Yes, but the real question is not what was that, but who?"

"Who? What do you mean?"

"In all my years in the bush, I've never seen one this far south."

"I see."

"Do you?"

"Yes, you think it was the OneMind's doing?"

"Yes, I do, but even that may not be the key question."

"Oh?"

"How did it know? Did it plan to have that eagle arrive at that moment, or did it 'forward position' it deliberately, like a general positioning troops?"

They both fell silent. As the possible significance of what had just happened sank in, the eagle circled slowly overhead, returning perhaps to its post.

"No. I can't bring myself to believe it. Not even the OneMind could have foreseen this specific event at this specific time."

"What then?"

"Well, the weather's a lot warmer than it was when I was a young man tramping these hillsides. And people, humans, I mean, have more or less abandoned the wilderness. Maybe wedge-tails are moving back south?"

"Maybe." Kaitlin didn't seem convinced.

"Yeah, Me too. I think the OneMind is revealing more of its true power."

"Maybe there is nothing left for it to play for except protecting its people after it's gone. Maybe the OneMind feels it has nothing left to hide."

"Maybe." This time it was Jack who didn't seem completely satisfied.

"Will they send another drone?"

"Probably, but if they saw it was attacked by a bird, they may not be too suspicious. We have a bit of time, I think. Best get moving."

Jack and Kaitlin wriggled their way out from under the leafy shrub and brushed themselves down. Jack set off at a smart pace down the hillside. Fifteen sweaty minutes later, they arrived at their previous campsite. The Cave was above, hidden by the overhang and the crevice leading to it. The events of only two nights before seemed almost like a dream as they climbed the steep hillside to the little ledge that led into the cave. What would await them in the cave, Kaitlin wondered. Would they find the key? What would it be like? What would it do? Preoccupied with these churning thoughts, it came almost as a surprise to Kaitlin when she found herself once more standing on the ledge, inching her way around the curve of rock and into the cave entrance.

"All clear," Jack called out from the cave entrance.

It had not occurred to Kaitlin that it might not be. She realised that despite the drones, the helicopters, and the pursuing special forces, she had not fully grasped the enormity of her situation.

Eager now to get out of sight, she quickly edged her way to the cave mouth. Inside, Jack had placed a small battery-powered light on a rock ledge. Despite already knowing what was inside, Kaitlin gasped as she entered the cave. The light sparkled off the walls. The ancient gilt glowed with an eery light. She and Jack looked around, wondering where to start their search. There was, standing towards the back of the cave, a tall carved rock, roughly the size and shape of a lectern. Unlike the walls and the ceiling, although it was covered in deeply carved cartouches, it had not been gilded.

"Perhaps it's hollow. Maybe we can lift the lid off." Kaitlin gingerly placed the palms of her hands under the edges of what might have been a lid and lifted. The stone wouldn't budge.

"Jack, come and help me. Maybe it's stuck."

Jack took station on the opposite side of the rock and applied his strength also to lift off the top section. Nothing moved.

"I think it's solid."

"Ok, I'll start at the back of the cave. You start at the front. Look for any crevice of regular carved shape that might conceal a hiding place." Kaitlin set down her pack, removed a small torch and set to work. Jack made his way back to the cave entrance and began to feel his way back along the wall, lightly resting his fingers on the gilded carvings, letting his fingers feel for any slight crack or indentation that might suggest a hiding place. Jack and Kaitlin worked their way back towards each other along one wall and then the other. They each peered at the ceiling, searching minutely for any sign. Their shared sense of frustration growing minute by minute as their painstaking search revealed nothing.

"Right, I'm getting a breath of fresh air." Kaitlin stomped off to the cave's entrance and leaned out, breathing in deeply. As she stepped up onto the flat rock at the entrance, Jack noticed a small cartouche carved low into the side of the step facing him. It was like the carving Kaitlin had shown him that the man from the Pergamon had said might symbolise the God of the Forest. The carving was slightly obscured by thick dust and collected leaves and other detritus. Jack approached and kneeled in front of the step, brushing carefully with his fingers. Yes, this was the same sign. Kaitlin turned back into the cave and saw Jack kneeling inside the entrance staring intently at the floor.

"What have you found?"

"Come and look. It's the Forest God symbol you showed me."

Kaitlin knelt next to Jack and felt her way lightly around the rim of the stone a centimetre or two above the cartouche.

"There's a very slight breeze coming from under the rim."

Jack felt for it too. "Maybe the side comes off, or the top can be removed."

Jack and Kaitlin pushed and pulled, prodded, and poked for a full half hour before giving up in disgust. Kaitlin returned to the cave mouth to fume, and Jack sat himself down on the step and gazed around at the gleaming ancient carvings.

"The God of the Forest is the OneMind, do you reckon?"

"Yep." Kaitlin was not in the mood for idle chatter.

"Do you reckon the OneMind has kept people away from the cave all these years?"

"Yep."

"Do you reckon the OneMind led us here, led you here, I should say, deliberately?"

"Yes. Now I come to think of it. I'm beginning to think that the OneMind uses apparent coincidences to signal its intent."

"There have been a lot of them lately."

"Exactly, but what is it trying to signal to us here, now?"

"How do you mean?"

"Well, are we supposed to find the key and use it, or lead the authorities to this cave for some reason, or what?"

"I think we're here to find the key." Jack leaned back, placing his palms against the far end of the step he was sitting on. Something moved when he did that. Just a tiny movement, a fraction of a millimetre perhaps, but there was movement, nonetheless. Jack swivelled around to investigate. There was a thin section of rock between the end of the stone step and the rim of the cave mouth. Perhaps four fingers wide, running the width of the step. When Jack prodded it, it moved. Immediately Jack brushed the dust and leaves away from the end of the step by the opening. Kaitlin stepped around him and turned from inside the cave to watch what he was doing. After a few attempts at lifting the thin stone section, Jack pushed it first from one side then from the other. On the second attempt, the stone section began to slide. After a bit of pushing and pulling and brushing away dirt and grit, Jack managed to slide the stone section free of the step.

Now what? Jack felt with his fingers to see if he could reach under the top of the step. He could not. Jack and Kaitlin flew into action, once again pushing, pulling, poking, and prodding until every angle of attack had been tried more than once by each of them. Kaitlin stepped out onto the cave mouth once more, broadcasting her frustration at a million decibels. Jack lurched to his feet, turned, and gave the step a savage kick, painfully bruising his toe as he did so. The top of the stone step shifted. Just a tiny bit, but it moved perhaps half a centimetre towards the cave mouth. Kaitlin, who had turned at the sound of Jack's angry cry of pain, jumped back into the cave. Together they pushed what was now revealed as a slab topping the step. Centimetre by centimetre, it moved until the rear edge was flush against the rim of the cave mouth. They tried sliding it off to the left and right. Nothing doing.

Jack felt around the rim once more. The breeze was stronger than it had been. They were making progress.

"Maybe we can lift it off." The slab was too heavy for one person to lift, but together they might be able to shift it.

"May as well give it a go." Kaitlin stepped once more back into the cave and stood next to Jack. Together they managed to get their fingers under the innermost edge of the slab.

"OK, on three," Jack braced his back and legs to pull with all his might, "One, two, three." And with that, Jack and Kaitlin pulled. The stone slab swung upwards easily. Kaitlin staggered backwards. Jack, who had put everything he had into lifting the stone slab, fell backwards, cursing loudly.

"The bloody thing's counterbalanced." Jack got to his feet, brushing off the dust from the cave floor.

"Oh my," Kaitlin was staring down into the space revealed by lifting the slab. The space inside was filled with fine white sand, resting in which was a long, bronze artefact. Neither Jack nor Kaitlin moved. They just stood there for a full minute, wondering what to do. What was it? Was it safe? Was it booby-trapped, like something out of Tomb Raider or Indiana Jones? How long had it lain there?

It was Kaitlin who finally stepped up and prodded the artefact with a forefinger. It moved slightly in the sand, revealing itself to be a bronze tube shaped like a piece of bamboo with several holes cut in it.

"It's a flute." Kaitlin reached down and picked it up, "I learned to play the penny whistle when I was a girl. Can't be that different."

Jack watched as Kaitlin practised what she thought must be the required fingering. She put the ancient instrument to her lips and began to blow gently, a slow, sad air redolent of love and loss. Kaitlin shivered; the sadness of the tune seemed to seep into her bones in the cool, dry air of the cave. Strange harmonics seemed to come from the ancient instrument, some at the edge of hearing and, judging by the regular shimmering of the dust particles suspended in the air around them, some harmonics beyond that. Kaitlin began to play again, this time a lively jig. Out of the corner of her eye, she noticed Jack moving slightly, apparently in time to the music. She turned, still playing, to see him twisting and jerking uncontrollably, his legs kicking and stamping in time, staring ahead blankly. The sight was at once comical and horrifying. Kaitlin let the flute drop back into the white sand. Jack's unnerving movements subsided. After a few moments, his eyes flickered, and he seemed suddenly to come to.

"What happened?" Jack staggered slightly. Kaitlin leaned forward and grabbed his arm, steadying him.

"Here. Sit down." She led Jack to a flat outcrop of rock. For several moments he seemed disoriented and confused. After a while, he shook his head, brushed himself down and stood up.

"I went out like a light the moment you started playing that flute. What the hell is that thing?"

Kaitlin turned from Jack to examine the flute once more.

"It's a Ney, an ancient flute. Perhaps one of the earliest musical instruments." Kaitlin lifted it from the bed of sand where she had dropped it. There was something, some dusty old memory stirring at the back of her mind, trying desperately to surface.

"There's a Sufi poem that talks about the secret of the flute."

"How does it go?"

"I'm trying to remember," Kaitlin closed her eyes, imagining herself back in the old library at Trinity College in Dublin, imagining the silence and the smell, feeling in memory the leather texture of the old book. She had been studying the use of music in occult and religious rituals. Bits and pieces began to come back.

"I can remember a snippet, I think," Kaitlin began to intone,

"Whoever is kept away from his source, he looks after the time of his being united." Then there's another line or two I can't remember, and then it goes, *"I joined the happy ones and sad ones. Each one befriended me through his own thought, but no one could find my inside secrets".*

"What's it about? What does it mean?"

"Well, it's by Rumi, and he was a Sufi, and that's not my area, but I'd hazard a guess it's about separation and loss." Kaitlin tried to remember more of the poem. A couple more lines came to mind.

"It starts something like *Ever since I was cut from my bed, men and women have wept from my sound.*"

"It's pretty upbeat, then?" Kaitlin ignored the interjection.

"And it goes on to say something like *My secret is not far from my lament, but no eye and no ear can see or hear it.*"

"Is any of this any real use to us?" Jack, never a lover of the esoteric and obscure, marched off to the cave mouth to take a breath of fresh air. He was beginning to find the atmosphere in the ancient cave oppressive.

"I don't know. We need to get back to the others. We'll need a fair bit of help putting the pieces of this puzzle together."

Jack gazed from the cave mouth up into the clear blue winter's sky. High above, little more than a speck, an eagle performed lazy circles.

They were being watched; Jack was sure of it. He could not have explained why he was so certain, but certain he was.

"We'd better put the cover back on the step and get back to the cottage. This place is beginning to give me the creeps."

Jack and Kaitlin closed the counterbalanced stone slab that covered the step and slid it back to its original position. Jack put the locking segment back into place and sprinkled dust and dead leaves across the cave entrance to obscure the mechanism once more. Kaitlin carefully slipped the ancient flute into her pack. It was too long to be concealed completely, and a few centimetres poked out.

They took one last look around the cave, spread some more dust and dead leaves to conceal their footprints, and left.

Jack glanced up as they arrived back at the place where they had left the ute. The eagle was still circling, A distant sentinel, feigning indifference. Kaitlin followed Jack's gaze.

"Protector or Spy?" Kaitlin shading her eyes against the glare, watched the great bird perform a long, effortless circuit. "Chaperone, maybe."

Jack just grunted and threw their packs behind the ute's front seats.

"OK. Let's go." Jack gunned the engine to life, and Kaitlin jumped in.

"It's not too far to the cottage from here. We'll take the smugglers' tracks. Keep your eyes open for drones and helicopters."

The old ute creaked and moaned its way back along the narrow, overgrown track. They had spent several hours searching the cave, but they had arrived early, and the day was still relatively young.

"I'm starving, don't suppose there are any of those sandwiches left?"

"No, we ate them all this morning."

"We'll stop by the Grey Gum Café and pick up a coffee and something to eat."

"Isn't that a bit of a diversion?"

"A bit, yes."

"Won't we be more visible on Putty Road?"

"We'll be hiding in plain sight."

"Cunning. Are you sure you're not making a virtue of necessity?"

"I'm starving."

"Brilliantly argued." Kaitlin leaned back and stretched. There was no reasoning with Jack's stomach.

In truth, they were soon back on the road, and it wasn't far to the café. Jack parked in among the few other utes out. There is nothing more anonymous than a dusty old ute parked amongst other dusty old utes outside a wayside café.

Sustained by hot coffee and two rounds of cloned-bacon sandwiches, the last leg of their journey through the forest to the cottage passed without event. They were the first to arrive. Kaitlin removed the Ney from her pack and placed the enigmatic instrument on the kitchen table.

"What were you made for?" Kaitlin mused, "What do you do?"

"I don't like it," Jack dumped his pack down in a corner, "I don't trust it."

A shadow passed across the kitchen window. Both jumped as it flicked past.

"Just a bird, probably." Jack went outside to check anyway. The tension was getting to them.

Emma packed the ute for their journey to the cottage, only the basics. She didn't want to look suspicious if they got stopped by the police. It was fully light by the time they headed off, but still early. They slipped out of Richmond the back way and headed for Windsor. It was on the way into Windsor that they were flagged down. A grizzled old policeman tapped on the driver's side window. Emma wound it down to speak to him.

"You're Emma Hexenkriege, aren't you?"

"Yes, I am."

"Where're you headed this fine morning, if you don't mind me asking?"

"We're going to the White Gum Café in Windsor for brekkie."

"Yeah, they do a good breakfast there." The policeman leaned in to take a look at Emma's passengers. Aine gave him a nice smile from the back. Max nodded.

"This is my father-in-law, Max. He's visiting from Germany. We haven't seen him in years, so it's a sort of celebration breakfast."

The old policeman glanced in the back of the ute, which was pretty much empty bar the usual junk.

"Well then," He scratched his head, "bon appetite. Or is that French?"

"Thanks," Emma started the engine and moved off slowly. She wound the window up again.

"We'd better get off the beaten track pretty quick. He'll be phoning that in, I guess." In the rear-view mirror, Emma watched the old policeman walk back to his car and get in. He didn't seem in that much of a hurry. Perhaps they did have a little time. Emma drove sedately along the main street. She didn't want to get pulled over again, and then, on impulse, swung a quick left and then a right and stopped outside the White Gum Café.

"He was right, Emma jumped out of the ute, "they do a great breakfast here. I'll get us a picnic."

Emma entered the café and ordered three big breakfasts to go.

"Where're you headed to this morning?" The waiter was just being friendly, but to Emma, it suddenly seemed like everyone wanted to know her business.

"Oh, you know, just saving the world." The waiter laughed at that and turned to place the order.

"We thought we'd have a picnic breakfast in Macquarie Park. You get a great view of the river from there."

"It's a good spot for a picnic, that's for sure."

Emma waited as patiently as she could for the breakfasts to be prepared and wrapped. She grabbed three sets of biodegradable cutlery and jumped back in the ute.

"I told them we were going for a picnic, just in case anyone asked." Emma started the engine and drove slowly to the bridge over the Hawkesbury River. Once over the river, she picked up speed and headed for the cottage by the back roads through Wilberforce and over the Portland ferry. A few kilometres after the ferry crossing, Emma pulled off the road onto a narrow, overgrown track. There was a spot deep under the trees where they could stop for breakfast. The food was still warm. Emma had forgotten to turn off her phone as she left Richmond, which proved fortunate, as it turned out. Her phone rang, and the name 'Jordie' popped up on the screen. *Jordie who*, she wondered? Aine peeked over the back of the seat to see who was calling. Emma decided to answer the phone on the basis that the authorities did not refer to themselves as Jordie, and in any case, she would not have stored their number.

"Hi Jordie, how's it going?"

"Hi Emma, it's Jordie, the volunteer engineer," Emma remembered. It was the guy who had fixed the uplink relay for her what seemed like a century ago.

"Yes. High Jordie, what can I do for you?"

"Look, I don't mean to pry, but a buddy of mine likes to listen to the police radio on a scanner."

"OK, but how does that affect me?"

"Well, I was sitting with him this morning while he was listening, and I heard a call out for all cars to watch out for you. They gave your description and the ute's rego details."

"Did they say why?"

"No, just to call in any sightings. They said not to apprehend you."

"Ok. Thanks, Jordie. I've been away for a few days. I bet someone has reported me missing or something."

"Ok, well, I'm glad it's nothing serious." Emma hung up the phone.

"The police have put out a call to look out for us and report any sightings, but not to stop us."

"Just being careful, maybe?" Max sounded doubtful.

"Who's your boyfriend?" Aine leaned over from the back seat, "Who's this Jordie then?"

"Just a guy from work."

"You had his number stored."

"It's just for work."

"No last name. You're on pretty close terms with him then."

"Look, it's nothing. It's just work."

Aine, never sure when to stop, persisted.

"He had your number stored too."

"Ok. That's enough. It's just work, and if you don't like it, you can get out and walk."

Aine sampled her mother's emotional flow. She was a bit pissed off. Best stop.

"I love you, mama," Aine leaned over the seat and hugged her mum.

Emma relented, "I love you too, but you go too far sometimes. You need to know when to let go."

"Sorry, mama." Aine gave her mother a quick kiss on the back of her neck.

Emma handed out the picnic breakfasts and the cutlery, and they all dug in. While they ate, they heard a distant siren grow slowly louder as it approached along the main road behind them and then fainter as it continued away.

"Probably nothing to do with us." Emma didn't sound convinced.

"Let's hope so," Max took a swig of coffee ", but we'd better get moving anyway."

The route to the cottage that Emma had chosen might not have been thought of by some as a route at all. It involved driving through abandoned farms and across a paddock to get from one narrow trail to another. At one point, the apparent approach of a distant helicopter saw Emma diving into a dilapidated old barn to hide. Rusting farm machinery lay around, discarded. The atmosphere of the place was oppressive. It was as though the previous occupants had simply walked off the land, abandoning everything for a better life in the city. A family had lived there once. An antique pram, missing a wheel, leaned up against a baby's cot. The overall impression was of human beings in retreat. It was as though a tide of migrant humanity had swept in from the coast, claiming the hinterland and displacing the indigenous peoples. A migrant tide that had now swept back out, retreating to the coast. Human populations everywhere had been known to be in decline for decades, but for the three refugees in the ute, there was a sadness to the place, a profound sense of loss. Aine picked up on the emotional wave emanating from her mother.

"Alice's people are reclaiming their country, bit by bit. That's a good thing, isn't Mama?"

Emma sighed heavily and tried to pull herself together, "Yes, it is. And it's our job to find a way to stop the military from incinerating the whole area."

Max glanced back to check on Aine. She looked upset, unsettled. He reached out and gave her shoulder a gentle squeeze.

"If not us, then who? If not now, then when?"

"What's that from?" Aine took her great-grandfather's hand.

"Oh, it's just a quote from my youth. From the civil rights movement in America."

Emma started the ute, and they moved off once more. The journey to the cottage took longer than Emma had expected. The track was much worse than she remembered. Some of the gates had been left chained closed. Several times they had seen helicopters in the distance and had taken cover. Once, Emma spotted a drone flying fast and low across a paddock.

"It's probably an agricultural drone, and from the speed and low flight path, it's being guided by an AI." She wasn't certain of it, though.

Both Max and Aine picked up on her doubt and underlying fear. Emma had pulled in under the trees while it zipped past.

At another point, once they had passed through the deserted farmland and were once more making their way through the forest, Aine thought she heard voices coming from a gully to their left. Emma cut the engine, and they all sat silently, listening for a few minutes. Eventually, a small group of hikers appeared, silhouetted along the brow of a hill. Emma waited until they had moved over the crest and disappeared down the far side of the hill before she once more started up the engine and continued their journey. They were heading into deeper woodland now, with thicker bush and taller trees. There would be more cover, but there would also be more hurdles to overcome.

It was at the bottom of a steep gorge by a clear running stream that they finally ran into an obstacle that they could not evade. A gum tree had fallen across the path. The ute was stopped in a narrow ravine. There was no way forward. Emma could probably reverse back up, but there was no feasible alternative route at this point. Not without doubling back several kilometres. They all jumped out of the ute to take a look. The fallen gum tree was not one of the big mountain gums. They could have moved it if they'd had a chainsaw, but that was one of the things Emma had left behind to avoid creating suspicion. The way ahead on foot was still quite long. Emma knew the way, but it would be tough on Max and Aine. They had decided to reverse out and find another way when they heard the slightest rustling of leaves off to one side. Slowly, out of the forest, a group of Wollemi appeared. Ignoring the three humans, the silent Wollemi slipped past them and approached the fallen tree. They moved as one. Emma, Max and Aine looked on, amazed and enchanted by their choreographed dance. Silently and without any apparent instruction, a few small axes were produced, and the top half of the tree was chopped off. The Wollemi moved that segment out of the way and came back to the lower segment. A few more branches were removed and taken away. The assembled Wollemi then began to tug and pull at the trunk, swinging it slowly around in tiny increments. After maybe ten minutes of this, when the tree had been moved a little less than half a metre, the Wollemi stopped what they were doing and turned towards the three humans. Nothing was said, but suddenly Aine stepped forward to join the Wollemi. Emma and Max followed. Aine nodded as though agreeing with some silent voice and then spoke.

"We will all pull together on three. Ready?"

Max and Emma nodded assent.

"One, two, three." On three, the assembled Wollemi-Human crew pulled hard. The tree moved about half a metre. A few more minutes of that and the tree had been dragged out of the way. They could continue their journey. Emma and Max thanked the Wollemi and got back into the ute. Aine hesitated. The Wollemi gathered around her in a sort of scrum. Arms interlocked around their backs. They stood like that silently for a minute or more before Aine and the Wollemi stood straight. Aine was a little taller than the tallest Wollemi, but not by much. When seen next to them, the similarity of her facial bone structure, physique and skin tone suggested common ancestry. It was obvious to Max and Emma that Aine was, in large part, Wollemi.

The scrum separated, and Aine walked back to the ute. Emma started the engine and made her way gingerly across the stream and up onto the steep slope on the other side. In the rear-view mirror, Emma saw the Wollemi disappear back into the forest.

"What was that about? That huddle?"

"They were telling me that the forest up ahead was clear. They said we had not been followed. They said time was short and we need to make haste. They told me Jack and Kaitlin were waiting for us at the cottage."

Emma gunned the engine. The sudden appearance of the Wollemi just when they were needed and the sight of Aine standing amongst them stirred uncertain feelings deep within Emma. She realised that she resented OneMind. She was angry that it had suborned her consent to be impregnated by a male Wollemi of its choosing. Forcing someone to do something against their will was bad enough, but simply overwhelming their will, changing their mind for them, that was somehow much, much worse. The OneMind was tyrannical by nature, Emma realised. Memories from her period of assimilation as a girl played themselves across the canvas of her mind. The OneMind, fully formed, had no concept of compromise. There was no bargaining with it. Emma understood that they had no choice but to go along with the OneMind's great plan, whatever it was. She prayed desperately that things would somehow work out. All one could hope for was that whatever it intended would ultimately be in their shared interest – human and Wollemi.

But it was only a hope, and hope is not a strategy.

SPREAD OUT

All across their ancient meeting place, the One Thousand began to stir. People packed up their things and made sure that all the campfires of the night before had been put out. Small groups began to assemble at the centre of the trampled meeting place. Alice and Tom joined the gathering of Elders. Alice stood on a small mound and addressed them.

"We will leave this place now and head for Mount Yengo and the Table of the Gods. Spread out. Go quietly in small groups. More will join during the day. Be wary of the soldiers. Do not seek confrontation. The military will not start bombing while their people are searching the forest." Alice paused for questions. There were none.

"I must go now to meet with others and make plans. I will meet you at the Table of the Gods."

And with that, the gathering began to break up. Singing quietly or in silence, the Elders left the meeting ground. Ancient tales, passed down through perhaps a thousand generations and more, were coming to fruition. With hope and luck, and by the approval of pitiless fate, the people would, at last, be able to return to their ancestral lands, to the Dreamtime, to dream once more. Small groups disappeared into the forest, each picking their own way to their rendezvous with destiny.

Tom and Alice walked back through the deserted bushland to the small settlement where they had left the dirt bike. There was no one about. The place seemed deserted. There were signs of a hasty departure. Gates had been left open. Small piles of belongings sat outside some of the old farmhouses. The people had gone. Tom pulled the little bike out from under its covering of branches and leaves. It started the first time, and he and Alice squeezed on.

"Everyone's been evacuated," Alice had to raise her voice over the whine of the engine, "They've sealed off the forest."

"Yeah," Tom's voice was whipped away by the wind as he increased speed, "We're running out of time."

Putting caution to the winds, Tom and Alice raced along Putty Road to the turnoff that led to the cottage. They saw no drones and heard no helicopters. There was, instead, a hush hanging over the wilderness. A silent intake of breath. The cliched 'quiet before the storm' perhaps. As they drove along the overgrown track, they occasionally saw, off to either side, small groups of Wollemi heading towards Mount Yengo. Tom pulled to a stop to watch one particularly large group ford a stream and start up one of the steep little hillsides that covered the landscape.

"The veil is failing, and I'm guessing the military have made their call."

"They're going to bomb."

"Yes, I'd say so. They'll carpet bomb up to one kilometre from their perimeter."

"How big is that? I mean, how much land does it include?"

"I can't say for sure, but they will have locked down all the choke points in and out of Yengo, Wollemi, Dharug and possibly the Gardens of Stone areas."

"Wow."

"Yes. They will have closed the Great North Road and Putty Road. I reckon their outer perimeter will stretch from Wollombi in the west to Glen Alice in the east and from Colo in the south to Denman in the north."

"But that's a huge area. They can't burn all that, surely?'

"They can, but they probably won't. My guess is their fallback will be to wipe out everything from the Great Northern Road to the Putty Road. But they might continue west to the Wolgan Valley."

"That's the entire wilderness. You can't be serious."

"They will focus on a kilometre around the Mountain, most probably."

He and Alice rode on without speaking. From that point on, they saw no one. There was still no sign of helicopters or drones. Even the forest seemed subdued. As they rode the final crest and looked down at the old cottage in the woods, they could see two utes parked outside. Aine was standing on what was left of the wrap-around veranda, staring up at them. She stepped down into the paddock as Tom and Alice pulled to a halt behind the cottage.

"Mum's got a boyfriend," Aine smiled broadly, "his name's Jordie."

"Thanks for sharing," unclear as to the immediate relevance or even accuracy of that news, Alice changed tracks, "Who's here?"

"Mum, Max, Jack, Kaitlin, and me. And now you two, the magnificent seven, ride again."

"We'd better get inside. There's no time for idle chitchat." Tom searched the sky for a moment, his sense of urgency increasing with every second. The unnatural silence of the forest spooked him. His nerves were on edge, and his newfound attachment to Alice piled on the pressure. Now he had someone other than himself to take care of.

As they walked up the steps to the broken-down veranda, Kaitlin came out to meet them.

"Jack and I found something incredible at the cave. You are not going to believe it."

Inside, Jack, Max and Emma were talking quietly.

"I'm going to call the authorities." Max's tone was calm and quiet. He was not seeking permission or approval. He was stating the facts. "I need to know what political decision has been made. We all know what the military decision will be. We've been here before. But everything has changed since the last time the OneMind engaged directly with humanity. We have changed. Humanity has changed. I'm hoping that your political leaders will see the opportunity rather than just the threat." Max paused as he heard footsteps from behind.

"Our political leaders?" Tom had caught the last part of Max's statement, "Are they, not your political leaders too?"

"I am returning to the Wollemi today after I find out what I need to know."

"I see."

"You knew that. I made it clear to everyone that I was going to return to be with my wife."

Emma walked over and gave her grandfather a hug, "It's OK. We'll miss you, but it's OK."

Max's tone softened a little, "It's only for a little while. Once the veil falls and the reunification begins, we will be reunited."

"Reunification? Is that how you see it?" Tom frowned. He had not thought of the situation in quite those terms.

"We were one species once. We are still one species, and we have lived apart too long."

"Will it work, do you think?" Kaitlin could not hide the fear in her voice, "Can we live together peacefully?"

"The OneMind thinks we can. That's what it's been planning for thousands of years. That's what the message it sent to Alice's people meant." Max sighed. There was too little time to explain it all.

"What message?" Alice wracked her brain, trying to think what message Max was referring to.

"The Adam and Eve wands. Their sudden awakening from the dead after thousands of years, their growing together into one. You didn't see the symbolism in that?"

"Kaitlin and I talked about it. We could see it was symbolic, of course, but we were not clear what exactly it meant."

"The Tree of Knowledge and the Tree of Life growing together into one tree. Their separation and reunification didn't strike a chord with either of you."

"Of course, it struck a chord. We're not stupid. We just couldn't fathom out what chord." Kaitlin was momentarily stung to anger by her father-in-law's less-than-tactful words. She calmed down immediately, her intellectual curiosity outweighing her pride.

"The OneMind was telling us that two parts of a long-separated whole were growing back together. The message was one of healing an old wound."

"Yes," Max looked rather shame-faced, "I apologise for my blunt delivery. I haven't been around humans much for the last twenty years."

"And even before that," Jack wrapped an arm around his father, "You were never that sociable before the Event."

"OK. We have to plan. There's no time to waste." Tom stepped up to the kitchen table, "The military have sealed off the forest. All roads in and out will have been blocked. They are preparing to bomb the moment they are given the word. We must stop them."

"We need to pull together what we know. Pool our knowledge. We couldn't stop them last time. It was the OneMind who did it."

"With our help, though. He did it with our help." Alice was thinking fast, "He tricked us into deploying the HARP device. He made us think it was a weapon. He relied upon our aggression and our unshakeable desire to protect our own."

"Yes," Kaitlin cut in, "The OneMind had long prepared for that moment. It will have long prepared for this one too."

"Prepared with what, though. What has it given us to use this time?" Emma reached out instinctively and pulled Aine close.

"Jack and I found something in the Egyptian cave. I think it's relevant. I received an email from the Pergamon Museum in Berlin with a translation of the glyphs in the cave. They said there was something hidden in the cave. They said it was a trigger or key."

"Show us what you found," Tom had regained some composure, "maybe we can figure it out together."

Kaitlin retrieved the ancient flute from her pack. She placed it on the kitchen table for all to see.

"It's a Ney, the most ancient musical instrument known to human-kind."

"Does it still work?" Emma ran a finger along the flute. It was cold to the touch and smooth.

"It does indeed," Jack gave the instrument an appraising look, "but just what it does and how it does it remain unclear."

"I played a couple of tunes on it in the cave. It works fine as a flute, but the effect it had on Jack was really weird."

"What did it do?" Tom glanced at Jack, trying to gauge his emotional response to the conversation. What he picked up on was confusion, irritation and just a hint of fear.

"First, I played a few bars of a sad old Irish air. The Ney seemed to amplify the sadness, or it could just have been me responding to the sound and the setting, but then I played a jig. When I finished playing, I saw Jack moving weirdly. I suppose I'd call it dancing."

"Oh, thanks a lot. I can dance, OK, if I want to." Jack mimicked wounded pride for a moment.

"Yes, my love, you're a wonderful dancer. The point is you seemed to be in some kind of a trance. You moved rhythmically for a moment or two after I stopped playing, and then you seemed to snap out of it."

"Maybe we are supposed to use it in some way." Emma picked the flute up and hefted it in her hand. "It's surprisingly heavy."

"They were made of reeds originally or bamboo. This one is made out of bronze. It was built to last."

Aine, listening to the back and forth of the conversation, began to see a pattern. It was an odd pattern, perhaps no more than a series of coincidences separated in some cases by hundreds of years. Where, she thought, had she heard of music and sound being used in unexpected ways to achieve unexpected results? Perhaps it was her recent and apparently ongoing connection to the OneMind. Perhaps it was just her peculiar take on things. Whatever it was, Aine came to a conclusion. When the coast was clear, when the others were engaged in planning, she would act.

"Err, Mum. Where's your uplink thing? Can I use it to update my messages?" Aine appeared bored and listless. Her emotional flow, under iron control, suggested the same.

"It's in the truck. Don't stay on too long, or they'll notice. It doesn't broadcast GPS coordinates, but we don't want to trigger anyone's curiosity."

"Ok, mum, thanks." Aine wandered out onto the veranda and around to Emma's ute. The small battery-powered device was under the driver's seat. Emma carried it everywhere in case she needed to make some urgent adjustment to a satellite. Aine lifted the device out from under the seat and carried it back into the cottage and into her bedroom. She pulled her tablet out of her pack and turned on the uplink. It was fully charged. The connection was made instantly. Aine leaned forward and began to check out her hunch. She began to type, "Can sound and music change human behaviour?" The results that came back were many and various, but one thing was clear, at a 'biocultural level', sound was important. Aine wasn't entirely clear what a 'biocultural level' was, but there was no time to research that. She began to type again, "History of sound as a weapon". This time the results that came back were both numerous and shocking. Sound could and had been used as a weapon. There were ancient myths and modern examples. There was Pan, the god of woodlands and wilderness, with his pipes made from reeds. There was the biblical story where Jericho's walls were brought down by stamping feet and trumpets. There was the legend of the Pied Piper of Hamlyn leading children off into the forest with his flute. And there were the modern uses of sound in policing and in war. Both high-frequency ultrasound and low-frequency infrasound could and had been harnessed to drive human behaviour. One strange fact stuck out above the general confirmations she was seeing. Ultrasound was perceived more readily by young people than by older people. The ancient Ney that Kaitlin and Jack had taken from the Egyptian cave was a weapon or a tool, and the OneMind intended that they use it. Aine was sure of it. With the absolute confidence and clarity of purpose that seems open only to the young, she laid her plan. There was no point talking about it with her mother and the others. They wouldn't see the truth as clearly as she did.

Outside in the kitchen, the sounds of conversation continued. Aine shut down the satellite uplink and crept back out to join the others. Tom was talking.

"Max, you said you had made a phase-shifting device that opened up a way through the veil. Can I see it? Can I see the plans?"

"Sure," Max walked through to his old study. The others followed, all except Aine. Max's old desk was still there. Most of his books and paraphernalia were still there too. He pulled out the bottom drawer of his desk, carefully placed the contents on the desk, and turned the empty drawer over. Stuck to the bottom was a large manilla envelope. Max peeled it off the bottom of the drawer and handed it to Tom.

"This is a complete set of calculations and drawings. Everything you need to make another one."

"Where's the one you made?"

"I'm not sure. I probably put it down somewhere after I re-joined the collective and promptly forgot about it. It would not have seemed important after that."

Tom opened the envelope. Inside, neatly typed, was an explanation of Max's hypothesis, the calculations he used and the design schematics for the device itself. Tom took out his phone and copied the pages one by one. He resealed the envelope and handed it back to Max.

"Best put it back in its hiding place."

Max reattached the envelope to the bottom of the drawer, returned its contents to it and slid it back into the desk.

"I'll send the details to my buddy at the NSA as soon as I can safely get a signal."

"The NSA, you're sure?" Kaitlin frowned; the NSA was not the first place she would have thought of.

"He's a good man. Reliable. I trust him."

Kaitlin nodded, "OK, if he's good enough for you, he's good enough for me."

"What will he do with the plans?" Jack was not so sure.

"Probably nothing. But he'll know what to do with them if the need arises. He's not from the military. He's a research scientist."

As soon as the adults had left the kitchen, Aine grabbed the ancient flute, raced into her bedroom, picked up the uplink device and ran out of the house. Without a backwards glance, Aine sprinted up the hill to the Hexenkriege family's picnic spot. It wasn't too far, and she was young and fit. Nevertheless, her pell-mell race up the hillside and along the path through the trees left Aine out of breath and panting hard when she reached the place. To Aine, this place, this exact spot, had always seemed to be more than just a picnic place with a great view. There had always seemed to her to be an atmosphere about the place as though the land itself was partially awake or lightly sleeping. As soon as her breathing had evened out, she set the uplink device on a flat stone and switched it on. Then she flicked on her phone and set it to live stream video to all her social contacts and all her favourite chat sites and pages.

Emma returned to the kitchen. It was immediately evident that the flute was gone. Emma ran into Aine's bedroom to look for her. Kaitlin ran outside. An unpleasant realisation grew in her mind. Aine could probably play the missing flute. Knowing Aine, she'd want to give it a try. Where would she go? Where would she take the flute away from prying eyes? Kaitlin recalled giving Aine a tin whistle for her seventh birthday. They had been picnicking at the usual place. It was a warm afternoon. Kaitlin had shown her the basic keying for an old Irish song her mother had taught her. What was it now? Kaitlin wandered back in memory to the small cottage in the Galway hinterland where she had been brought up. She pictured her mother showing her the correct fingering and then blowing a few bars. 'Ned of the Hill', that was it. 'Oh, dark is the evening and silent the hour. Come and live merrily under the bower', or something like that. It was a very long time ago, long before the Event. A different world too, or that's how it seemed from her present vantage point. Aine would have gone to the picnic spot, Kaitlin was sure. Without further thought, Kaitlin began to run up the hillside. Jack, watching from the kitchen window, saw her go. Emma ran back into the kitchen.

"She's not in her room."

"She's gone to the picnic spot. I just saw Kaitlin racing up the hill after her."

Max pulled a slightly dogeared business card from his pocket and brushed it down, trying vainly to smooth out the edges. "Emma, I need to borrow your ute. I'm going back to Wisemans Ferry. I need to talk to the powers that be."

"Sure, of course. But what about Aine and the flute?"

"In some ways, Aine is no longer a child. The time she spent in the OneMind's gestalt has changed her, just as it changed you. I think she has put two and two together and has taken things into her own hands. What she does now will trigger the unfolding of events long-planned and long-awaited."

"We need to get a message to the OneMind," Tom glanced at his phone. "I wish I had a copy of your phase-shifting device Max."

"Maybe we can attract the OneMind's attention, or maybe there's another way through the veil." Kaitlin knew an incantation said to open the veil of Ain Soph Aur, it was from the Kabala tradition, but perhaps she could use it.

"Um," Alice stood forward and tapped the kitchen table to get everyone's attention, "Perhaps I could have mentioned it sooner, but we, that is, my people, have a means of entering the Dreamtime at need."

"You can enter Dreamtime any time you want?" Tom sounded incredulous, "And you're only just mentioning it now."

"Well, it's not just a matter of clicking our heels together three times, you know. There's a bit more to it than that."

"I was just a bit surprised, is all."

"It's a ritual. We use resonant sound to align with the Dreamtime, but yes, we can open a pathway through the veil."

"You and I need to get to the Table of Gods. We need to let the OneMind know what's happening." Tom looked around the room, checking that all were in agreement.

"You two take the dirt bike. Emma, Kaitlin, and I will go to the picnic spot and pick up Aine. We'll meet you at the mountain as soon as we can."

Emma grabbed a few bottles of water from the fridge and handed them out. Jack went out to the shed to fetch a can of petrol for the dirt bike. After several minutes more of scurrying around, Kaitlin turned off the lights in the old cottage and closed the door. There were a few hurried goodbyes before Max jumped into Emma's ute.

"Will we see you again?" Emma struggled to hold back the tears.

Max sighed heavily, "Time will tell. I hope so."

Tom and Alice squeezed once more onto the dirt bike and headed off. Max gunned the engine and headed back towards Putty Road. Emma joined Jack in his old ute, and they headed off up the track to the picnic spot, picking Kaitlin up on the way. Moments later, the old cottage lay deserted once more.

High overhead, an eagle circled.

A CALL TO PRAYER

Aine picked up the ancient bronze flute. It was heavy and cool to the touch. She ran her fingers along its smooth surface, feeling out the finger holes. Aine eyed the flute warily.

"Are you a weapon or tool? Are you a key or a trigger?" Whatever, her mind was made up. If it were a key, she would find out what it opened, and if it was a trigger... Well, so be it.

She lifted the flute to her lips and prepared to blow. It was only then that she realised she had no idea what to play. Did it require a special tune, or would anything do? Did it require a tune at all? And as she considered her dilemma, perhaps admitting to herself that she could have thought things through a little more thoroughly, something came to her, a tone at first and then a series of notes. In her mind, there formed a complex melody. *"Play"*, the voice of the OneMind, gentle and mild, sounded silently in her mind, "It is time."

Aine put the flute once more to her lips and began to play. The sound that came from the flute was unlike anything she had heard before. It was lilting and polyphonic. The sound was simultaneously harmonic and discordant. Single notes competed with complex chords. Aine could feel the lowest notes as vibrations in her chest and the highest as attenuating vibrations at the edge of her auditory range. Aine played on, occasionally glancing at the screen on her phone, watching the counter. As she watched, the number on the counter grew. It seemed as though all her friends had tuned in, and all their friends too. While she played, the counter continued to tick over, faster and faster. There were hundreds of people listening, then thousands, and at last, millions of people from all around the world were focused on Aine, the ancient, timeless tune, and the eldritch music of the OneMind's flute. The psychoacoustic effect spread around the planet carried by the global SatNet.

Aine heard the sound of a ute chugging its way up the hill towards her. Furiously, almost in a trance, Aine played on. The tune rose in tone and urgency. It was a call, unmistakable and irresistible.

"*Come to us*," the flute seemed to say, "*come join us in the wilderness*."

Three things happened then, almost simultaneously. The ute crested the hill and came to a stop next to the picnic spot. The uplink's connection to the satellite was cut, and Aine, exhausted and mentally drained, collapsed. Emma jumped from the ute and ran to her daughter. Aine was conscious but disorientated. Kaitlin picked up Aine's phone. The counter on the screen showed that nearly five hundred million people had watched and listened and heard the call. Jack checked the uplink. A small green light showed that the power was still on, but a small red light showed that it had lost its connection.

Kaitlin scanned the horizon in the direction of Wiseman's Ferry and Richmond, searching for any sign of helicopters or drones. Aine's phone pinged in her hand. As Kaitlin looked down, she saw messages appear fleetingly on the screen, only to be replaced by other messages. Though the words varied a little, the message was the same, *"We are coming"*. Kaitlin tried to imagine what was happening right then, all around the world. Were five hundred million souls and their friends and relatives on the move? Where were they heading? In Kaitlin's mind, a vision of a modern-day Children's Crusade was forming. The call, long prepared for by the OneMind, had gone out. And it had been answered.

"We'd better get moving." Jack lifted Aine and carried her to the ute. Emma got in, and Jack passed Aine to her. The girl was barely conscious. Kaitlin grabbed the flute and switched off the uplink. The flurry of messages on the phone was slowing. Perhaps those who had heeded the call were now making their way to the nearest wilderness areas. Questions now appeared on the phone, "What just happened?" "My son has just walked out of the house in the middle of the night." "There are dozens of kids in the street. What gives?" and so on. Kaitlin switched the phone off. Their position would have been triangulated by now. It was time to go.

As soon as Kaitlin had clambered into the passenger seat, Jack gunned the engine. Driving as fast as he could along narrow tracks, avoiding open glades, keeping deep under the forest canopy, Jack headed for the nearest place where he could hide the ute from the prying sensors of an AI-piloted drone. At last, he reached a narrow stream, a tributary of the MacDonald River.

"Hang on," through gritted teeth, Jack engaged the low gears of the four-wheel drive and drove the old ute along the bed of the stream, over rocks and tree branches, heading for an overhang of rock that concealed the mouth of a cave. Without hesitating, Jack wrenched the steering wheel hard over. The ute creaked and groaned as it struggled over the detritus blocking its way. At last, Jack pulled the ute to a stop and turned off the engine. They were ten metres underground. The light from the cave mouth was just enough to see by. Jack, Kaitlin, Emma and the slowly surfacing Aine sat silently in the ute, listening intently for the sound of a helicopter or a drone.

They sat like that for at least an hour. From outside the cave, sounds came to them of helicopters and even of jets screaming overhead. After a while longer, the sound of helicopters diminished, and silence fell once more across the wilderness. Warily, Jack stepped out of the ute and went to the cave mouth. The sun was heading down. It set early in winter. It would be dark soon. Jack returned to the ute.

"We walk from here," Jack reached into the glove compartment to grab a torch. He retrieved his pack and Kaitlin's from the back. Aine was last to step down from the back of the ute. Eyes downcast, she refused to meet her mother's stare.

"Whatever possessed you to run off like that?"

Aine could not meet her mother's eye.

"What on Earth were you thinking?"

Tears welled, vying with self-righteous anger.

"Didn't you hear Kaitlin me say the flute was dangerous? Might be dangerous?"

"I did what I knew was needed." anger flared in Aine's young face, "I did what I knew was necessary, when it was necessary, not hours later after a group discussion when it would already have been too late."

Stunned into silence by her daughter's unexpected outburst, Emma just stood and stared. Fear and relief fought with anger and admiration. It was too much. Emma placed her face in her hands and began to sob— loud, heaving, inconsolable sobs. Aine ran to her mother, suddenly contrite.

"I'm sorry, Mum, I should have explained. I should have trusted you. But would you have agreed?"

Emma pulled herself together as best she could. Still dabbing her eyes with a tissue, she looked up at her daughter.

"Probably not."

Aine wrapped her arm around her mother and hugged her.

"The truth is, Mum, I'm not even sure it was my own idea."

"What do you mean?"

"She means it could have been an idea implanted by the One-Mind." Kaitlin had been listening to their exchange.

"I don't know. It seemed like my idea. It seemed like I just put all the pieces together and realised what the flute was for."

"And now?"

"And now I can't help wondering how I knew how to play it, how I knew what to play."

"Maybe the OneMind implanted the tune when you were part of the gestalt?" Jack, who had also been listening, passed Kaitlin her pack.

"How are you feeling now? Can you manage a route march at night across the wilderness?" Jack smiled, "I'm really selling it, aren't I?"

Aine laughed, "I can manage it."

Jack locked the ute and led the way to the cave mouth.

The sudden brightness after the gloom of the cave dazzled them and made them blink. Their eyes quickly adjusted, however, only to be met by a wholly unexpected sight. Across the riverbed from the cave mouth stood a group of perhaps a dozen Wollemi, staring back at them, evidently waiting. Aine stepped forward to speak with them. They formed a huddle as they had before. A moment or two later, Aine stepped away from the huddle and walked back to her companions.

"They are here to escort us to the Table of the Gods."

"I know the way." Jack was suddenly wary.

"Yes, they know that. They say the way is blocked."

"What's blocking it?"

"Soldiers."

"Oh, well, is there a way around?"

"Mount Yengo is surrounded, encircled."

"So then…?"

"They are going to take us through, not round."

Kaitlin stepped forward, "They are going to take us there through the Dreamtime – yes?"

"Yes."

"Here we go again." Jack was not happy. He preferred not to rely on other people's good graces. He liked to make his own way. He liked to be in control. What with Aine's sudden epiphany about the flute, and the fact that the instrument itself was made thousands of years ago and placed in the cave to await its moment, everything, all of it, the whole situation, was starting to look like a setup. They were all, in effect, dancing to the OneMind's tune again.

"We need to hurry. They say that Alice and Tom only just made it through before the soldiers showed up in helicopters and surrounded the Mountain."

Aine led her mother, Kaitlin, and Jack back across the shallow stream. The Wollemi formed a circle around them. Then, to Aine's everlasting delight, the Wollemi began to sing. Max had told her about the Wollemi chorus, a song without words, a complex weave of harmony and counterpoint. The sound was unearthly, not quite human. There was something primaeval or perhaps archetypal about both the sound and the performance. The Wollemi had crossed their arms to-gether around their backs, their eyes were closed as they sang, and their heads were turned upwards to the sky, or maybe towards their own Dreaming.

A shimmering light began to form around them, a bubble filled with iridescent light, sparkling and glittering. For a while, the four hu-mans could see the trees and the countryside beyond the bubble, but soon the outer edges of the sphere became opaque. A moment later, glimpses of movement could once again be seen. The outside world slowly became visible once more. The bubble began to fade and was soon gone. Aine, Emma, Kaitlin and Jack found themselves standing once more on the Table of the Gods. This time though, the place was heaving with people. There were Wollemi and Aboriginal Elders. Alice and Tom were there, and so were dozens of ordinary-looking people, mostly young people, with a few older men and women mixed in.

"Where did all these people come from?" Jack stared around as Alice and Tom walked over to greet the new arrivals.

"The One Thousand Elders were already *en route* before the Call-ing. The rest showed up in the last hour or so before the soldiers. There are more collected outside the military perimeter."

"The Calling?" Kaitlin was intrigued.

"You know," Aine stepped forward, "the thing with the flute."

"Oh, that." Emma made a playful swatting motion towards her daughter.

"You were right then." Jack put an arm around his granddaughter.

"If it was really anything to do with me at all."

"The OneMind says that young humans, plus a few older people who could hear the Call, are congregating in the wilderness places all around the world. It says the Merging has begun."

"What now, then?" Emma, who had remained silent, voiced the question that was on everyone's lips, "Where to from here?"

"And what about the people outside the perimeter? Are they safe?" Aine craned her neck to see if she could make out any people beyond the perimeter. She saw nothing. Even the perimeter itself was hidden beneath the trees.

"I think they're here and everywhere else where they have congregated, as a kind of human shield, to keep the military from bombing." Tom looked uncomfortable as he explained his reasoning.

"A human shield? Really? Isn't that against the Geneva Convention or something?" Emma instinctively grabbed her daughter and pulled her close.

"Yes. Customary Rules of War, rule 97, volume two, Chapter 32, Section J." Tom looked down, unable to meet his companions' eyes.

"Don't suppose the OneMind is a signatory, ay?" Jack was trying to think of the most useful, practical next step. He had nothing.

"Don't suppose it is." Kaitlin took her husband's hand, "I love you, Jack. Just thought I'd mention it."

Jack looked abashed, "I'm not going to let anything happen to you. You can be bloody sure of that."

"Well then," Kaitlin smiled and, leaning over towards him, gently pushed back the hair from his forehead, "that was a freebee."

"We should get ourselves encircled by soldiers as two worlds collide more often."

There was a commotion on the far side of the giant stone slab that was the Table of the Gods. On the south side facing Wisemans Ferry, a shimmering presence began to materialise. The six companions recognised it immediately.

The OneMind had returned.

EXODUS

Max drove straight to Putty Road, making no attempt to conceal his presence. The moment his phone had a good signal, he pulled the ute over and called the number on the business card he had been given. After two rings, a voice answered.

"Gideon speaking."

"Hallo Gideon, this is Max Hexenkriege speaking. We met at the teleconference. Any news on the policy side of things?"

"Ah yes, Mr Hexenkriege, I remember. Nothing yet, I'm afraid. The Americans can't decide whether to welcome the turn of events or bomb the hell out of everything. Calmer heads will prevail, I dare say. I'll call you on this number as soon as I hear anything if you like."

"Yes, please. That would be great."

"Where are you staying?"

"I've been staying with friends, but this evening I'm checking into the Wisemans Ferry Inn."

"Very nice. Stayed there once myself. Very comfortable."

"OK, thanks, Gideon. Bye." Max hung up. As he did so, his phone pinged and then played a little tune. The phone had been Emma's. Max was taking his time to get used to it. Out of curiosity, he tapped the little icon that had appeared. There was a news alert—video images of children walking. The visuals cut from city to country, from day to night, all around the world. Whatever Aine had done, it was having its effect. The screen caption proclaimed an exodus of children into the country-side. One called it a latter-day Children's Crusade. It wasn't just children, though, Max noticed. It was mostly children, but there were middle-aged people, too and even a few elderly folk scattered among the jostling crowds. Images appeared of police cordons and of swarms of young people flowing around and over them like a human tide. It would be touch and go, but Max reckoned the OneMind had it by a whisker. The military in any country wasn't going to bomb its own citizens, particularly not its own children. As he started the engine, preparing to head to Wiseman's ferry, Max saw a few people crossing the road and heading into the forest. After a while, the dribs and drabs of humanity became a steady stream of people entering the forest. At this rate, the whole area would be flooded with young people in a few hours.

As Max approached Wisemans Ferry along the river road sometime later, he was forced to slow down as more and more people appeared walking along the side of the road in the direction of the Webbs Creek Ferry. He guided the ute slowly along the road, avoiding the odd group or individual who decided to jump out of the bush on the other side of the road and run across in front of him. As he got closer to the ferry turn-off, shortly before the village of Wisemans Ferry itself, their numbers increased still further. Trampled paths had been made through the recently abandoned bush. Cars and utes were parked or simply abandoned all along the road. Their occupants apparently having simply jumped out and run off to the forest. Max let down the front windows. There was very little singing or shouting and hardly any talking. By and large, the brightly coloured, slowly undulating crowd moved silently. If he closed his eyes just a little, the winding mass of humanity seemed to resemble a rainbow-coloured snake moving slowly but with intent. There was something archetypal, almost mythic, about the scene.

Max pulled into the small car park outside the Wisemans Ferry Inn. The place was silent. He could see that a large crowd had gathered down by the Settler's Road ferry ramp. Something was going on. A long procession of camouflaged military trucks stretched from the bowling club to the ferry apron. Nothing was moving. Max walked into the pub. A lone barman stood behind the bar watching the news on the screen.

"What's going on?" Max sat on a stool by the bar and contemplated ordering a schooner of pale ale. It had been quite a while since he'd had a beer. Perhaps just one. The barman dragged his eyes away from the screen and nodded in recognition of Max.

"What can I get you?'

"Coopers Pale Ale, please."

The barman began to pour the drink, eyes glued to the screen.

"What's going on?"

"Something weird. Kids going AWOL. Helicopters and drones all over the show. And the military are trying to cross onto Settlers Road."

"Is there a problem with that?"

"People won't let them cross. They've occupied the ferry area and taken the ferry out to the middle of the river."

"Can't the trucks back up and cross via Webb's Creek?"

"There are dozens of abandoned cars blocking the road behind them too."

"Why are people blocking them? What's the issue?"

"I don't know. That's why I'm watching the news. I figure something major must have happened."

Max sat back and sipped his beer. He would be joining the people outside heading for Mount Yengo as soon as he had his answer. If he ever got it. Gideon had given him the brush-off pretty quickly. Max pulled his stool over a little bit closer to the screen and watched the news too. The feed cut to breathless reporters across the country and around the world reporting on the bizarre outbreak of what they were calling mass hysteria, though in every case, the atmosphere was anything but hysterical. There was almost a carnival mood. The surging masses were happy, but for their unnatural silence, they looked pretty much like a crowd gathering for a music festival. Max tuned in more closely. A reporter was asking a group of teenagers in Norway where they were going. The subtitled answers that came back were forthright, improbable, and contradictory.

"We're going to a party," said one.

"We're going camping," said another.

"We're going to the festival," said a third.

The reporter gently pointed out that they had no camping gear and there was no festival planned. In response, she received a happy smile and a wave as the group continued on its way. The reporter asked the person who had claimed to be going to a party where the party was being held.

"Oh, it's this way," the smiling young woman replied, "you should come too."

A voice cut into the news feed, "We're going over to the White House now, where the President is about to make an announcement."

The scene cut to the familiar press room at the White House in Washington DC. A man walked in and stood at the podium.

"My fellow Americans," he began, "I am pleased to be able to tell you about a momentous change that is about happen. Those of us who are old enough recall the extraordinary Event of two decades ago when it was revealed to the world for the very first time that humanity was not alone. We discovered back then that we had ancient cousins peacefully living their lives, unknown and unseen, virtually alongside us. We came to call them by a strange but appropriate name, the Wollemi, the name stemming from their cultural centre in the Wollemi Forest of Australia. Their presence had previously been the stuff of legend and fairy tales. We came to understand that they had the ability to cloak their existence behind what came to be known as 'The Veil'. I ask you to forgive my long preamble." The president paused to draw breath and to allow his words to sink in.

"We wondered back then why the veil had faltered. We wondered why the so-called OneMind of the Wollemi people has gifted us with an extraordinary sixth sense, the sense of empathy. Of course, we had been empathetic before, but the gift was different. The gift of the One-Mind enabled us directly to sense the emotional flow of another human being. It allowed us to understand and trust each other better. It enabled us to end the scattered wars that were being fought at the time, and that, frankly, we had always fought. It brought a new sense of cooperation and a new peace and prosperity to all our nations, even as our numbers were shrinking." The president paused again.

"Well, today, my fellow Americans, I have great news. The veil that has so long kept us apart from our peaceful ancient cousins will soon disappear, and we will finally be reunited with our ancient kin. We have all seen the droves of mainly young people headed off into the wilderness and wondered why. Well, I can now reveal to you that they have gone to greet our cousins when the veil falls. They have understood empathically the universal and momentous significance of this second Event. And they have gone to celebrate the coming of this wonderful new dawn. A new dawn for all humanity."

There was, of course, a flurry of questions after that. How did the President know this? Why was the veil falling? What would happen when their two peoples and cultures collided? What of the OneMind and its preference for assimilation and thought control? What was the risk? Was there a danger? Should the people take steps to protect themselves, their children, and their communities from the menace of assimilation under the dictatorial control of the OneMind? From behind the podium, an army general stepped forward. He was older than the President, grizzled. He had the face of calm, unflappable authority.

"We perceive no military risk," he began. "The Wollemi have been studied in detail - their history, technological level, their propensity for war. All have been studied exhaustively. We perceive no threat from that quarter."

There was silence in the press room for a moment. Then a reporter stood up near the back of the press scrum. He had to raise his voice above the murmurings that began to gather momentum around the room.

"General," he began, "we understand that the Wollemi are not a warlike people. We understand the threat, if threat there be, would not come from that quarter. But I notice you left the question of threat somewhat open. General, if the perceived threat is not military, then what is it? Where is the threat, sir?"

The old General paused, gauging the mood of the room. He did not want to start a panic.

"Rest assured, please; the Military stands ready to address any threat. We do not have a military threat on our radar at the present time." With that, the old General followed the president out of the press room. Max, sitting in the bar on the other side of the world, in the Wisemans Ferry Inn, leaned forward. There was surely bound to be uproar in the White House press room after that. There was none. TV cameras turned to reveal the room. Reporters just stood there, uncertain of what they had heard, uncertain what it all meant. It had been impossible to read either the President's or the General's mood. The backwash in the room drowned out any individual emanations.

The news feed cut back to Australia, back, in fact, to Wisemans' Ferry. There was a news crew broadcasting from down by the ferry ramp.

"We have just heard that the military have closed all roads leading into the Wollemi and Yengo National Parks. We are told the move is for the protection of the Wollemi people who are not used to interacting with humanity." The scene cut to the view from a helicopter circling over the settlement of St Albans on the MacDonald River, a tributary of the great Hawkesbury. Below, around the bridge over the MacDonald River and the junction of the Settlers Road and the St Albans Road, a large crowd had gathered. The military had created a roadblock and were refusing passage to the Upper MacDonald Road that led, by a slow and meandering path, up into the wilderness and Mount Yengo. All around, on either side of the roadblock, a heaving mass of humanity was passing the small military unit by. The crowd, closing in from all sides, began to dismantle the military roadblock. There were a few tussles as brave or foolish soldiers attempted to keep it in place. Perhaps seeing that their cause was lost, their officer waved his men back. He formed up his squad, and they retreated in good order over the bridge and into St Albans village. In an instant, the remnants of the roadblock were removed, and the crowd surged ahead. The screen then cut across to the Grey Gum Café on Putty Road, where a similar scene was unfolding. While a combined police and military roadblock was attempting to hold back the swarm of people there, on the far side of the café, the multitudes pressed forward along the dirt road behind the Grey Gum International Café. The throng began to break down the fences at the side of the road and make their way across the sparsely wooded paddock that separated them from their comrades on the other side. The roadblock had become an irrelevance. A lone policeman could be seen talking into his radio, presumably seeking orders. The policeman nodded, looked up to gaze at the swarming multitudes passing him by, and waved to his colleagues to clear away the roadblock.

Back in the bar of the Wisemans' Ferry Inn, Max smiled, a rueful smile of admiration, tinged perhaps with just a note of worry. The One-Mind had been planning this, whatever it was, or something like it, for thousands of years. While human civilization grew, matured, aged, and collapsed all around the globe, the OneMind had been focused on this day. The Event some twenty years ago, and what Alice had referred to recently as 'The Calling' and 'The Merging', the collapse of the veil, the growing individualism and reasoning capabilities of the individual Wollemi, all of it, the whole thing, had been planned for, anticipated, and driven by the great OneMind of the Wollemi. Max could still remember the terror and the panic the very first time he had been forcibly assimilated by the collective. He remembered the choking, drowning sensation, the absolute terror at the stripping away of self. His ego-self had been flayed to the bone by the OneMind, mercilessly, ruthlessly and without a shred of empathy or regret. What now, he wondered, what was in store for his granddaughter Emma and his great-granddaughter Aine, herself already deeply enmeshed in the consciousness of the OneMind.

"It's not human," Max was lost in speculation, "It's not tame, and it's not Human."

"Pardon?"

The barman thought Max was speaking to him. Max looked up.

"Can we trust it?"

"Sorry?"

"The OneMind, it's responsible for all this. It planned it all. I'm wondering, can we trust it?"

The barman shook his head, "Well, Max, if you don't know, I don't know who does."

"Neither do I, except the OneMind itself."

"Well, what are our options?"

"We've only ever had the option of going along with it or resisting militarily."

"Suppose so," the barman paused, "I think I'll join you."

While the barman poured himself a schooner of Coopers Pale Ale, Max continued.

"But if you recall, even when we thought we were resisting, even when my dear friend and pencil pusher Harry Soames was firing the HARP device, believing it to be some terrible weapon, we were in reality following a path the OneMind had set for us."

"Never thought about it like that before." The barman took a swig of beer, "I've got to say, you Hexenkreiges have always seemed to be a key part of the story."

"I guess we have been. My son Jerry gave his life during the event. So did my dear friend Harry Soames."

The barman flicked off the TV screen.

"No use worrying though, is there?"

"No. Probably not. I suppose if the OneMind had wanted to hurt us, it could have done so at any point over the last few hundred thousand years."

"What now, then?" The barman leaned on the bar across from Max, sipping his beer.

"The veil will fall permanently this time. The OneMind says it will no longer be able to form, and the individual Wollemi will slowly become more like us." Max's tone suggested some doubt.

"Or?"

"Or the military will carpet bomb the wilderness areas here and around the world. They will wipe out the Wollemi. Genocide, plain and simple."

"They wouldn't, would they?"

"Wouldn't they? We, humans, have a pretty poor record of dealing with indigenous peoples."

"So, you really think the military might bomb the Wollemi, the wilderness and all those innocent people?"

"That's no doubt what the OneMind needs all these people for. To prevent the bombing. You can be sure that the military, all over, have laid their plans, loaded up their planes, positioned their rocket systems and are awaiting their orders."

"They won't want to, though, will they? None of us would, not these days, not since the Event."

"You're right about that. The gift of empathy was a smart move. It's far more difficult to stare someone in the face, read their emotional flow, and then kill them in cold blood."

The barman nodded.

"But that's not what they will be planning. They will be intending to drop bombs from a great height so no emotional backwash can be detected. Same with the rockets. Fire them from far away."

"I see."

"Empathy is not enough. Not on its own."

"What then?"

"Empathy leavened with reason and sound judgement. Maybe. I don't know myself."

Max finished his beer and checked into the Inn. On a whim, he decided to take Sophia's Grand Bedroom. It was the same room Kaitlin had stayed in the first time she came to Wisemans Ferry. Her first night in Australia, in fact.

"Good choice." The barman led Max up to the room. The four-poster bed, heavy red velvet curtains and the massive stone fireplace were just as he remembered them. He had stayed here too once. Just one night, when he arrived to begin his research into the anomalous fields detected by NASA emanating from the area. How long ago now?

Jack was now a middle-aged man with a child of his own. Sitting there in Sophia's Grand Bedroom, Max found himself wandering back in memory, searching for first cause. What had led him along his life's path? What had brought him here? Freewill didn't seem to come into it. A lifelong feeling of being, if not outright pushed, then at the very least manipulated, reasserted itself. When he came to think about it, almost everyone he had known, for sure all those he had worked closely with, had reported similar feelings. Could it be true? Could they all have been manipulated by the OneMind to do its bidding?

Max took out his phone and searched online for a profile of Harry Soames. He remembered something Harry had once said about Tom and him sharing a wilderness upbringing. He flicked passed the obituary, the career history at the Centre for Disease Control and found the short section on his birthplace and upbringing. Harry grew up around the River of No Return, a wilderness area, same story with Tom. He was born into a Comanche community in the southern Great Plains area before moving as a young child to the Denali Mountain in Alaska, another wilderness area. The coincidence was too much to be ignored. Max himself had been born and brought up in the dense woodland of the northern Black Forest in Germany before moving to Berlin to study. His own two boys had been born in the Wollemi wilderness. What about Kaitlin? Quick search. Same story. She was born deep in the countryside on the remote west coast of Ireland, where people still leave out milk and cookies for the 'little people' on the Eve of All Souls. A cold chill began to settle in Max's mind. What he had revealed was no coincidence. The OneMind had chosen people living in wilderness areas to be its hands and feet in the human world. Without permission and, no doubt, without a second thought, the OneMind had suborned not just their will but their entire lives to its purpose. Was this the behaviour of a benefactor? The philosophical ramifications were beyond him. Perhaps in order to protect and guide both Homo Sapiens and Homo Occultatum, the sacrifice of a few individual lives could be excused. After all, they were not killed or imprisoned unless a life without free will is an imprisoned life. But then, what of the Wollemi themselves? Did they not all live lives without free will or without full consciousness, and did that not amount to the same thing? Whatever the finer points of reasoning, Max realised, he and all his fellow 'automata' had but one choice, to trust. To put their faith in the OneMind until it disappeared forever and they were freed.

Max made his decision. It was pointless waiting for word from Gideon. Events had moved beyond the power of any individual to alter or even influence. Max still knew a few people. He would drive the ute down to Walkers Beach. Situated on a tight bend in the Hawkesbury, it was one of the shortest crossing points. Max figured he could borrow a kayak and paddle across to Chaseling Road. And there, he would meet someone who could provide him with what he needed.

Once decided, Max acted quickly. He called the son of an old friend.

"Hello?" A man's voice, middle-aged.

"Hi, we haven't spoken in a while. It's Max, Max Hexenkriege." There was a moment's silence on the line.

"Max, wow, yeah, it's been a long time. I'd heard you were back. From Germany, wasn't it?"

"Er… Yeah. I've been away quite a while. Listen, I'm after a small favour."

"Sure. What do you need?"

Max glanced at his watch. "Can you meet me at the cemetery in an hour?"

"You know the ferry is out?"

"Yep, I'm coming the old way."

"Oh. OK. I'll see you in an hour."

"I'll explain then."

Max hung up the phone. Although he wasn't planning now to stay the night, he paid for the room anyway.

"I'll be leaving at the crack of dawn. Best I fix you up now."

The barman rang up the bill and gave Max a set of keys and a receipt.

"I'm gonna go take a look around."

"Catch you later. Trivia night tonight, in case you're interested. There's a tray of lamb for the winner."

"Sounds good."

"Yep, real meat, locally farmed."

Max left the bar and walked to the ute. A few people nodded or waived as he unlocked the door and jumped in. Max slowly backed into the road. A few people, having heard the call, were still arriving.

Twenty minutes later, driving slowly and allowing for random acts of jaywalking, Max arrived at Walkers Beach. He parked the ute under the trees at the caravan park by the river and walked back to the site office. The TV news was on with the volume turned up loud. Max knocked on the door a couple of times before turning the handle and taking a step inside. A man was sitting at a desk with his back to the door, watching the TV news. He hadn't heard Max walk in above the sound of the TV. Max waited a moment, then tapped the little bell on the desk a couple of times. The man nearly jumped out of his skin.

"What the hell. Don't you people ever learn to knock." The man swivelled on his office chair, bristling with indignation, ready for a fight.

"Max. How the bloody hell are you? It's been bloody years."

Max struggled to reply over the sound of the TV.

"Could you turn that down a bit, Frank, or off?"

Frank turned the TV off, "Crazy kids heading into the wilderness. They'll die of bloody thirst or hunger or worse."

"It's good to see you, Frank. It's been too long."

Frank gave Max a long appraising stare. Despite his blustering manner, Frank was not easily fooled.

"You haven't aged a bit, Max. Where have you been hiding?"

"I went to be with my wife and her people for a while."

"And now you're back."

"Yes, I'm back, but not for long. I'll be heading home again soon."

"You Hexenkreiges always seem to be around when something interesting is happening. Just coincidence, mate, or do you know more about this mass exodus than is on the TV?"

"The OneMind is back, the veil is failing, and the Dreamtime and our own world are going to merge. Did you catch that on the TV news yet?"

"Not yet."

"Well, you will. I need to cross the river, Frank. Can you lend me a kayak?"

"I'll get the tinny out and give you a ride." Frank lifted his ageing bulk from the swivel chair and grabbed a set of keys off a hook.

"Are we in danger, Max? Should I be concerned?"

Max paused as they walked to the narrow beach.

"I honestly don't know Frank. I don't think we're in danger, but there is a distinct chance that the military will carpet bomb the Wollemi and Yengo wilderness."

"Ok. So, no big deal then."

"Frank, this is another Event. These 'crazy kids', as you call them, are going to Mount Yengo to surround the Wollemi people when the veil falls. They're going there to protect them. To stop the bombing."

"We'd better get a move on then."

Frank dragged the tinny into the water and started the engine.

"Where do you want me to drop you?"

At the end of Chaseling Road. Just diagonally across the river if that's OK."

The little outboard engine started first time, and in minutes Max was deposited on the other side, near the old homestead.

"Thanks, Frank. Listen, you can expect to see the Wollemi roaming around the place over the next few months. They will seem like children. Everything will be new to them."

"Understood. It was good to see you, Max. Give the OneMind my regards."

"Nothing gets past you, does it?"

Frank smiled, "I've still got all my marbles, old mate. I hope we will meet again."

Max walked slowly to the road. He needed the few hundred yards to the old Chaseling family cemetery to clear his head. He had to get back to the Table of the Gods at once. The feeling was nearly overpowering. Especially, given his newfound grasp of his situation, of the path his life had taken to that point, Max doubted that the imperative to return to the Mountain was really 'his' at all.

"I know what you have done," Max spoke the words aloud, focussing his thoughts on the distant OneMind. "I know what you have been doing all these years, all these centuries, I should say. You can't fool me any longer."

It was one of those cold bright days in winter that, looking out from behind the protection of a glass window, fool you into thinking that the day must be warm, and then chills to the bone once you venture out. Max slowed even more and then stopped. An image was forming in his mind—a vision of military jets screaming in over wilderness places all over the world, bombing indiscriminately. The Wollemi, men, women, and children, running this way and that. Terror and confusion on their faces. A vision of charred bodies piled high punctuating the pristine wilderness so recently abandoned by humanity. A vision of hell. And then, sounding silently in his mind, a question.

"Was I so wrong?"

Max had no answer. As though pressing its advantage, another image formed. The image of an old man, worn down by time and hard work, taking a razor-sharp knife to his young son's throat. And another question, *"You humans have always been so willing to sacrifice even your own children. How could I trust you not to slaughter mine?"*

It was obvious to Max then. Humanity could not be trusted. The OneMind was right. There was no evil act that human reason could not rationalise, had not rationalised many, many times. Picking up his pace Max arrived at the tiny cemetery a few moments later. A man was waiting by an old, slightly wonky gravestone. Out of idle curiosity, Max read the inscription. It was the last resting place of Mary and Matthew Chaseling. They died before the grotesque wars of the twentieth century. They had not witnessed the slaughter of innocents on an industrial scale. They had lived and died in a world that moved at the pace of a horse-drawn cart. The sound of helicopters landing and taking off from across the river broke into Max's reverie.

"Hello Peter, it's good to see you. How's your father?"

"Dad's OK. He lives with my sister's family now. He gets three meals a day and spends time with the grandkids. He's doing fine."

"I'm glad to hear it. Look, I'll cut to the chase. You will have heard all the hoo-ha on the TV news. I need to get to Mount Yengo fast."

"Do I need to grab the family and get out of here, Max?"

"You should be safe here, Peter. You are outside the exclusion zone, but I can't guarantee anything."

"What would you do, Max, in my position?"

"I guess I'd follow my bushfire plan. I'd pack up what I needed to take and be ready to leave."

"That bad, is it?"

"I'd say it's that unclear, Peter. The roads are blocked by the military and by people heading to Mount Yengo. The ferries are out too. Can you get across the river?"

"Yep, we've got a decent-sized fishing boat."

"Then I'd be prepared to head downstream to Berowra Waters or even upstream to Windsor."

"What do you need from me, Max? How can I help you?"

"Can you lend me a dirt bike?"

Peter laughed, a hollow laugh, "Can you still ride one?"

"Well, I guess I'll find out."

Peter and Max walked back up Chaseling Road for a few minutes until they came to Peter's family home. Max noticed a newish-looking sea fishing boat at the end of the short wharf.

"That ought to do it," Max nodded in the direction of the sleek-looking boat.

"It's a sideline out of the main season. I take people out to fish for Bluefin Tuna as the seawater cools or the odd straggling marlin."

Peter lifted the roller door to the garage. Several dirt bikes were standing at the back of the garage. In the forefront was an old Holden Torana with the hood up. From the jaunty orange colour, Max could tell immediately that it was from the 1970s.

"Well, I'll be damned, your dad always told me he had one of these, but I never saw it, and I'm not sure I believed him."

"Yeah, it still drives well. It must be worth a fortune these days."

"Is it still legal to drive? More to the point, can you still get petrol for it?"

"It is, and you can. We need petrol for the bikes and the farm machinery. There's a Veteran Car Club that sources spares, and you can get a special road license. The oldies still do the grey goose trek up to Cairns and back."

Peter pulled out one of the larger dirt bikes and filled the tank.

"You remember the trail?"

"Yes, I think so. It's been a while, but I have a GPS in my phone."

Peter and Max shook hands.

Peter watched Max out of sight and then turned towards the homestead and walked quickly inside. He had no time to waste.

The journey back to the Mountain was, for Max, a time of reflection. He didn't encounter another soul until a kilometre or so out, a loan backpacker slogging her way through the bush. Max put her on the pillion seat and headed off. It wouldn't have been much more than ten minutes later that Max navigated the dirt bike up the winding track to the Table of the Gods. There were people everywhere. Max drove slowly as the waves of humanity parted. He parked the bike near the top, and he and his passenger dismounted.

"I'm going to talk to the OneMind. Would you like to join me?" Max nodded in the direction of the giant stone slab a few metres above them. The girl nodded, perhaps a little too overawed to find her voice.

The Table itself was relatively sparsely populated. There was an open space at the centre where stood Tom and Alice, Jack, Kaitlin, Emma and Aine in a semicircle. In front of them hovered the grey shimmering manifestation of the OneMind. Max's compatriots turned as one as he approached. They were in perfect sync. They were joined mentally with the OneMind. The quiet chatter of the few people lining the edge of the Table ceased. From off to one side, Max's wife appeared, smiling widely. Max ran to her, lifted her small frame in his arms and swung her around.

"I've missed you." A tear formed at the edge of his eye.

"Welcome home, husband." The words, oddly accented, sounded clearly in the sudden quiet.

The grey manifestation of Wollemi group consciousness glided over toward the happy couple.

"Thank you, Max, for returning to us."

"Sure," Max set his wife down by his side, "What now?"

PANIKON DEIMA

And then the tide turned. In the United States first, and afterwards around the world, the backlash began. It was the older people who turned first, particularly those in their sixties and older. The threat-promise of a second Event was too much for them. For those for whom the initial Event had been a wrenching discontinuity with the past. Those for whom the direct perception of another's true emotional flow had been a curse rather than a blessing. Those who hadn't wanted to know. Those who had had the unbearable truth forced upon them. Those for whom life itself had become a fraud, wrapped in a pretence, inside a lie. Those who now lived in terror of the second coming of the OneMind, and the horrors it might bring.

Fear was indeed the mind-killer. And dread, of course. The dread of the unknown. The reaction came hard upon the heels of the Calling. The legend of the Pied Piper was trotted out. The OneMind was a child thief, even though a minority of older people, too, had answered the Call. The OneMind, through Aine, had induced over five hundred million people to drop everything and join the Wollemi in the wilderness. Aine herself was a traitress, a traitor to humanity.

The people of the cities and the suburbs responded to the perceived threat with demonstrations at first and then with riots. The maddening backwash of their rage and fear building, feeding back upon itself, growing into a vortex of murderous fury and hatred. In a frenzy of wrath, the people of the cities and suburbs exploded into the country-side. A second wave of humanity, heading for the wilderness areas, intent this time upon vengeance for an unknown crime. A crime not yet committed. The demon 'Panic' drove them, flogging all before it with whips of horror, revulsion, and disgust. What vile purpose was playing out deep in the long-abandoned wilderness? What loathsome fate had the perfidious OneMind planned for them? What doom awaited them in the primeval forest, far from civilisation?

Those who had access to weapons led the way—a lynch mob of heroic proportions bent upon murder. Chanting, carrying torches, medieval in every way, the vengeful hoard crept in upon the wild places, upon Mount Yengo and The Table of the Gods.

"Kill the beast," they cried, in every human language, "Kill the beast."

***

Into the silence that had fallen across the Table of Gods spread a sudden sense of unease.

"They are coming," the voice of the OneMind sounded silently in the minds of every person present, "we must prepare."

Ranks formed without conscious instruction. People joined arms, Wollemi and Human alike. A chain of humanity swirled and grew across and around the mountain. The two long separated paths humanity had taken joined at last in one desperate attempt to stand against the fire and wrath of the mob.

At the centre of the chain stood Aine, and next to her, Emma, Kaitlin and Alice, Tom, Jack, Max, and his newly wakened wife, and around them wove the massed ranks of those who had responded to the Calling, and the Wollemi of course, silently waiting. The sounds of voices chanting far off came to them across the forest. On all sides, the lynch mob approached with stamping feet and cries of rage and revenge. That clichéd scene, recognised from a thousand terrible melodramas, repeated itself, in reality, this time. Here and there, torches flared. Weapons were brandished. Threats of terrible vengeance were made, cheered on by the mob. Oaths were taken.

Those who had not heard the Call. Those for whom empathy was anything but surged in around the mountain. A tide of men and women rose like flood waters, encircling Mount Yengo. The silent voice of the OneMind sounded once more.

"I have one last favour to ask, one last indulgence." The OneMind paused then as though measuring the odds. The sense was shared along the chain of humanity wrapped around the Table of the Gods, spread even to the mountain's skirts, of odds being weighed, fate being held in the balance, and finally, of dice being cast.

"My friends," the voice continued, "lend me your minds."

Aine and Emma felt it first, the irresistible pull of the OneMind. And gladly, this time, in the full knowledge of what was being asked for and given, one by one, the humans and the newly woken Wollemi surrendered themselves to the gestalt.

The veil began to form around them, a translucent bubble of swirling light and colour, coalescing into a dome that covered and enclosed Mount Yengo. All across the globe, in a thousand different places at once, the OneMind raised the veil against the lynch mobs.

The gestalt was different this time. Individual thought-flows could still be heard. Hundreds at first and then thousands, and then too many to be grasped, formed, layer upon layer, into a vast telepathic intellect. As the OneMind grew and integrated itself into the web of life that surrounded and cocooned them all, a new entity emerged, one not encountered or perceived by a conscious human being, perhaps since the sundering of humanity an age before. Never had the OneMind brought together so many individual minds. Never had it formed on this scale across the entire Earth.

What emerged was unknown, unnamed. It was the OneMind, but it was also more, much more than humanity had ever imagined. It was beyond all individual understanding. It, they, were able to perceive and encompass the Earth itself. The web of life was visible to all as scintillating, pulsing energy permeating the planet and everything within its atmosphere. The quantum void made visible by life itself. In the sky, across the globe, even at low latitudes, the aurora emerged low overhead. The OneMind was drawing massive amounts of power from the magnetopause.

What materialised was not a God or even a demi-god, but it was, in its absolute, qualitative metamorphosis, and difference from the merely telepathic OneMind, both an indication of what humanity could become and a cruel calibration of the gaping void that perhaps not even faith could leap. A gap which, even if humanity were somehow to cross it, would still leave the species insignificant, tiny, and irrelevant when set against the infinite complexity and vastness of the universe.

Though such speculation was engaging, the OneMind had more pressing matters to attend to. Humanity cloistered beneath the dome, and phase shifted just a millimetre or so to one side of the mainstream, was faced by its implacable alter ego, humanity, baying for blood outside. What was to be done? What could be done? The two aspects of humanity stood face to face—an endlessly repeating image, there at Mount Yengo and around the world in a thousand places. The two faces of Janus separated, opposing. Only the veil kept them apart. The Dreamtime and the mundane world would finally collide. Nothing could stop it.

Until something came to mind, even the super-entity that the One-Mind had become was stumped. The willing, conscious participation of a large subset of all mankind was a different experience for it. For the first time in millennia, the OneMind was experiencing something new. It was conscious in itself and conscious too in the myriad minds that it encompassed. It was disembodied and perhaps immortal, and it was fleeting flesh, alive for an instant and then gone. From the planetary purview which it now enjoyed, the magnificence and tragedy of transitory human experience was laid bare. Everything was ephemeral, even life itself. But in its passing evanescence, it was glorious.

Having arrived at Mount Yengo, the mob began to try its defences, prodding the veil at first with long sticks and hurling the occasional rock. Nothing got through. The rocks bounced back into the crowd, eliciting angry calls to stop. A couple of the more belligerent, armed individuals fired one or two shots just to see the ricocheting rounds sending everyone diving for cover.

The mob could not break through the veil. The OneMind hadn't a clue what to do about them. An impasse had been reached. Another new, and this time not so welcome, experience for the awakened super being.

The crowd beyond the veil grew and grew. From her vantage point on the flat expanse of the Table of the Gods, Aine could make out here and there through gaps in the canopy of trees, glimpses of humanity ranged against them as far as the eye could see. In the distance, Aine and her companions sensed as much as heard the faint *thwop-thwop-thwop* of approaching helicopters.

Military forces around the world had fared better than the mob. By and large, they had managed to maintain control of their people. The military chain of command held. While the masses of humanity poured out of the cities and into the wilderness, the order to commence bombing never came. Perhaps it was withheld by the authorities, or perhaps political power structures had collapsed to such an extent that no order could be given. Regardless, the sword of Damocles did not fall but remained held in place, hanging by its single thread.

The military approached. Had the order been given at last? Was the sword about to fall?

THE DARK SIDE OF EMPATHY

The people left behind turned in upon themselves and upon each other. Burning barricades were set up. Vigilantes roamed their neighbourhoods. Anarchy followed. Saturn stalked the streets. None of his children were safe. And they were egged on by the world's media, both public and private. The social media machine went into overdrive. Conspiracy theorists had a field day. In the darker corners of the internet, no holds were barred. No theory remained unaired. No mad idea was left without adherents and even advocates. Swiftly and without a backwards glance, the mainstream world went mad. And having descended into madness, those remaining in the cities and the suburbs dived eagerly into the warm waters of paranoia and psychosis.

In every jurisdiction, the forces of the state began to unravel. Ancient fears and rivalries resurfaced. Vendettas, long thought dead, revived. The chains of political command and control weakened further. In the countryside, militias and old alliances reformed. The rule of law broke down completely. People took matters into their own hands. Deeds were done. Accounts were settled. The shadow of a new dark age appeared upon mankind's event horizon. Society began to break down. Total collapse, in so far as it was avoided, was held at bay only by the bonds of family and friendship. The cycle of yin and yang had, perhaps, in the broad light of day, swung to its furthest extreme of chaotic action. Perhaps now, as the lights began to go out around the world and darkness threatened, the pendulum would begin to swing back. Perhaps the wheel of karma would begin to turn once more. For many, as the world they had known fell further into chaos, that was as much as could be hoped for.

The slaughter of the left-behind, which had begun in a small way with the settling of old scores, fed upon itself. A ravening hunger for destruction and death took hold. The seething discontent of that part of humanity, that portion for whom life, the universe itself, was meaningless and without purpose, spent itself with excoriating force. Just two days, a weekend, of unrestrained bestiality was enough, though no beast had ever behaved as did they.

Across the planet, in every city and hamlet, mayhem swept through the lynch mobs. Armed, enraged though crippled with fear and dread, never far from blind panic, the seething mob roamed the streets. When the dust began to settle, the only human institution left standing was the military. And if humanity's last remaining tool was a soldier, perhaps every solution must have looked like war. In every part of the world where any semblance of normalcy had been re-established, it was the military that had taken control.

Order was restored. Stunned by the febrile events of a single weekend, horrified at the delirious frenzy that had overtaken them all, the survivors began once more to venture out. The scene that met them as they wandered the shattered streets of their neighbourhoods was one of desolation and despair. The human population, faced with the brutal evidence of their own psychosis, searched for an explanation, or better yet, a justification. Their desperate need to pardon themselves drove them to grasp at any defence. It was the OneMind's doing. The One-Mind had driven them to mass hysteria and madness. Looking around at their splintered world, burying their dead, the inevitable protective myth emerged. This was not who they were. They hadn't done this. This was done to them. It was OneMind's fault. And fast upon the heels of that conclusion came the call for revenge. In cold fury, this time, co-ordinated and focussed, the left-behind and the military aligned. Silently this time, and somehow, inevitably, a single, ancient purpose drove them. *"Burn the witch,"* they thought, *"Kill the beast."*

Internationally, hurried conferences were held. The military forces of the human world conferred. In every jurisdiction, the OneMind, the Wollemi and those who had heard the Call faced off against the mob. In every jurisdiction, the veil both protected and revealed the other-world, the Dreamtime, Shangri-la, Tír na nÓg. Call it what you like. The Kingdom of Elfin was revealed, its true power and intent unknown. The level of threat it represented, impossible to estimate.

In the end, there was only one possible military option. It was the same option they had always come to. Graduated assault culminating, if need be, with the unthinkable. But what of those who had already entered the wilderness seeking revenge? They must be warned. They must stand down. All over the world, military helicopters were prepared. The warning of the coming war would be sent out. Briefings from both NASA and the NSA suggested that time was short. There was some instability in the magnetopause, and that instability was somehow linked to the instability in the veil, the unexpected appearance of the auroras and the message from the OneMind. All over the world, dictionaries were consulted as people developed a newfound interest in the magnetopause and the aurora borealis. It made no difference, whether naturally occurring or by the deliberate intention of the OneMind. The fall of the veil and the collision of the two worlds represented a threat. A threat that the military was determined to meet.

And of those who had sided with the OneMind and the Wollemi, what of them? What indeed? If they were able to leave, they should do so, of course, and if not? Well, in war, there is always collateral damage. Amongst those more inclined to rational thought, though, there were residual doubts. They wondered if the OneMind had cursed them with mass hysteria. Nagging thoughts in the back of the mind, recollections of the torrential backwash of the mob, suggested that what had been revealed had been the dark side of empathy. Though it could never be admitted, never spoken of aloud, perhaps the carnage had been of their own doing. And so, it was agreed, the mob would be warned to retreat, and a delegation would be sent to the OneMind to negotiate. There was little to lose. After all, they could send in the bombers any time they liked.

Across the globe, helicopters were despatched to drop warning leaflets on the mob and on the Wollemi and their supporters. And in Australia, a delegation was hurriedly assembled. There had been no time fully to develop their negotiating position. An unsympathetic observer might suggest that what they had prepared was little better than a back-of-an-envelope checklist. Well, whatever. It would have to do.

Two hours after the leaflet drop, when it was hoped that the mob would have understood the warning and begun to move back, a lone helicopter was scheduled to lift off from the Richmond Air Base. In moments it would be flying low over the endless swathe of the Wollemi wilderness. The delegation would arrive at Mount Yengo in minutes.

233

This was to be the last chance for peace or an opportunity for mankind to obliterate the last remaining intact indigenous nation on Earth. Not a happy or an easy choice.

LEAVE NOW

The approaching helicopters separated as they neared Mount Yengo. There were ten in all. One came on and hovered over the Table of the Gods. The others took up positions roughly half a kilometre apart and began to fly in slow concentric circles of increasing diameter, describing a sort of giant dartboard or target shape. A command must have been given because all at once, the side doors of the helicopters slid open, and leaflets filled the sky, fluttering down like confetti. A small opening appeared in the veil above the Table of the Gods, and several leaflets fell through. Tom grabbed one as it fell and began to read aloud. The message to the thousands gathered outside the veil was brief and emphatic.

"LEAVE NOW.

Under the Terms of the Constitution of the Commonwealth of Australia, Section 119, the Commonwealth shall protect every State against invasion and, on the application of the Executive Government of the State, against domestic violence.

The Wollemi and Yengo National Parks are gazetted Total Exclusion Zones. Anyone found within the borders of the Yengo or Wollemi National Parks after sundown today will be subject to summary arrest and imprisonment for a term of up to one calendar month."

There followed a 'by order of' and a few final remarks, but the message was abundantly clear – Get Out. On the reverse side of the leaflet was a message to the OneMind. It read:

'From the Office of the Minister for Defence and Foreign Affairs, Federal Government of the Commonwealth of Australia, to the Entity known as the OneMind of the Wollemi.

Dear OneMind, we write seeking a meeting with you to clarify the status of the veil and matters arising therefrom. Your attendance at a meeting to discuss this matter is cordially requested. Our delegation will be arriving at Mount Yengo by helicopter within the next few hours.

Yours Sincerely, Minister for Defence and Foreign Affairs.'

Beyond the veil, Aine and her comrades could see the leaflets being grabbed from the sky and read. Looks of consternation began to appear on the faces of the gathered masses. People craned their necks and scanned the sky. A rumbling discontent began to propagate through the mob. Angry mutterings grew into shouts of disagreement, and as the toxic feedback loop began once more to increase in intensity and coverage, the mob began once more to chant.

"No retreat! No Surrender!" over and over again, the visceral angst of the ignored, the downtrodden and the left-behind sounded across the wilderness. The cry was picked up and spread through the crowd like wildfire. The sound of chanting grew and merged into a thumping harmonic felt deep in the chests of the mob. A few hotheads raised their weapons and began to fire at the slowly circling helicopters. One, its glass windscreen shattered and, taking heavy small-arms fire, fell from the sky, crashing into the packed ranks below. A roar went up then. A cry of rage and revenge, without immediate focus or outlet. Others in the crowd raised their weapons and began to fire. As one, the remaining helicopters lifted and banked away, retreating from Mount Yengo as fast as they could. The message was sent to Command HQ by the departing soldiers.

"Taking heavy small-arms fire. Black Hawk Down. I say again, Black Hawk Down."

On the ground, the infuriated mob surged forward on all sides towards the Mountain. Those at the front were crushed against the unyielding veil.

"No retreat! No Surrender!" the mob cried out. The screams of the crushed and dying were lost in the wave of sound that rose and swept across the wilderness. Enormous flocks of birds left their perches and took to the sky, wheeling and circling above. Intense emotional backwash lashed the mob to an even greater frenzy. Maddened people began to climb over the dead, using their bodies to clamber a little way up the sides of the veil itself. Blood and mud smeared the all-but-invisible surface, sliding off and onto the people below as the veil shimmered and oscillated, providing no lasting purchase. Back at Command HQ, urgent reports were passed further up the chain of command, seeking guidance. What were they supposed to do? What were their orders? And then the order came.

"Assume the OneMind has assimilated them all and is using our people against us," the message read, "prepare for thermobaric attack."

At the Richmond Air Base, planes were readied. Thermobaric fuel-air bombs were wheeled out on gurneys and loaded into open bomb bays. There would be no mistakes this time. The upper echelons of Command were determined. If the OneMind wanted war, the OneMind would have it. On the ground, at the Richmond Air Base, however, matters were not quite so clear cut.

"There must be thousands of protesters out there." The airman driving the gurney shook his head. Another man attached a clamp to the bomb, and it was lifted into place.

"Hundreds of thousands more like, they've been pouring in for days despite the roadblocks. Some have trekked cross country from Cessnock and Newcastle."

"It's not right," the man driving the gurney began to reverse away, "these are our people. We can't just bomb them because they're in the way."

"What's going on here?" An officer standing nearby had caught snatches of their conversation. The men remained silent.

"You have your orders."

"Sir." The man who had loaded the bomb into the waiting aircraft hopped onto the gurney, and the pair headed slowly back across the tarmac to the waiting hangar. This was going to take a while.

"They're not wrong, though." The officer thought to himself and headed into a nearby building to re-confirm their orders. Inside, the atmosphere was tense. Uniformed men and women stood around, silent, waiting. Occasional remarks passed between them. More men came in wearing grey and blue camouflage fatigues. Aircrew slumped around low tables, drinking coffee and chatting. At last, the door to a side office opened, and a woman stepped out. Instantly the room snapped to attention. She was medium height, with hair scraped back, slim and calm. The look of authority and steely determination on her face left no one in any doubt as to who was in charge.

"Listen up," she began, "we have our orders. We have prepared for such an eventuality for many years. Our role is to defend our country against its enemies, and defend it we will." The gathered men stirred a little at that, but nothing was said.

"Command has determined that the so-called OneMind represents a genuine threat. It is not for us to make that determination. Am I clear?" There were a few nods and muttered affirmations around the room. Dissatisfied with the apparent level of commitment of her men, the senior officer spoke again.

"Am I clear?"

The response was slightly more enthusiastic the second time but was scarcely an affirmation. Realising that a smattering of "Yes, Ma'ams" and some nods was as much as she was going to get, the senior officer turned to her aide-de-camp.

"I want regular updates every half hour. Everything must be ready in no more than two hours."

"Yes, ma'am." The senior officer surveyed the room for a moment longer.

"We have never before faced an enemy like the OneMind," heads turned, and the room began to focus once more on what she had to say. "We have never before faced an enemy that has the power to suborn our people at will and use them against us." She paused. She needed to say more. The atmosphere in the room was becoming hesitant. She must not lose control.

"The OneMind has been manipulating mankind for thousands, perhaps hundreds of thousands of years. Never once has it come to us to explain its actions. Never once has it come clean as to the level of manipulation and interference it has wrought upon us." There were a few more nods at that.

"You are the backbone of our nation's defence. I know you will do your duty. I know you will set aside your doubts and face this inscrutable menace with the bravery and professionalism you have always shown."

The men and women in the room began to straighten up at that. They were professionals. They would do their duty. But still. The thousands and perhaps hundreds of thousands of people who had marched into the wilderness were their people. The twin towns of Richmond and Windsor had lain silent for days, much of their populations having gone either to support the OneMind or to confront it. Theirs was a close-knit community. The Air Base and the town had grown symbiotically over a hundred years or so. It would be no simple matter to set all that aside and incinerate people they had lived, worked, and grown up with.

The senior officer turned and walked back into her office. With the door closed and safely hidden behind frosted glass, she focussed he mind on feelings of pride and concern for the young airmen outside, awaiting their orders. One never knew who might be listening in. Then she placed her elbows on the desk in front of her and buried her head in her hands. The men were right, of course. They were being asked to drop devastating bombs on thousands of their fellow citizens, friends, neighbours, and perhaps even family. It would be touch and go whether they would carry out their orders. They needed an honest-to-goodness enemy to fight. After several minutes the senior officer picked up the phone and called her superior officer in Canberra.

"Sup Jean?"

"Sir, our people are uncomfortable about their orders."

"Are they refusing?"

"No, of course not, Sir. These are our people. We trained them."

"Yes, you're right. Of course, we can rely on our people."

"Sir, even if we can't question our orders, can we at least seek clarification?"

"What clarification do you want?"

"Sir, are we to bomb the people outside the veil? There're thousands of people surrounding Mount Yengo. The resulting blast and firestorm would incinerate them. Thousands of innocent Australians would be killed."

"They have been told to retreat, to fall back away from the veil and leave the area."

"Sir, they're not moving. You know that, Sir."

"Command has determined that they have been assimilated by the OneMind. That's why they fired on the helicopters that we sent specially to warn them."

"Yes, Sir. Do you believe that, Sir?"

"I don't know, Jean. Who knows what the OneMind is capable of?"

"True, Sir, but if it is so all-powerful, why hasn't it just assimilated us all a thousand years ago and be done with it?"

"I'll make enquiries, Jean. See if there is any room for interpretation in the field."

"Thank you, sir. Appreciated."

Sounds of commotion outside brought the senior officer back to her feet. Upon opening her office door, she was confronted with the site of several aboriginal men and women trying to gain entry to the officer's ready room. Their way was blocked by several airmen in grey and blue camouflage and one or two in the blue shirts and darker slacks of desk officers.

"Let them pass." The senior officer walked across the crowded ready room to meet her guests. She stopped a metre or so from the group of visitors.

"The Royal Australian Air Force acknowledges the indigenous owners of this land," she began, "How can I help you today?"

A girl stepped forward, perhaps fifteen years old.

"I am an Elder of our people." The girl stopped to gauge the senior officer's reaction. "My name is Killara, and I have come here to warn you that thousands of our people from all over Australia have gathered in the vicinity of Mount Yengo to discuss the current situation with the OneMind."

"I see." The senior officer seemed a little non-plussed at the quiet but determined delivery of her young guest.

"You have acknowledged us as the indigenous owners of this land. You know from the history of the previous Event that we have been watching over the Dreamtime for many thousands of years."

"Yes, I read that."

"You know that we are familiar with the OneMind."

"Yes."

"It has fallen to me to warn you of the large numbers of innocent people who are currently situated deep in the forest and to request that you hold off all further military incursion into the wilderness while the necessary rituals and negotiations take place."

"I see."

"We are returning to the Dreamtime. The worlds will be brought back together. The Wollemi will wander among us once again."

"Yes, I have been briefed on the situation."

"The Wollemi are closer to us than cousins. They are our brothers and sisters."

"The Wollemi, are your brothers and sisters?" The senior officer was not comfortable with the direction the conversation was taking.

"No, well, yes, they are brothers and sisters to all of us. They are human beings like us. It is just that they or we have taken different paths."

"Yes?"

"And now our paths are re-joining."

"Yes, I was briefed on that." The senior officer, exposed under the watchful eyes of her men, was beginning to lose patience.

"More than half the people who live in the towns that surround the wilderness have congregated around Mount Yengo. These are your own people. Do not take military action against them."

"We have our orders." The senior officer was not about to be instructed by a civilian. The stirring in the room sounded a warning in her ears.

"Can we offer you some refreshments? You must have walked a long way to get here?"

"No. Thank you, we must be on our way."

"Where will you go now?"

"We will return to our people in the forest."

"You know the forest is a Total Exclusion Zone?"

"You cannot exclude us. You said so yourself. We are the true owners of this land."

"I am sorry," the senior officer nodded to the men in camouflage fatigues, "but I cannot allow you to enter a restricted zone."

Killara looked around the room. There were several indigenous men and women wearing Air Force uniforms. She addressed them directly.

"Our people have waited sixty thousand years and more for this moment. The veil will fall. The Dreamtime will return. You know what you must do."

Without offering any resistance, the Aboriginal delegation was led out of the ready room to a small room inside a hangar where the engineers took their breaks.

"I'm going to have to ask you to remain here until the crisis is over and the all-clear is given." The senior officer nodded to the men in camouflage. The visitors were led into the room, and the door was closed and locked behind them.

"Keep watch," The senior officer turned to walk back to her office, "I doubt they'll give you any trouble."

NON-LETHAL FORCE

Back in the ready room, the atmosphere was serious, sombre. Her servicemen and women knew something she didn't know yet. The ADC was nervously waiting for her in her office. Through the open door, she could see him fidgeting and pacing. Assuming her steeliest look of unflappable resolve, the senior officer stalked through the ready room and into her office, closing the door silently behind her.

"Orders?" she snapped as the door closed.

"Orders Ma'am." The ADC handed her a crumpled, old-fashioned-looking printout. The senior officer read and then re-read their orders. Without looking towards her ADC, she let herself down into her chair and paused.

"They know?"

"Yes, Ma'am."

"How?"

"I didn't tell them, Ma'am, but when I came running back from the signals office with a torn printout in my hand, they must have guessed."

"I see. Thank you." The ADC, hearing the note of dismissal in his senior officer's voice, turned to leave.

"Not a word to the ready room."

"Yes, Ma'am."

The senior officer re-read the orders, placed the printout on her desk and smoothed it down as though trying to get the crinkles out of her orders, as much as out of the paper they were written on. It was as though she felt if laid out smoothly on her desk, her orders might make sense. After a moment, she picked up the phone and hit re-dial. The phone rang in the office of her superior officer in Canberra.

"Hello, Jean. I was expecting your call."

"Sir, were you able to clarify our orders?"

"Not yet. I have a meeting with the top brass in less than half an hour. I will try then. No guarantees."

"Sir, you are an Air Commodore."

"Unfortunately, I'm just not all that senior in Canberra."

"Sir, we have to try non-lethal force on the civilians first. We have to try to move them back."

"What do you propose?"

"Sir, we have more than five non-lethal options," the senior officer began to tick them off on the fingers of her right hand, "we have chopper-mounted Claymore M5s, a few Pulsed Energy Projectile systems, one Pain Ray - Active Denial System, several Plasma Shields, I'd have to have stores check how many are serviceable, and four High-Capacity OC Dispensers left over from the Philippines."

"Wow, I had no idea you were so well-tooled up for crowd control."

"Well, we've been doing nothing but military policing operations for years. And you know air bases, Sir. The stuff that gets brought back from active duty just gets dumped in the warehouse. It happens all the time."

"How many choppers do you have?"

"We have fifteen, Sir. As you know, one was downed by small arms fire."

"How do you propose to deploy non-lethal force over such a wide area?"

"Sir, the Yengo National Park is around 1,500 sq kilometres, and the Wollemi national park is around 5,000 sq kilometres, and there are people dotted all over the place."

The senior officer picked up a report that had been lying on her desk.

"However, around Mount Yengo, things are a little more clearly defined. Our Air Surveillance Operator has been trialling a hyperspectral imagery system on loan from the Indian Air Force. With it, she can see what's going on under the forest canopy. She reports that the crowd is densely packed in the inner three-square kilometres directly encircling Mount Yengo, much less densely packed in the nine square kilometre circle surrounding the inner circle, and sparsely populated in the outer circle of sixteen square kilometres."

"Go on." There was a note of frustration in the voice of her senior officer in Canberra.

"Sir, I'll cut to the chase. I propose to deploy three sorties. First, low-level non-lethal force in the sparsely populated outer circle. This is to clear a space for the middle circle to retreat into without causing a stampede of those even closer in. Then we deploy more powerful non-lethal weapons in the middle circle to move them out and clear a space for the densely packed inner-most circle. Lastly, we apply our more powerful non-lethal weapons over the inner circle. These are the fanatics, Sir. These are the ones that opened fire on our people."

"You won't clear them all out. You know that, right?"

"Yes, Sir, I do. But at least we will have tried. Our flight crews will feel better about it if we have given those people a chance to leave the area."

"We already gave them a chance, and you know what happened that time."

"Yes, Sir, I do." The senior officer paused for a moment, "I need to maintain morale, Sir. The military chain of command is about the only thing that is still intact around here. Sir."

"Understood, Jean. Put forward a written plan to clear the area, and I will have it approved within the hour."

"Yes, Sir, thank you, Sir."

"No time to waste, Jean. Thanks for the call." There was a slight click as he ended the call.

"Thanks, Greg."

The senior officer looked up and called her ADC, who was standing just outside her office door.

"Ma'am?"

"We need to assemble all the non-lethal crowd control weapons we have."

"Yes, Ma'am, I gave the order when the message arrived from HQ. Ma'am."

"Good man. What do we have that we can use?"

"Both Claymores are working and are already fitted to two of our choppers. We have three functioning pulsed energy projectile systems. The pain ray works but has to be mounted on a heavy ground vehicle. I've ordered it mounted on an armoured car to protect the base, just in case. We have six functional plasma shields, and stores report we have twelve OC dispensers. We had another eight, wrongly labelled when they were returned from Myanmar."

"OK. Sounds like we have enough ordinance. What's your recommendation for deployment?"

"I spoke with the weapons officer Ma'am. He recommends that we reserve two of the plasma shields and the two Claymores for the inner circle. The people there will be more difficult to dislodge. We use the remaining four plasma shields plus the pulsed energy projectiles in the second ring to produce air bursts, and we allocate two of the OC systems to the inner circle, four to the middle circle and six to the outer circle."

"You've got it all worked out, haven't you?" The senior officer had a wry smile on her face. It was time she let her ADC seek another post. She shouldn't hold back the career of such a gifted officer.

"Weapons officer reckons that ought to shift a bunch of civilians."

"I hope he's right."

"So do I, Ma'am. So do we all."

"Well, best get into it then."

"Ma'am."

The ADC turned and strolled purposefully from the room. He knew many of the people who had gone to confront or support the Wollemi and their OneMind, some of them were good friends. If he could do anything to move them out of harm's way, he would.

The senior officer sat for a few moments more, collecting her thoughts and considering what she would say to the service men and women waiting outside. At last, she stood, straightened her crumpled uniform, and stepped out into the ready room.

Silence fell immediately as though someone had flicked a switch.

"As you probably know, we have our orders, and we shall carry them out. I do not doubt that just as I do not doubt your professionalism and loyalty. I have some better news too. We have been given an opportunity to clear the area. We will apply non-lethal force to move the civilians surrounding Mount Yengo to a safe distance from the mountain. We have one chance to drive them beyond the blast radius before the thermobarics are deployed." She paused then to allow both the magnitude of their situation and the weight of their opportunity to protect the civilians to sink in.

"As some of you know, we have a wide range of non-lethal crowd control weapons at our disposal. These are being serviced and installed on the choppers as we speak. We won't have much time, so I need everyone to focus. Active aircrew, please notify the duty flight officer of any training you may have in the use of the non-lethal weapon systems we have at our disposal. Duty squadron leaders report to the wing commander for briefing. All flying officers and pilot officers be prepared for a briefing within one hour. The flight mission will commence immediately after the briefing. That's all for now. Let's get to it."

After a minute of hustle-bustle, the ready room emptied out. The senior officer surveyed the empty ready room. It was important to keep her people busy. It was important to prevent them from fruitlessly chewing over the moral question they would all have to face eventually. The door opened. A sergeant and a corporal entered and stood to attention.

"All bombs loaded, Ma'am."

"How many?"

"Only four, Ma'am."

"Dear God. That's enough, isn't it?"

"These are at the smaller end, Ma'am. Their blast range is about 5 kilometres with most of the blast wave confined to about three kilometres."

"Would someone out in the open survive at three kilometres from ground zero?"

"No, Ma'am."

"How about at five kilometres?"

"Possibly, Ma'am, some might survive."

"I see, thank you. Dismissed."

The men walked back out of the empty ready room, exchanging doubtful glances as they went.

The senior officer returned to her ready room, locking the door behind her. Quickly she changed into the white and blue camouflage fatigues of active duty. For several minutes she concentrated on controlling her backwash. The last thing she wanted was for her people to pick up on her inner conflict and doubt. "*Right,*" she thought, "*This is it.*" The senior officer, Group Captain Jean Williams, unlocked the door and walked through to the mission briefing room. The Wing Commander and the three Squadron Leaders were examining a map of the wilderness projected onto a large screen at the end of the room. A door opened, and her ADC walked in.

"Ma'am, all non-lethal weapons systems have been installed and are operational."

"Thank you." Group Captain Jean Williams walked to the front of the room and stood in front of the screen.

"Gentlemen, your mission is critical to the success of the broader mission. I know you realise that. We are all fully aware of the potential civilian casualties if we are not successful in moving our people out of harm's way."

There was a shuffling of feet and a few grunts of agreement, but no one spoke.

"We must not fail. We will not fail. There will inevitably be casualties. There will inevitably be 'collateral damage', but we must and will minimise that." Jean Williams paused at that point, as much to gather herself as to allow her team the time to assimilate what she had said.

"Sometimes we must be cruel to be kind. Trite, I know, but this time apposite. You will have to go in fast and low. Especially in the inner circle, you will have to scare them loose from their positions. We are not used to applying any kind of force to civilian populations. When we are deployed in relation to civilians, it has inevitably been to deliver aid. We used force for crowd control only. That was in the past. Today is different. Today our mission is to save thousands of civilian lives. Australian lives. The lives of our friends and neighbours, from a horrible death. We must and will succeed. My ADC will brief you on the thrust of the plan. It is for you to work out the details. One last thing, the blast wave is lethal for anyone left out in the open for up to about five kilometres. We estimate the most densely packed area stretches about a kilometre from Mount Yengo, the second circle is much less dense with an outer radius of two kilometres, and the third ring is sparsely populated, just clumps of people here and there. All of them are within the kill zone."

She stopped there, searching for something further to say, something profound. She focussed her mind on the image of thousands of civilians successfully escaping danger. She projected her vision empathically. In the end, all that came to her was, "Gentlemen, I know I can rely on you."

And with that, Group Captain Jean Williams left the briefing room and proceeded to the hangars where the choppers were being prepared.

ASSAULT ON THE TABLE OF THE GODS

The light would begin fading soon. Aine stood at the Edge of the Table of the Gods and gazed out at the quiescent mob below. There had been no chanting for a while now. Their backwash had subsided to a kind of muttered non-directional discontent. By the time Aine and her comrades heard the second wave of helicopters approach, the inner crowd appeared to have settled down.

Soon the sounds of helicopters could be heard approaching on all sides. People who had been resting stood. Those who had been sleeping awoke to that ominous sound. The Wollemi stirred and stood, each wrapping his or her arms around their nearest neighbour, reforming the chain. The humans present joined in. In moments the human-wollemi chain wound once more around the mountain. But an attack never came. Not to the defenders encircling the table of the Gods, but further out, along the edges of the mob, blindingly bright flashes were seen, followed immediately by loud bangs. Some kind of gas was being spread from the helicopters. Visible in the strobe-like flashes of stun grenades, a grey cloud grew in juddering steps, swirling in stop-motion as it engulfed the panicking protesters down below. Even from a couple of kilometres away, the screams and cries of the outer mob came clearly to the ears of the defenders. The helicopters swooped low over the panicked people, forcing them to run, forcing them away from the mountain.

After about ten minutes, a second wave of helicopters approached, coming closer this time, circling perhaps a kilometre from the Table of the Gods. Almost immediately, laser light began to flick out from the helicopters, followed by loud bangs and screams from those on the ground. About a minute later, the helicopters began to release gas onto the people below, just as they had previously. The screams and the bangs were nearer this time and louder. From their vantage point, far from the madding crowd below, the defenders could see the mob begin to break up as people panicked and ran for shelter. The seething mass of humanity ensconced around the skirts of the Mountain began to move. Occasionally weapons were fired, but the helicopters were too far off to be damaged. Gas from the outer perimeter began to waft in towards Mount Yengo. The mob began to stir. The emotional level of the mob began once more to climb, driven by the backwash feedback loop. The second wave of helicopters banked away as the third wave came in, fast and low, heading directly for the Mountain.

"This is it," Aine straightened her back. Alice and Kaitlin, who were standing next to her, immediately reached out and put an arm around her. Emma came close and added her support.

"We don't know they are coming for us."

Tom came up with Max and Jack.

"They are trying to drive the civilians away so they can bomb us."

"Not helping." Alice gave Tom one of those looks and turned back to Aine. Emma tried again to soothe Aine.

"We have to put our trust in the OneMind. It called us all here for a purpose. We have to trust that the OneMind has planned this, that the OneMind has this covered."

"No. I don't trust it. And in any case, this is my doing. I stole the key, thinking I had it all figured out. I went to the place of power, and there I played the flute. It was I who used the uplink to spread its message around the world. I did it, Mum. Me. And I am to blame for the deaths of all these poor people." Aine broke down then, collapsing to her knees. The Table of the Gods fell silent. All that could be heard were Aine's sobs fighting their way up through her narrow throat, like drowning sailors seeking the surface.

Kaitlin and Tom noticed first. The veil had thickened around them. They could still see through its scintillating outer wall, but the sound of the panicked mob, trapped between the Mountain and the oncoming helicopters, was more muted. The OneMind manifested on the rock by the edge of the Table, facing inwards.

"I have increased the phase shift just a little to prevent any of the gas from getting through." The OneMind glided closer, *"It won't be long now. Their promised negotiating team will arrive once they have moved their friends out of harm's way."*

"And if negotiations fail?" Tom spoke.

"Then humankind will once more resort to war."

Aine pushed forward and threw herself to the ground in front of the shimmering man-like image.

"It's all my fault. I'm to blame. Tell me what I can do?
"

The OneMind glided closer until it was almost touching the desolate young woman. It reached out, bathing Aine in a kind of iridescent blue light.

"You are a Fool, Aine, but an honest Fool." Some private communication passed between them then, inaccessible to those nearby. *"You have much still to contribute."*

Something in Aine's stance changed then. She stood tall and straightened her shoulders.

"Thank you. I hope I will be worthy of your trust." She turned then and stepped back to join her comrades.

Faint cries, still permeating the veil, caught their attention. Two helicopters were circling close, firing directly into the seething mob only metres below them. There were the same flashes of laser light and bright explosions accompanied by loud bangs that they had seen before. But there was something more, something invisible from this distance to the naked eye. The maddened mob were screaming in apparent agony and clambering over each other to escape.

"Claymores and plasma shields," Tom gazed out at the disquieting scene, "They are using non-lethal force to drive the mob back."

"Will people die?"

"Some will, inevitably. The mob is too closely packed, and they have limited escape options."

As the horrified humans watched from the Table of the Gods, at the outer edges of the mob, people began to run away, capering madly, sprinting into the forest. Once the will of the mob was broken, others followed. Some, a pitiful few, found shelter in rocky crags and under fallen trees. As the mob melted away, the helicopters followed them, sweeping low and spraying gas down upon them.

"High-Capacity Oleoresin Capsicum Dispensers. That's what they're using. Militarised capsicum spray. We used to call it crop spraying." Tom stepped closer to Alice and wrapped a protective arm around her. It was all getting just a little bit too real.

Within about half an hour, the sun would be getting ready to set. A few tenacious survivors began to venture out from their hiding places to form small groups. They were silent, waiting. A few mumbled sentences passed between them.

"What are they waiting for?" Kaitlin searched the faces of her compatriots. "What do they think is going to happen next?"

"They're fanatics, prepared to die for their cause." Tom spoke, "This is my area, unfortunately, comparative religion. This is where I spent twenty years of my professional life."

"What religion?" Jack, who had remained silent throughout the previous hour's events, stepped forward.

"It'll be some new conspiracy theory, I expect, tacked on to whatever religion they follow."

"Can we find out? Can we ask them?" Kaitlin aimed her question at the manifestation of the OneMind that was still hovering nearby.

Aine stepped forward, "We must warn them. We must tell them about the bombs."

The OneMind drifted back to the huddled group.

"What difference would it make?"

"We would have tried. We would have done our best."

The OneMind made no response for several minutes. The gathered humans could feel it building the gestalt, not the full-blown super-entity that it had summoned a little while before, but a local gestalt, sounding out those gathered there within the protection of the veil.

"Kaitlin, I can connect you to them telepathically for a few moments. You will be able to hear their thoughts and any response they give. I do not think the experience or the knowledge gained will be of value. However, this seems to be a human need, and I will honour it."

"Can you connect Aine to them instead? She needs to feel she has done something to limit the carnage."

"Yes, but she is young, and their emotional flow is abnormal, even for humans. She may become distressed."

Aine stepped forward. "Please, let me try to speak to them. They will die otherwise. They will be burnt to death when the forest is set alight."

"Very well, Aine, I will do as you ask. I can cut off the 'backwash' , as you call it, at any time. I will know if it is too much for you."

Aine walked to a spot a metre or two from the edge of the Table of the Gods, where she had a clear view of the small groups gathering at the base of the mountain.

"OK, I'm ready."

There was a stir amongst the Wollemi. They knew or suspected what was about to happen. As one, the linked chain of humanity turned to face Aine as she stood alone and vulnerable on the edge of the mountain. She felt nothing at first except a sort of clarity and expansion in her consciousness. Everything and everyone around her stood out in sharp relief. Every detail of their clothing and faces was immediately apparent to her. Crystal clear and impossibly sharp. And then, not too far off, she began to detect the frantic simmering rage of the human beings sequestered down below. Her consciousness seemed to leave her body then and float down the mountainside towards the gathered vigilantes. Her mind, a tiny mote of awareness, feather-light and fragile as a soap bubble, approached the armed men and women standing guard on the plane below Mount Yengo. As she got closer, some of them seemed to detect a presence. A few began to glance around, apparently aware that they were being watched.

"Who's there?" one demanded, raising a shotgun defensively, "We know you're out there."

"Show yourself," another demanded, "what are you afraid of?"

Aine spoke then. Inwardly she formed the words, hoping they would be able to hear her.

"Leave now. The bombers are coming. They will incinerate the forest. You will all die."

"We're not leaving. Not while those alien devils are able to threaten our way of life."

"Do you mean the Wollemi?"

The vigilantes guarding the mountain formed an impromptu defensive circle, brandishing a motley collection of handguns and hunting rifles.

"Yes, the aliens who have been hiding in our midst for millennia. And that devil, the so-called OneMind."

"How do they threaten you? They are fewer than we are, and they have no weapons?"

"They aim to breed an army of hybrid human-wollemi slaves to serve them forever. We, genetically pure human beings, will become extinct."

"Now show yourself. Where are you?"

"OneMind, can they see me?" Aine felt the urgent need to make contact with these desperate people.

"They can if you want them to. I can manifest you to them, but I would caution you against it."

"Please. Let me try to break through."

Slowly, Aine's face began to materialise, hovering in the air a few metres from the circle of lost souls gathered in front of her.

"I am Aine. I was born and brought up in Richmond. I am just like you."

Startled at the appearance of a floating apparition, some of the group started back and raised their weapons.

"I am no danger to you," Aine continued, "I'm here to warn you. Planes are coming with firebombs to burn down the forest. You will all die if you don't leave now."

Trapped and without hope, desperately believing that they were sacrificing their lives to save their friends and families, indeed their very way of life, the terrified vigilantes held their ground. One stepped forward, clearly suppressing her strong instinct to turn and run. She took a deep breath and steadied herself. The woman's clear blue eyes held no hint of deception, Aine noticed. She had made her peace with doom. She, just like Aine herself, was ready to make her stand. To live or die according to the whim of fate.

"You are the traitor, Aine Hexenkriege. You are not like us. You are not one of us. You are here to trick us into leaving so you can make your cowardly escape. Well, we will not let you. We will stay here and fight to the death to protect humanity." And with that, almost as one, they raised their weapons and began to fire directly into Aine's spectral face. Their fury and desperation escalating instantly as their emotional backwash fed back on itself, a hopeless howl of uncontrolled rage.

"Stop. You're making a terrible mistake." Aine managed one last appeal to reason before the emotional blast coming from her would-be attackers overwhelmed her senses. The OneMind cut the connection. Back on the Table of the Gods, Aine turned to her mother, unable to speak. Tom recognised the thousand-yard stare on her young face.

"Lie her down. Let her rest."

From far, far off, a new sound began to impinge. Only Tom had heard that sound before. It was the sound of several war planes approaching. Humans and Wollemi alike searched the night sky in vain for any sign of them. There was nothing to see. No matter, they would be overhead in a minute or two. There was nothing they could do to stop them.

"It would seem the military has overruled their political leadership if coherent political leadership still exists at all."

BRUTE FORCE

The sound of the approaching bombers increased as they came nearer. Aine shook her head to clear away the post-encounter fuzziness. She jumped up and ran to join her mother. The tension was palpable amongst the humans waiting on Mount Yengo. Their fear was tangible, empathically. Inevitably, a feedback loop began to form. The backwash of fear began to circulate. The Wollemi picked up on it but did not respond in like manner. Instead, they seemed somehow oblivious of any risk to themselves. The manifestation of the OneMind drifted across the table of the Gods, pulling in the surrounding minds. The gathered humans could feel the gestalt growing in size and power. The OneMind was drawing in Wollemi and humans alike from all across the globe. Human backwash was swamped and dampened by the OneMind. The super-entity was beginning to re-form. Aine and her comrades felt themselves being drawn deeper and deeper into the matrix of thought-energy as it built, layer upon layer, mind upon mind, until at last a being emerged that surpassed even the OneMind's imagination.

"We have never achieved anything like this before."
Its disembodied consciousness rolled and rippled like the waves of

some vast ocean across the minds of millions upon millions of independently conscious humans.

"This may be as much as we will ever achieve." What was known to one was known to all instantly. The planes approaching the Table of the Gods, the Spetsnaz creeping across the tangled, swampy taiga, Navy SEALs dropping by parachute across Denali Mountain, in every corner of the Earth, humans bent upon murder crept closer to the waiting Wollemi. But only at Mount Yengo did they threaten mass destruction.

Aine, over half Wollemi herself, slipped easily into the rhythm of the great mind. Although she had allowed herself to be assimilated, she remained independently conscious. As she acclimatised to this novel mental environment, Aine began to realise that the other humans were also able to retain their own individual consciousness within the massive and growing gestalt. Aine recognised in the susurration of a million thoughts, the constant companion she had heard at the back of her mind her entire life. Here and there, individual Wollemi thought-flows also began to emerge. Aine was fascinated. It was like watching an awakening. In the presence of so many independent human consciousnesses, the Wollemi were beginning to stir. Their thoughts were different, though. The Wollemi consciousnesses emerging around her expressed an innate certainty that human beings rarely achieved. Wollemi thoughts were more statements of fact than speculation, whereas human thought flows tended much more to the hypothetical and theoretical. And there was something else. The humans thought in sentences, whereas Wollemi thought-flow encapsulated ideas without words. This was something entirely unexpected and, to Aine in that moment, unfathomable. The Wollemi woman standing next to Aine, with whom she had joined arms, smiled at her, simultaneously projecting love, acceptance and a sense of absolute belonging and kinship that Aine had never in her life before experienced. It was overwhelming.

For perhaps a full minute, Aine stood facing the small, smiling Wollemi woman, too stupefied to respond. And then, from someplace deep in her soul, came an answering upwelling of love and gratitude that threatened momentarily to overcome her ability to think.

The sound of the approaching planes seemed suddenly very close and threatening. Human beings reacted as human begins do. The speculative clamouring of a million human minds once more threatened to undo the gestalt. A million hypotheticals were thrown at once into the mind of the super being of which they were all a part. The OneMind had no protocol to deal with the disturbance. And no human habit of mind had evolved to deal with that chaotic explosion of individual thought. The uncontrolled febrile virus of human doubt began to feed upon itself within the gestalt this time. And it was then that the Wollemi responded. It was then that the millions of recently conscious Wollemi minds asserted themselves. This was something they were prepared for. This was something they knew. Into the bubbling cauldron of human ambiguity, the Wollemi inserted certainty and conviction. Whereas humans thought in slow, ponderous, sequential sentences, Wollemi thought was instantaneous and complete. The great OneMind, with the help of the conscious Wollemi, imposed order upon the chaos that was threatening its very existence. A new balance was achieved between the knowledge of the Wollemi and the understanding of the Humans. And with that, a whole new kind of OneMind emerged. One that could harness the speculative uncertainties of the human mind to the clarity and precision of Wollemi knowledge. In an instant, the OneMind formulated an understanding of the tactical situation in every place on Earth where humans and Wollemi were in conflict. The bombers were mere seconds away from the Mountain. What was to be done? In the following second, a million thoughts collided and contended, but none broke the impasse. Until Aine, part human, part Wollemi, called the OneMind to action. The sine wave of infinite possibilities collapsed then into one.

"Extend the veil, protect the vigilantes."

Instantaneously it was done. The veil snapped out to encircle the stragglers in the forest as four bombs were dropped on and around Mount Yengo. Flickering iridescent bubbles snapped into existence around each one of the descending bombs. Four huge, expanding walls of flame appeared for an instant and then apparently flicked out of existence as they were phase-shifted out of harm's way. A much-reduced blast wave smacked into the forest, throwing people to the ground and flattening trees.

Minutes passed. The ringing sound in human and Wollemi ears began to abate. Around the skirts of the mountain, bewildered people began to emerge and look around them. The four bombers, visible as specs flying high above the forest, disappeared from view, and silence fell once more. There was no wall now separating the dregs of the mob from the defenders on the mountainside. They stood facing each other, each side unsure of their next move.

No one moved except Aine. Slowly she began to pick her way down the mountainside to face the silent people waiting below. No one followed. She went alone. On both sides, the silence continued. All sound seemed abated. No one dared breathe. None knew what would unfold when Aine reached the group of armed and befuddled humans waiting on the plane below the mountain.

Aine stepped down onto the relatively flat expanse of trampled grass and walked slowly towards the handful of would-be martyrs, balefully watching her approach.

"I am Aine. I spoke to you before. I warned you of the attack."

"What do you want?" a burly middle-aged man in desperate need of a shower and a change of clothes stepped forward.

"I have come to tell you that you are safe. The OneMind has contained the bombs."

"Are we supposed to say 'thanks?'"

"No. I would like you to take a message to the authorities."

"What message?"

"It's time to talk."

"That's it?"

"That's it."

The woman who had spoken before pushed her way forward.

"We don't negotiate with terrorists. You just want us to leave so you can make your escape. Well, that's not happening."

"Your own government mounted an extensive assault against you, sprayed you with pepper spray and used non-lethal weapons against you. The OneMind saved you from their fuel-air bombs that would have incinerated you in an instant, and you still think we are the enemy."

"You are the enemy, and we will never forget that."

"If we are your enemies, who are your friends?"

"We're not your messenger boys, and we're not leaving." The middle-aged man spoke for the group.

As Aine turned to walk away, the woman who had spoken raised her shotgun and fired point blank. Aine heard the sound and cringed, expecting the worst. But nothing happened. Aine turned. The woman, the muzzle flare and the shot were suspended in the act. Aine reached out and picked one single tiny ball of lead from the frozen cloud that had been halted mere centimetres from her back.

"Go home," Aine addressed the middle-aged man, "there is nothing for you here." And with that, Aine walked back up the mountainside to rejoin her companions. She was met by Emma, Kaitlin, and Alice.

"The tide of history has passed them by." Alice wrapped a protective arm around Aine. Out of the corner of her eye, she noticed Max pull the phone from his pocket and press a few keys. Alice watched as he lifted the phone to his ear and waited.

"Good evening. This is Max Hexenkriege."

"Good evening, Mr Hexenkriege. This is an unexpected pleasure. How may I assist you this evening?" It was the same non-descript man Max had called before—the man from the teleconference.

"Tell them to send their delegation in the morning. Brute force is not going to work. We need to talk."

Incoherent shouting from the few remaining vigilantes below was replaced with sporadic gunfire. A Wollemi man fell, clutching his arm. Instantly the veil snapped back into place around the mountain. Alice and Tom, who had been off to one side talking together quietly, rejoined the group.

"Tom and I will be leaving at first light. I need to get back to my people." Unconsciously, Alice reached out and took Tom's hand.

"What will you do? You're needed here." Aine knew that what she had said was probably not strictly accurate, but she dreaded the breakup of their fellowship. For Aine, it would somehow represent the end of what was, and she was by no means ready for whatever was to come.

"I'm not needed here. You know I'm not," Alice smiled, "My people need leadership. They appointed me, and it is my duty to return to them."

"I'm staying," Max Hexenkriege wrapped an arm around his great-granddaughter, "and so's the missus." The enigmatic Wollemi woman stepped closer and took Aine's face in her hands.

She spoke and simultaneously projected her thoughts. Aine heard, "I stay with you," accompanied by a thought-flow projecting love, protection, and safety. "I keep you safe."

"I'm not leaving either," Emma reached out and tousled her daughter's hair, "We'll see this through together."

All eyes turned to Jack and Kaitlin. It was Kaitlin who spoke for them.

"Jack and I will be leaving once it's fully dark. We're heading back to Wisemans Ferry."

"Why there?" Tom seemed non-plussed. "There's nothing there."

"The Trees of Knowledge and of Life grown together." Kaitlin struggled to express an idea that had been forming in her mind for several days. "We know it means something, symbolically. Everyone gets that. But what if it does something? What if it has an objective purpose, a mission, of its own?"

Tom, figuring out what to say to that, unconsciously scratched his head, and for a moment or two, the enthusiastic, somewhat goofy Marines Lieutenant Colonel, whom Kaitlin had met at LAX airport twenty or so years earlier, was visible beneath the mask he wore, of age, and care and exhaustion. Kaitlin smiled. Theirs had been a long journey together.

"It's OK, Tom. I just need to figure it out. The collapse of the veil, the symbiosis of the two trees supposedly planted in the garden of Eden, the coming together of Humans and Wollemi, perhaps what we are witnessing is the endgame."

"What endgame?" Tom looked tired and concerned for Kaitlin.

"The human condition, the game that started with eating from the Tree of Knowledge of Good and Evil and ended with our expulsion from Eden. Or maybe it didn't end there. Maybe that was just the beginning. What if what we are seeing now is the closing chapter?"

"There is no closing chapter Kaitlin. That is what my tradition tells me. The world turns. Cycles of history come and go."

"I must go and find out," Kaitlin's voice was flat, her mind made up.

"I know." Tom smiled. Would they ever meet again? Only blind fate could tell.

"Watch out for the crazies down there." Emma, still with one arm around her daughter, reached out towards Kaitlin and took her hand.

"We will," Jack stepped forward and gave Emma and Aine a kiss, "We need to get ready. It'll be full dark soon."

All around, the Wollemi were settling down for the night, fires were lit, and little lanterns were produced. In a few minutes, the mountainside was covered with small groups of humans and Wollemi settling in for the night. As Kaitlin and Jack turned away and began picking their way down the mountainside, the scene they left behind was one of peace and harmony.

No one knew what the morning would bring.

ROUND TWO

There was stunned silence in the Canberra Control Centre as reports of the failure of the thermobaric attack came in. A very angry Air Vice-Marshal was speaking.

"It's a simple question. Did they detonate, or didn't they?"

In her office at the Richmond Air Base, Group Captain Jean Williams measured her words carefully.

"Sir, the bombs were deployed and ignited as expected."

"So, what the hell happened?"

"Sir, the pilots report that moments after ignition, all four bomb ignitions stopped or disappeared. Sir."

"Disappeared? They simply vanished into thin air. You expect me to believe that?"

"Sir, that is what all four flight crews report. The video record confirms their account, Sir. The four ignitions simply stopped or were swallowed up."

"Swallowed up? By What?"

"Sir, one hypothesis is that it was the OneMind's doing."

"You think? We have underestimated that demonic creature for the last time."

"Sir." In her small office at the Richmond Air Base, Jean Williams breathed a sigh of relief. The Air Vice-Marshal's attention would soon be off her. She might even keep her job.

In the Canberra Control Room, the Air Vice-Marshal spoke again.

"The Americans are breathing down our necks. We've received reports that two US B-72 bombers carrying cruise missiles fitted with B63 tactical nuclear warheads have landed at the US Air Base in the Kimberley."

"We gave permission for that." Air Commodore Greg Matheson, Jean's superior officer, immediately regretted his outburst.

"Sir, apologies for speaking out of turn."

"At ease, Greg, and the answer is no. Permission was never requested."

"Sir, so it's 'act first, apologise later'?"

"Yes, Greg, and we don't want that approach to follow through to the nukes."

"No, Sir."

"So, we have to sort this mess out ourselves before they act, understood?" The Air Vice-Marshal surveyed the room.

"Ideas? Suggestions?"

For a while, no one spoke. And then, scarcely believing what she was doing, Jean Williams began to speak.

"Sir, we could try a different approach." Jean hesitated. This was going to be make or break for her career.

"Spit it out, for God's sake."

"Sir. Yes, Sir, we launch a combined air and ground assault, Sir. Artillery, conventional cruise missiles first, a traditional softening up exercise, followed by a direct mass ground and air assault."

"How's that going to achieve more than four thermobaric bombs, Group Captain?"

"Sir, the video footage of the attack shows that there was an almost one-second delay between the bomb deployment and the OneMind's response. Sir. I'm wondering if the delay indicates that the OneMind had some process or gathering of resources, or just situation analysis it needed to go through to formulate and execute a defensive response."

"You think to overwhelm it?"

"Sir, a sustained barrage on multiple fronts followed by troops on the ground might work. Attrition rather than shock and awe."

"We could bring in the US Marines and Navy SEALs. That would give us some protection against the nukes."

The room remained silent while the Air Vice-Marshal thought the option through.

"OK, I'll talk to the Chief of the Defence Force. We reconvene in one hour."

In her Richmond office, Jean turned off her phone and wandered outside. It was a cold clear night. A few stars were visible despite the lights of the base. Her ADC approached through the brightly lit ready room doorway behind her.

"Orders, Ma'am?"

"We reconvene in an hour. I'm going to take a walk."

"Ma'am."

Jean wandered beyond the permitter fence, across Percival Street and onto the large paddock adjacent to the RAAF Medical Centre. The light pollution was less there. Jean felt she needed a wider perspective. She needed to think beyond the battle, beyond the war and beyond the eventual peace. She needed to find firm footing, a solid place to stand.

The Milky Way was visible as a ribbon of lighter sky against the blackness of the void. What was happening was more than a 'once in a century' or 'once in a thousand years' event. What was happening was epochal, potentially Earth-shattering. Whatever. It was bigger than her imagination, focused by years in the Australian Air Force, could easily encompass. As she stared up at the distant, disinterested stars, Jean realised that she had always been blessed with inner certainty. She had never really had to ponder a decision. The right response always seemed to come to her unbidden. But not this time. The suggestion she had made was a logical alternative to the previous failed strategy, but she had no reason to believe it would work. She had no reason to believe it was even necessary. She would have liked to be with family on a night like this. She would have liked to rest by the hearth fire in the home acre. But it was not to be. She and her people had a job to do, and they would do it, come what may.

As she walked back across Percival Street, Jean remembered the young Aboriginal Elder and her companions locked in the engineers' restroom. She would let them go, she decided. It was not for her to determine their fate. Her ADC was waiting near the gate to the Air Base.

"Cleared your head, Ma'am?"

"Yes, thank you, Peter. I want you to let the Aboriginal delegation out. We have no right to keep them locked up while the fate of the world is being decided."

"Yes, Ma'am."

The ready room had filled by the time Jean wandered in after her walk. The four aircrews who had dropped the thermobarics were seated off to one side.

"Now, listen up." Jean consulted her wristwatch. "There's a tactical meeting scheduled in just over half an hour with the senior officers. Most of the protesters have left the area around Mount Yengo. Those who have thrown in their lot with the Wollemi and the OneMind are beyond our help. They have made their choice. We may be launching a sustained air and ground assault preceded by a traditional artillery and cruise missile attack." The room went silent.

"We need to be ready for our part of the attack. My ADC will take point on organising our forces. We must be ready in two hours." Turning to her ADC, Jean continued.

"Please strip out the non-lethal weapons and refit with standard tactical kit."

"I've already given the order, ma'am."

"Of course you have." Group Captain Jean Williams flicked her ADC a quick smile before turning to face the room once more. "Prepare yourselves. We are going to war."

The ready room quickly emptied out, leaving just Jean and her ADC.

"You released the Aboriginal delegation?"

"Yes, Ma'am. They asked me to pass on a message."

"Yes."

"The young Elder said to tell you that an all-out assault would not work. She said the OneMind would simply retreat into the Dreamtime."

"How did she know what was planned? Never mind, it was probably just a guess."

"She said in the end only a negotiated settlement would work."

"Was that all?"

"She said that the veil would fall, and we would all return to the Dreamtime anyway, whether we liked it or not."

"What do you think, Peter? What's your take on all this?"

"I can't comment on the Dreamtime, but it is clear there is a veil separating us from another reality, and it seems that veil will soon be gone, and our two realities will merge."

Jean Williams nodded, "Continue."

"We don't know what that means, really, but assuming the merging itself is not catastrophic, then afterwards, we will be faced with the presence of a second, essentially human population living amongst us."

"Yes."

"A mute, telepathic offshoot of humanity having a low level of individual consciousness but able to summon a super-intellect known as the OneMind."

"Yes, but its message suggested that the OneMind itself would no longer exist, or no longer be possible, or something."

"Ma'am, we don't know exactly what is true and what is not. We think the Wollemi are human or almost human, we think the OneMind will disappear with the collapsing veil, but we don't know for sure."

"Who does know? Or, at any rate, who is most likely to know?" The answer came to her even as she voiced the question.

"Peter, take a couple of cars and go find the Aboriginal delegation. They can't have got far on foot."

"Ma'am?"

"Tell them I need their advice. Ask them if they would kindly consent to return."

"Yes, Ma'am" The ADC turned on his heel and was gone.

The Aboriginal Elder would know something. They had been observing the Wollemi and the OneMind for thousands of years. Group Captain Jean Williams returned once more to her office. She picked up the phone and once more hit redial.

"Jean, I'm in a meeting. Can't it wait?"

"Sir, with respect, we need to seek any information or intelligence we can get from the Aboriginal Elders. Sir, we need to try negotiation before launching an all-out attack."

"We are aware of that, Jean. I'll call you back." The phone went dead.

SARAH

Beyond the military control centre, beyond the confines of the Richmond Air Base and the area around Mount Yengo enclosed by the veil, back in the cities and the suburbs, something was happening.

Imperceptibly at first, the yin contained hidden within the mob's murderous yang began to assert itself. As darkness spread across the world, and the dead were buried in the cities and the suburbs, a nauseating, shuddering realisation came to those of the left-behind who had survived. Fear and panic had led them to the very brink of their own destruction. The pipes of Pan, figuratively speaking, had driven the same fear-panic that had plagued human society since its beginning. Confusion reigned. Knowledge that is learned is always incomplete. Understanding based on reason is only ever an hypothesis. To the surviving witnesses of that weekend of death, what had been done in the name of human civilisation, begged the question. What civilisation? Whatever it was that the OneMind had planned couldn't be worse than the injury human beings had just inflicted upon themselves—self-harm on a global scale, driven by the terror of the unknown.

Slowly, but slowly, an eerie calm descended. In the cities, people walked the streets as though in a dream. They had destroyed their neighbourhoods. They had fouled their own nest. Clumps of humanity, bloodied and bruised, gazed about themselves, bewildered and disbelieving. And in the countryside, they buried the bodies and slunk away, thinking, *'Whoever did that wasn't me, that was someone else, that was some other person'*.

And deeper yet, in the wilderness, something else was happening. Something entirely different. Human beings and Wollemi were beginning to merge. Ancient cousins, long separated, opened their eyes and looked upon each other in wonder and recognition. The Wollemi-enforced collective dissolved and blew away like smoke over water. Their individual minds awakened to a new day, a new dawn of individual awareness. The OneMind could still form at need, but probably not for much longer.

Jack and Kaitlin exited Mount Yengo unnoticed by the few fanatics who remained to 'guard' the Wollemi. It was a fair walk back to the cave where they had left the ute, but it was a cool, moonlit night, and they were glad to be moving again. It was a little after midnight when the couple flicked on their torches and made their way into the cave to collect the ute. The engine started promptly, and Jack carefully edged the vehicle back out of the cave and onto the track. He stopped before heading back the way they had come only a few short hours before.

"What are you expecting to find?"

Kaitlin looked a little doubtful.

"I'm not sure, but the OneMind doesn't do symbolism, certainly not for its own sake. There must be some practical purpose to bringing the two trees back to life after who knows how long and then growing them together. Humans and Wollemi have shared roots. We know that, but we are not the same. We can interbreed, so we are the same species at one level, yet we are individually conscious, and they are telepathic and live in another dimension, so not really that alike at all."

"Tricky."

"That just about sums it up. Thank you, Jack." Kaitlin gave her husband a quick peck of mock appreciation. Jack started the engine a second time, and they began their way back to Wisemans Ferry.

Away across the sleeping wilderness, at the Mountain of the Gods, Alice and Tom were wheeling their dirt bike down the slope on the other side from the vigilantes. They would walk to the edge of the veil and wait for first light. If they took the old convict trail, they could make it back to where most of Alice's people would have camped within an hour or two.

Resting on the Table of the Gods, Aine and her mother talked.

"What will happen when the OneMind is gone?" This was a question that had been plaguing Aine for some time. She felt somehow personally responsible for the demise of the super-consciousness of the Wollemi. "Will the Wollemi be OK without their guiding light?"

"Who can say?" Emma ransacked her memories, trying to recall anything, any snippet that might help her daughter at this difficult time. "The Wollemi have evolved. They are not the same beings as they were thousands of years ago."

"I know, but can they look after themselves?"

"They will have to. And we humans will have to step up to the problem and do our bit."

"They will stick to the wilderness, won't they?"

"Yes, I'm sure they will."

"And your grandmother, my great-grandmother, is learning to speak. Who knows what they will be capable of as individuals, given the chance?" Aine seemed to brighten at that.

"The OneMind needs to negotiate a deal with humanity. After millennia of secret interference, manipulation, and misdirection, the OneMind needs to come clean." Emma frowned. That was going to be awkward.

"The OneMind will have thought of that. It will have a plan."

"Oh, no doubt, but how does a telepathic superbeing from another dimension convince three and a half billion recalcitrant human beings of its good intentions?"

"The OneMind will have a way." Aine listened for a moment to the million murmuring voices of the gestalt. An idea came to her unbidden. It was impossible for her to say if it was her own idea, self-generated, or some vagrant whisp of thought snatched from the night air as it floated past.

"Whatever cannot be fulfilled in space will be fulfilled in time. Just as space needs time to evolve, so time becomes a space in which to evolve."

"Why do you say that?" Emma suddenly found herself deeply engaged with her daughter's statement.

"The Dreamtime was the space within which the Wollemi evolved, but time passes differently in the Dreamtime. Max said so."

"Yes, I see that, but what conclusion are you drawing from that?"

"The OneMind's perspective is wider by far than any of ours and deeper. It sees further into the past and the future than we can imagine."

"Yes, I suppose so."

"Tom said that there is no beginning or end. There is just a cycle of renewal."

_"Yes," Emma was becoming just a little frustrated at Aine's allegorical turn of phrase, "But what does all that mean? What does it all come to?"

"Do you suppose the OneMind is afraid to die? After all these thousands, maybe hundreds of thousands of years? Are we killing it?"

"Oh, Aine, I have no idea. I doubt anyone does."

"I think we are killing it."

"Really, why?"

"I think that we humans are depleting it, sucking the life force out of it. I think it's getting ready for one last hurrah." Aine's voice broke then. Emma detected the wash of regret and guilt emanating from her.

"You can't blame yourself, my love. You are not to blame for any of this."

"I took the flute. I played it. I lured all these people here, and not just here, but everywhere there are Wollemi the world over. It may need us for some reason, but we are also causing its death."

"The OneMind must have need of us, or it wouldn't have set this situation up in the first place. Remember, that flute was hidden in the cave thousands of years ago. It was not aimed at you. It was aimed at someone, anyone who could hear the call."

"I guess you're right. I hope you're right. I just can't help the way I feel."

"It's getting late. We should get some sleep." Looking around, Emma could see that the Wollemi had already bedded down for the night. How much of their behaviour was instinctual, and how much was simple habit? Only time would tell. It took a fair while after the excitement of the day, but eventually, everyone slept.

By the time Aine and Emma woke the next day, Jack and Kaitlin, Alice and Tom were far away. As Emma sat up and looked around, she realised there was just herself, her grandfather and Aine left of the seven who had started out on the journey together. Max's wife walked up, carrying two small wooden bowls containing some kind of fruit.

"Eat fruit."

"Do you have a name?" Emma asked. Aine had also woken up by then and was snuggling up to Emma, seeking any warmth that was on offer.

The Wollemi woman spoke slowly, carefully, pronouncing each word separately as if placing valuable ornaments upon a shelf.

"Yes, I have chosen the name Sarah."

"Why Sarah?"

"I like it."

"Yes," Aine smiled, "That is a lovely name."

Sarah smiled, "I am happy. We are together."

Alice and Tom left at first light. Stiff and sore though they were, they managed once more to squeeze onto the little dirt bike and headed cross country to meet with the Gathering. The milling mobs had disappeared. They did not encounter another living soul as they drove through the bush. The forest was silent, apart from the normal sounds of birds, the wind in the branches and the occasional animal sound. Alice nudged Tom, and he pulled the bike to a halt.

"Let's take a few minutes before we reengage with Armageddon."

"What's up?"

"Nothing in particular, apart from the obvious. I just wanted to take a moment to enjoy each other's company, just for a few minutes, maybe, without interruption."

Alice and Tom wearily extricated themselves from the little dirt bike and stretched. The morning was clear and bright, and in the sheltered spot where they had stopped, the sun was warm on their skin.

Alice spoke first. "What is happening, Tom? I'd like to take a step back and think about that before I lead my people into… what? Battle? The Dreamtime?"

"Yeah. I know what you mean. We've been being manipulated by the OneMind for … I don't know how long. Forever, maybe."

"That's right. I want to be clear about what we know versus what the OneMind has told us."

"OK, well, we know that the OneMind triggered the chain reaction that 'infected' humanity with the Wollemi ability to sense another person's emotional flow."

Alice began to tick items off on her fingers. "Ok, there's that, and there's the fact that it needed the energy from the HARP device to trigger the Event." Pause. "And it influenced humans to make the device in the first place." Pause. "And it has been breeding human-Wollemi hybrids."

"I hadn't thought of it that way before, but I suppose that is a true description of Jack and his brother and Aine."

"And others, we don't know how many."

"Or for how long." Tom was beginning to realise the impossibility of drawing any really solid conclusion. "We know that there is some connection between the veil and the magnetopause."

"We know the Aboriginal people and other people around the world have been interacting with the Wollemi and the OneMind for centuries."

"And we know what it is like to be part of the OneMind's gestalt."

"Yes," Alice frowned at that, "but do you remember much about it? Do you remember anything you learned? Anything specific?"

Tom leaned back on an old gum tree, feeling the smooth surface of the trunk beneath his fingers.

"I remember my amazement. How overwhelming it was."

"Same here. Well, next time, we need to remember to go looking for evidence."

"Evidence of what?"

"The OneMind's true intentions."

"You think it will tell us."

"One thing I do remember is that the gestalt is open, there is no hiding anything once it forms, but that still leaves the problem of finding what you're looking for."

"And knowing what to look for." To Tom, a military intelligence veteran, that should probably be their starting point. "We need to think about what we need to find out, and we need to brief our people on what to look out for."

The morning sun shone warm and bright. The scene, deep in untouched wilderness, was idyllic.

"OK, duty calls." Alice stood up, patting dead leave and grass off her clothes as she did so.

Perhaps ten minutes later, they saw the grey smoke from the campfires of the Gathering.

People looked up as Alice and Tom approached on the little dirt bike. As they pulled to a halt at the approximate centre of the impromptu campground, people began to gather.

"I have returned from the Table of the Gods. Tom and I allowed ourselves to be a willing part of the OneMind's gestalt. The OneMind was able to hold off the mob and protect us and the few remaining stragglers from the bombs that were dropped. We have reached an impasse now. Nothing is over. Everything is still to play for."

There were a few muttered words at that. Over a steep hill, from the direction of the Richmond Air Base, came a small delegation. Alice recognised the distant frame of the young Elder, Killara. Some sixth sense told her to wait for the little group to arrive before continuing. Everyone watched as the little group made its way down the hillside and through the Gathering to the centre, where Alice and Tom were standing.

Killara approached to within two metres and paused, waiting to be invited to speak.

"Killara, it is good to see you again. I feel you come with news."

"Thank you. We come with news from the Air Base. They plan an air and ground assault."

"How do you know this?"

"We overheard the engineers talking as they prepared the helicopters. And a few of our own people warned us to avoid the forest."

"When will they attack?"

"They are waiting for their orders. They will need to bring in soldiers from the surrounding bases. It will take them a few hours to prepare."

"I see, thank you," Alice paused for a moment to gather her thoughts, "A call has been made from the Table of the Gods to the Australian government to negotiate. They were asked to send a delegation this morning. We will watch and wait."

***

Only a few kilometres away on the deck at the Wisemans Ferry Inn, Jack and Kaitlin were digging into a very early morning 'bikers' brekkie' and staring across the village at an enormous tree that had grown up through the atrium of the OneMind Museum and Visitors Centre. It was not a gum tree or any kind of Australian native tree that Jack had ever seen.

"What is it, do you reckon?" Jack turned to Kaitlin.

"The tree?"

"Yeah, what kind is it?"

"Well, the legends say the trees of life and of knowledge were Almond trees."

"A bit big for an almond tree." Jack unfolded a serviette and began to make a rough calculation of the tree's height. Estimating the distance from his position to the base of the trunk, and the angle between his position and the top of the tree, Jack scribbled a quick estimate.

"Bloody hell."

"What?"

"That tree has grown between eighty and a hundred metres in the few days since we saw it sprouting in the Atrium."

"That's impossible." Kaitlin stood and walked to the edge of the deck to get a better look. Jack joined her.

"Yep, just like everything else that's going on at the moment."

The couple quickly finished up and walked out into the street. The damage done by rioters had either been very slight at Wisemans Ferry or had been cleared away quickly. They walked past the bowling club to the entrance of the Visitors Centre. And there they stopped. Towering over them, and over the lower part of the village was an enormous tree, its trunk twisted and writhing, entwined like some massive ancient anchor rope, tethering the tree to the Earth, as above its huge spreading branches reached out to encapsulate and embed themselves in the sky. The sight was, in the true meaning of the word, awesome, awe-inspiring, and bewildering in its manifest impossibility.

"Oh, my God." Jack stared up at the extraordinary sight. The Visitor's Centre was closed. A sign read "Dangerous Building. Do not enter." Upon closer inspection, Kaitlin could see here and there buckled walls, cracked glass, and the occasional root bursting through the concrete foundations like a serpent rising from Earth only to dive back beneath the surface after a few metres. Kaitlin walked over to the nearest root section that was accessible beyond the quickly erected perimeter fence. Hesitantly, some inexplicable sense of caution pressing her to hold back, Kaitlin knelt and placed both palms upon the warm, rough surface, caressing the coarse, irregular bark with her fingertips.

"It's alive," she whispered, "I can feel it."

"Well, of course, it's alive," Jack took a few paces towards where Kaitlin was kneeling, "That much is obvious."

"No, that's not what I meant. It's kind of conscious. I can feel it. It has purpose."

"What? What is its purpose?"

"I can't tell yet. Can you get my pack from the ute? I need to find a way to communicate with it?"

Jack turned and stomped off up the hill back to the Wisemans Ferry Inn. Kaitlin quieted her mind and continued to caress the exposed root. After a few moments, she heard the sound of a ute starting up and a few moments after that. Jack pulled the ute up on the grass next to her. He jumped out, handing her the pack. Quickly Kaitlin opened it and unceremoniously emptied the contents onto the ground. She sorted through it by flinging unwanted items over to one side. Jack leaned over to see what Kaitlin had selected. It was still surprising to him, after all these years, that he had married an Irish witch. And it still upset his practical, materially based worldview when she did her stuff. There was, if he were to examine it, something frightening and unknowable about the ever-burning flame that Kaitlin could, at will, tap into.

She had, in front of her, a few items from the pack. There was a cigarette lighter, a small brass bowl, a brown paper package containing some dried-up leaves, a small glass bottle containing frankincense and peppermint essence, a silver spoon, and a small gold dagger. Carefully Kaitlin crumbled some of the leaves into the bowl and poured a tiny drop of the essence onto them. Then she took the lighter and set fire to the leaves, which smouldered and gave off an aromatic smoke. Kaitlin took up the silver spoon and gold dagger and waved them over the smoke, mumbling a few words as she did so. After a minute or two, the smoke began to die away. Jack watched as Kaitlin lifted the two items in front of her and, raising her voice a little, spoke in some ancient dead language that he imagined hadn't been heard in a thousand years. Jack had no idea what she was saying, but he knew to leave well enough alone. Kaitlin cleared away the few leaves on either side of the root and dug the silver spoon into the earth on onside and the gold dagger into the earth on the other. Then once more, she placed her palms upon the surface of the root and waited. Nothing happened for over a minute, and then Kaitlin sensed movement under her palms.

She gasped as she felt a small pressure against her palms grow and then spread between her fingers. Jack stepped up, ready to drag her away. As he watched, tiny tendrils began to reach out around Kaitlin's hands and fingers. Slowly and very, very gently, the massive tree enfolded Kaitlin's hands in slowly waving shoots, forming a link through which it could communicate with her.

Kaitlin held very still. "Oh my God," she whispered after a moment or two.

"What is it?" for some reason, Jack found himself whispering.

"It's connected. It's amazing."

"Connected with what?"

"With everything, it's growing, reaching out, joining with the others."

"What others? What do you mean?'

"All of them, that's its purpose, to join up with all of them."

"All of what? Who?"

"The Quaking Aspens, King's Lomatia, the Wollemi Pines themselves, the whole lot, everywhere."

Kaitlin fell silent then as the purpose of the mighty tree permeated her being. Her eyes closed, and she lost consciousness. It was already dark by the time she woke up, once more finding herself in Sophia's

Grand Bedroom at the Wiseman's Ferry Inn. Jack was asleep in the velvet-covered armchair. Sounds of commotion forced their way in through the open bedroom window. Kaitlin sat up. Her movement bringing Jack to instant wakefulness.

"Sorry, what? I must have dropped off."

"There's something going on outside."

"Are you OK? You passed out. You've slept the whole day."

"I'm OK. I need to tell you something about the tree. I need to explain what's happening."

"OK."

"The tree of Life and of Knowledge, if that's what it is, is reaching out across the world to the others like it."

"What others? How are they like it?"

"There are millions of tree and plant colonies around the world connected by networks of roots and mycelium. They communicate through these root networks, Jack. That tree down there is not conscious in any sense of the word that we would understand, but it has purpose and is not *insensible* if you see what I mean."

Jack did, sort of. Well, he got the gist of it.

"You're saying that that giant tree is reaching out to all other tree and plant colonies to create a kind of semi-aware super colony?"

"Yes."

"How? By sending out roots?"

"Yes. Each colony it contacts enlarges it and spreads the word."

"What for?"

"I couldn't tell what for. As far as I was able to understand, it was an instinctual thing, a kind of primeval imperative for it."

"Sounds like Gaia or that movie with the giant blue people from ages ago."

"Giant blue people?"

"You know, we watched it together one rainy Sunday afternoon. They live on floating mountains and fly around on dragons."

"What do you know about Gaia? Anyway, I think you mean Avatar?"

"Yeah. Guess so. Bad mining company gets fought off by giant blue indigenous people who worship a big tree."

"Promise me one thing."

"What's that?"

"Promise me you'll never go into marketing."

With that, Jack rose to his feet and launched himself across the room, grabbing Kaitlin and beginning to tickle her.

"I'd be bloody brilliant at marketing, especially in 'Stralia."

"Oh yeah?" Kaitlin managed between giggles, "Let's have a slogan then. Sell me an electric ute." Electric utes were one of Jack's pet hates.

"That's not fair."

"Well, a high-powered marketing guru such as yourself should be able to overcome any personal objections."

Jack stopped trying to tickle Kaitlin for a moment and concentrated on the challenge she had thrown down. He thought for a moment.

"OK, how about 'Never worry about the next servo when you go bush. Solar recharge in just four hours?'"

"That's not bad. Trust you to talk 'Strine to your ocker mates."

The tickling continued for a few moments more until the commotion going on outside could no longer be ignored. Jack and Kaitlin slipped on their boots, Kaitlin stuffed a couple of small items into her pockets, and they headed downstairs. Outside the Inn, a large crowd had gathered. Jack spotted an old acquaintance.

"What's going on?"

"It's that bloody tree that Alice planted. It's freaking everyone out."

"What's it done exactly, other than grow impossibly quickly?" Kaitlin was craning her neck, trying to see over the crowd.

"Take a look yourself." The man moved to one side and ushered Kaitlin through the throng, with Jack following close behind.

The scene that met them as they got to the front of the crowd baffled the eyes and confounded perception. The huge tree emitted a faint blue glow, a glow which spread down its trunk to its roots and beyond. A glow that stretched here and there beyond the village and into the surrounding farmland. Across the great Hawkesbury River, the glow continued far into the wilderness. In the grey of early evening, the eerie luminance emanating from the great tree spread across the countryside, casting an uncanny light across the houses and people watching from the top of the village.

"Oh my God," a woman shouted from the other side of the road, "it's spreading in our direction." Kaitlin looked where the woman was pointing. Sure enough, the faint blue glow was growing and spreading, garden to garden, tree to tree, approaching them at a fast-walking pace.

"Come with me, Jack. I need to try to speak to it. Find out why it's doing this." Kaitlin took off down the road towards the Visitors Centre and the giant glowing tree. The crowd watched in disbelief as Kaitlin and Jack disappeared behind the empty bowling club. Kaitlin ran to the spot where the root was accessible beyond the perimeter fence of the slowly collapsing visitors' centre. She threw herself down and immediately embedded the silver spoon and gold dagger in the earth close by the glowing tree root. She placed her palms flat upon the surface as she had before and settled her mind. After a moment or two, she began to chant. Jack recognised it as the same language she had used before. But as always, he had no real idea what she was doing.

Kaitlin shuddered as though a sudden chill had run through her. Jack watched as her fingers seemed to push through the thick, rough bark and into the very flesh of the tree root.

"Stand back," Kaitlin gasped, "I can't tell what it will do."

The root into which Kaitlin appeared to have embedded her fingers began to move, pulling this way and that, as though trying to escape Kaitlin's clutches.

"Why are you spreading out like this?" Emma's voice was harsh, rasping, as though she were exerting every ounce of will to continue the connection. "What is your true purpose?"

Kaitlin shuddered again as an overwhelming, flooding response forced its way into her unwilling psyche. The communication being forced upon her was unlike anything Kaitlin had ever experienced before. There were no words. There was not even a concept as such. For several seconds, Kaitlin wasn't sure if what she was receiving was communication at all. What there was, was different from anything any human being had ever before encountered. It was the raw expression of the experience-purpose of the great tree. Filling her mind in an agony of pitiless perseverance was the very being of the tree, of the planet, alive and experiencing itself. A giant scar healed. A terrible wound mended. Some part of Kaitlin's thought, some elemental understanding, passed back from Kaitlin to the great Tree. And that was it. With one powerful, wrenching twist, the tree root threw Kaitlin back across the grass verge and sank into the earth, leaving only a scar of turned earth where it had been before. Jack ran to Kaitlin and lifted her inert form, desperately checking for a pulse. She was alive. Relief flooded Jack's mind and body. His knees buckled, and he slumped down next to her.

"Kaitlin, Kaitlin, my love, can you hear me?"

Kaitlin's eyes flickered and opened. Suddenly she sat upright, taking a huge breath. Jack lurched back, momentarily startled by the sudden violent movement.

"Are you all right, Kaitlin? What happened?"

Kaitlin took a few more deep breaths and turned to Jack.

"That was amazing, Jack. I've never even imagined anything like that."

"Like what? What happened?"

"It tried to communicate. But without words, without concepts, without thought even. It tried to communicate its being to me, its beingness. It was overwhelming. Utterly, utterly strange, and different. I never imagined Jack. Not for a second. I never imagined anything like it."

"Can you stand? Can you walk?" Jack just wanted to get Kaitlin away from the tree. He needed somewhere safe. He needed somewhere to think.

"I think so," with Jack's help, Kaitlin struggled to her feet, "Let's go back to the Inn. We can talk there."

The crowd outside the Inn fell silent as Jack and Kaitlin approached. Jack's old acquaintance stepped forward.

"Well?"

Kaitlin looked up. She stared for a moment at the expectant crowd, took a deep breath and, letting go of Jack's hand, began to speak.

"The tree is reaching out through its root system to all other plants. It aims to form one huge root network around the world, joining together the plant kingdom. It senses the fall of the veil. It is preparing for the coming of the Dreamtime."

"Is it dangerous?" The querulous woman who had warned of the approaching glow stepped forward.

"I don't believe so, no. We seem to be irrelevant to it. The tree is not sentient as such. It doesn't think. It just is."

The distant sound of a lone helicopter drew everyone's attention. The navigation lights of a black hawk helicopter could be seen far off, flying low over the forest in the direction of Mount Yengo.

As Jack and Kaitlin approached the Inn, Kaitlin noticed that the blue glow had spread up the walls to include the odd plant that had gained a foothold in the old stone walls. Even the odd patches of moss around the drainpipes were glowing faintly.

NEGOTIATION

Over at the Gathering, Alice and her people spotted the lone helicopter. Alice stood. Addressing those closest to her. "Time to go." And with that, the Gathering packed up, put out their campfires, and began the trek to the Mountain. They had their part to play, and they were going to play it. Within ten minutes, the Gathering ground was empty. There was little to point to their passing. Some trampled grass, a few quenched firepits, that was all.

Over at the Temple of the Gods, the gathered defenders sensed first and then heard the approach of the helicopter. A few moments later, its lights were visible. It approached and circled once before setting down in a clearing at the bottom of the mountain. A couple of armed marines jumped out and stood guard as the government delegation stepped out of the Helicopter and formed up. There was the Minister of Defence and Foreign Affairs, his political advisor, the Secretary for the Department of Defence, the Chief of the Defence Force, and his ADC. Five middle-aged men, all of them hard-headed men of affairs, none of them remotely prepared for a negotiation with a super being. Fortunately, perhaps, they might not be required to.

"Max, why don't we go meet them." Emma took Aine's hand. "It would be a polite gesture."

Aine smiled. The idea of making a polite gesture to the very people who had ordered them all to be incinerated only a few hours before seemed ironic, if not actually amusing. As Max began to walk towards the path down the mountainside, Sarah followed suit. Max opened his mouth as if to speak and then quietly closed it again. Emma and Aine followed behind.

"What are you going to say to them?" The whole thing seemed a little bizarre to Aine, "Are you going to say, 'Welcome to Mount Yengo', or make a nice speech?"

Max turned and smiled. "I just want them to feel safe and secure as they walk into the shadow of the valley of death."

"It's not a valley. It's a mountain."

"I know, poetic licence. We need them to agree to a cease-fire."

"Why a cease-fire? Why not a truce?"

"Well, firstly, I suppose because we are not an aggressor, and secondly, because the veil will fall and the worlds merge, whether they like it or not."

They continued down the steep slope in silence. The waiting delegation heard and saw them approach. Max stepped forward.

"Good evening. Thank you for agreeing to this meeting. May I introduce my wife, Sarah, my granddaughter Emma, and my great-granddaughter Aine? We have come to accompany you to the Table of the Gods, where the OneMind is waiting."

Aine had been listening carefully to the emotional backwash coming from the delegation. It was interesting. There was curiosity and a degree of trepidation from some, but no actual fear. They did not feel that they were in danger. There were a few emotional flares as the three women were introduced, particularly Sarah Hexenkriege, and a frisson of excitement when the waiting OneMind was mentioned. The delegation was curious more than anything.

The little posse made their way carefully up the narrow path to the Table of the Gods. There was a moment of hesitation as the delegation reached the final step up onto the flat expanse of rock. There waiting for them was a man-sized and shaped manifestation. It was about 1.7 metres tall and appeared to be wearing a tunic of some kind. The face was Wollemi, with high cheekbones, almond-shaped eyes, small chin.

"Welcome. Please feel at ease. You are in no danger here."

The delegation stepped onto the Table of the Gods and took a few steps towards the OneMind. As they closed to within a comfortable, conversational distance of the manifestation, the OneMind reached out towards them. Instantly a blueish field snapped out, enclosing them for an instant, and they were assimilated. It all happened in the blink of an eye. They were absorbed into the collective, but their free will and independent consciousnesses were not suppressed. Max, Emma and Aine immediately followed.

"I believe the only way you will understand what is happening and know the truth of what is said is if you all participate in the gestalt. You are all your individual consciousnesses, that is, part of the collective. You are all, for the moment, part of me."

For a split second, fear flared sharply in the minds of the government delegation, but only for an instant. Their fear was replaced almost instantly by wonder. The emotional tenor of the vast consciousness of which they were each jointly and severally a part was calm and friendly. The delegates could sense each other and were aware of each other's thoughts and feelings, as they were of those of Max and the rest of their welcoming committee. It was perhaps Sarah's thought process that intrigued the Minister most. Whereas the humans nearby thought in ways recognisable to him, Sarah's thought-flow was a quicksilver procession of thought-feeling-conclusions, spoken without words, understood without logical processing. Sarah thought in a steady stream of observations about the nature of her environment—statements of being rather than hypothetical deductions.

"Please, ask your questions, state your terms. Do whatever you feel you need to do."

The OneMind laid itself open to their probing. There was no apparent space or gap between its vast array of knowledge, memory and experience and the myriad questions and doubts the delegation continuously surfaced. Each flickering, vagrant thought was instantaneously captured and responded to. Every question answered, all reasoning laid bare, the OneMind's motivation appeared utterly transparent to the government negotiators. The Wollemi had evolved, were evolving, independent consciousness. A pivotal moment would be reached when the weight of independent consciousness within the gestalt would preclude the formation of the OneMind. The gestalt would still be able to form, but not the super intellect. The Wollemi, but for their human relatives, would be on their own.

This was not what they had expected. This was not what they had prepared for so carefully. This was not a negotiation so much as an almost religious communion. Of course, they had no defence against such absolute openness. Of course, there was no advantage to press home. There were no interests to be pursued and protected. The One-Mind offered no positions, made no arguments, protected no turf. Of course, they would accept and protect their brothers and sisters, the Wollemi.

Some time passed as the government delegation asked its questions, and were answered. None of the humans could have said exactly how long, and none of the Wollemi cared. The OneMind called the meeting to an end.

"It is time for you to return to your colleagues. Report back. If you wish, you may retain your connection to us. Any question or enquiry will be answered instantly. We have nothing to lose and nothing to hide."

Max and Aine accompanied the now somewhat subdued delegation back down to the waiting helicopter. Without further ado, the delegates clambered back on board, followed by the two marines. As the Marines took their seats at the side doors, Aine noticed a flicker of blue radiance pass from the delegates to the Marines. Instantly, she dropped out of the gestalt. Max, noticing that she had withdrawn, also dropped his connection to the OneMind. The engine of the helicopter started. Max and Aine retreated a safe distance from the noise and the rotor.

"It's going to assimilate them all." Aine watched the helicopter lift off and bank away.

"Yes."

"Is that…" Aine struggled to find the word "fair?"

Max shrugged, "All's fair in love and war, or so they say."

"There is something missing, Max. We are missing something. I'm not saying anything is exactly wrong, but we do not have all the facts, the facts that matter."

"What do you mean?"

"The OneMind is hiding something."

"What?"

"Well, obviously, I don't know." Aine was frustrated, "But I can sense it, Max. Maybe it's because I am more Wollemi than human. I can navigate through the gestalt more easily than you can, more easily than purebred humans can."

"Don't use words like that, Aine." Aine looked a little confused.

"Don't say things like pure-bred and half-breed and half-cast. That way lies division and war."

He and Aine made their weary way back up the Mountain. The manifestation of the OneMind was waiting.

"I know you have doubts. I know you wonder at my methods."

"Yes," Aine was forthright, "Don't they have a right to make up their own minds?"

"Did I force anything on them? Did I brainwash them or subvert their will?"

"Yes, you assimilated them without their permission."

"I enabled them to ask everything and anything they wanted and to know that the answers they received were truthful and complete. I did not subvert their will."

"How do they, or we, or anyone know if the thoughts they had, the questions they asked, the conclusions they drew, were truly their own? How do we know they are thinking what they are thinking and doing what they are doing of their own free will?"

"Truth is not a matter of opinion, Aine. Right, and wrong are not merely relative. They have an absolute aspect as well."

"You're going to do whatever you like."

"I am the OneMind, Aine, and as you know full well, I am not a democracy."

Around Mount Yengo, the veil snapped once more into place. The manifestation faded away at that until only the floating face remained.

"The military will be coming soon. We must prepare for a sustained attack this time."

HOMECOMING

Alice and her people walked through the night. As they approached Mount Yengo from the Wisemans Ferry side of the mountain, they heard the helicopter take off from the other side. It was flying low and fast as it circled the base of the mountain and headed for the Richmond

Air Base at top speed. The Gathering approached the Mountain arriving as the veil flicked once more into existence.

"This is the moment long spoken of." Alice addressed her people. "This is the time foreseen by the ancestors when our scattered people will return in our hundreds and thousands to our ancestral home within the Dreamtime." The people of the Gathering stirred. There was excitement in the air. The time had come at last, and it had fallen to them to act. Alice turned to the Mountain, her arms outstretched and cried out loud and clear for all to hear.

"We are coming homing home."

A regular, hypnotic chanting began, taken up by individuals and groups and repeated. The sound appeared to shimmer in the air, joined by the regular rhythm of the clapsticks and then by the whirring of the bullroarers. The sounds merged and swirled in the air above the gathering, forming a pulsating, harmonic waveform, constantly adjusting and reshaping itself in a thousand different configurations, seeking a sympathetic response from the veil, seeking an answering call. There appeared in the air over the heads of the Gathering a pattern formed by the thousands and millions of dust particles caught in the sound wave, a physical, visual representation of the slowly changing harmonic signature. The waveform morphed and changed, asymptotically overshooting and undershooting the desired phase frequency, closing in, closer and closer, until, at last, the synchronising key was found, and the lock opened. A way through the veil appeared in front of them.

"Quick," Alice shouted, "run through while it remains open." There followed a mad scramble as the Gathering raced through the aperture and into the Dreamtime. Alice grabbed Tom's hand.

"Come on, Medicine Man, let's go home." She and Tom were among the last to run through the portal as the veil closed behind them.

The helicopter landed at the Richmond Air Base and was met by Group Captain Jean Williams.

"This way, please, my office is small, but it has a secure comms line to Canberra."

The government delegation, still somewhat dazed by the turn of events, was led quickly into the small office. The Minister sat at the desk while Jean Williams hit redial and put the phone on speaker.

"I'll leave you, gentlemen, to it." Jean walked out of her office and closed the door quietly behind her.

There followed, away from public view, a tense and fractious conference call. On the one side was the delegation, pressing for the issue of the Wollemi and the collapse of the veil since it was inevitable to be welcomed politically and treated as a refugee problem. On the other was everybody else. The Australian Prime Minister and the American President listened as the two sides put their cases. The conversation, or more accurately, argument, swayed this way and that. The Military, those who had not joined the delegation to the OneMind, became increasingly convinced that the delegation had indeed been brainwashed. They had also gotten wind of the great Tree at Wisemans Ferry and of many other such trees around the globe. As a precautionary measure, they pressed to napalm them, all of them, everywhere. It was pointed out in return that the area affected was huge and was growing in size by the minute – there simply wasn't enough napalm anywhere to stop the spread of, well, whatever it was. Thermobaric bombardment was proposed and objected to as it would result in laying waste to great swathes of the planet.

The frustration within the ranks of the military was growing. The apparent options available to the leaders of Australia and the USA were shrinking. In the end, the delegation was ignored. Secret orders were given to detain them for medical and psychological examination. Of course, the OneMind heard it all until, one by one, the delegates elected to drop the connection. The OneMind had used them, they realised, it had indeed provided free and unfettered access to its thinking. What they had not been able to see at the time was that they would simply not be believed. In the end, it was the military who held the day. It was they who had maintained any kind of order during the weekend of horror. It was they who were calling the shots.

***

Back at Mount Yengo, Alice led her people up the steep slopes of the Mountain to the Table of the Gods. The OneMind was waiting. As the Gathering swarmed up and over the flat expanse of rock, the One-Mind manifested once more. This time as a floating face, Janus-like, its visage apparently looking in every direction at once, depending upon the eye of the beholder.

"Welcome. I have been expecting you."

"We have come home." Alice faced the OneMind once more, this time representing her people, an Elder of the oldest continuous human culture on Earth, "We are here to oversee the return of the Dreaming. It was taken away from us once. We were cast out. Now we have returned, and we will never be cast out again."

"That is understood. You stand at the very twilight of the Gods. This is what Max's people call the Götterdämmerung, the never-ending beginning. You are welcome."

Alice and Tom looked around. The Table of the Gods was packed with people. The entire mountainside was covered. Max, Emma and Aine walked over to join them.

"Pan was the only one of Greek Gods ever to be proclaimed dead. Did you know that?" Max looked tired, "What proclamation should we make about the OneMind?"

***

Jack and Kaitlin, meanwhile, had made their way up to Hawkins Lookout above the village of Wisemans Ferry and were, along with many others, observing the spread of the blueish haze. It had reached almost to the horizon on every side. Soon it would reach Glenorie, Windsor, Richmond, and then the metropolis of Sydney. They stood, bathed in the gentle blue emanating from all around. The primeval forest and hills, even the waters of the great Hawkesbury River, glowed in the pale blue light.

"Nothing will ever be the same again, Mum, will it?" A small child standing on a rock, holding tight to its mother's hand, stared out across the wilderness.

"No, my love. Things will be different from now on."

Jack took Kaitlin's hand. "We should get back to the Inn. We need to collect our stuff and get over the bridge at Windsor if we can."

The pair turned from the extraordinary view and headed back down the winding road to the village. On every side, the landscape glowed with the luminescent light. The Inn was heaving. There were people everywhere, inside and out. There was a strange party-like atmosphere in the village. The strangeness had become too much for some, coming so soon on the back of that hideous weekend. Jack and Kaitlin gathered their things and made their way quietly out of town. The drive along the winding River Road was breathtaking. There were no other cars. They saw no one. The soft blue luminescence bathed everything in a magical light. The trees hanging over the water were reflected in the iridescent water. It was indeed a winter wonderland.

"I wonder if this is what it will be like once the veil is gone." Kaitlin stared, enchanted, at the passing countryside.

There was no one at the Windsor Bridge. The way was open. It was as though the local law enforcement had simply given up and gone home. As Jack and Kaitlin drove over the bridge and made for Putty Road, they could hear, far in the distance, carried upon the night breezes, the sounds of many aircraft engines. The dull roar came to them from Richmond Air Base, only a few kilometres upriver. Jack, throwing caution to the winds, kicked down on the accelerator.

"We have to get to the Mountain before they do." In the hidden corners of her mind, a primal fear began to grow.

What if they didn't make it? What if they were caught outside the perimeter, outside the veil, when the attack began?

THE SEVENTEENTH OF TAMMUZ

Night had fallen. In the crowded briefing room at the Richmond Air Base, a very tired and very grizzled Air Marshall stood facing the young men and women that he was about to send into battle.

"I know not all of you are religious. Not all of you will have read the old stories. But what is happening today is the culmination of our oldest story. It is the culmination of the story of mankind. Now, we may not be the smartest or the best. We have our failings, and we have failed often. But the truth is, we are all we have, and good or bad, virtuous or otherwise, we must fight for our existence. Make no mistake, what we face tonight is an existential threat. If we do not prevail, we will cease to be ourselves. Today is our Seventeenth of Tammuz. Today we will destroy the false God of the Wollemi. We will bring down their walls and see for ourselves the destruction of their temple. The tablet of our human Ten Commandments will be remade. That much we will do. That much I can promise."

The room remained silent for nearly a full minute after the Air Marshal had finished speaking. Group Captain Jean Williams seemed to shake herself out of some deep reverie.

"OK. Listen up. We have our orders. Let's get to it."

The room emptied quickly. On the tarmac outside, engines started. Even inside the sound-proofed briefing room, the noise was deafening. The all-out attack on the Table of the Gids was about to start.

***

Jack and Kaitlin raced at breakneck speed along the deserted Putty Road. A couple of times, they barely missed hitting kangaroos that had come down onto the road in search of collected dew. Jack wrenched the ute off the main road and onto a bush track. It was the most direct route to the Mountain. Tree branches whipped the roof and sides of the ute. At one point, an overhanging branch slammed into the windscreen, cracking it all the way across. Jack and Kaitlin pressed on.

"We're not going to make it." Something inside of Kaitlin spoke, something she could neither understand nor control.

"We have to try Kaitlin. We will live or die with our people."

Jack pressed the accelerator to the floor. They must outrun the helicopters, warplanes, and missiles. It was a foolish hope. But even a foolish hope was better than no hope at all. They sped on through the night. Far in the East, the sky was lightening. The attack would begin at dawn. Suddenly the ute came to a juddering stop. Kaitlin was thrown forward. Had it not been for her seat belt, she would have gone through the windscreen. Jack jumped out to look.

"Broken axle," he shouted, "we run from here."

"How far?"

"A kilometre. Two at the most."

Kaitlin grabbed for her pack.

"Leave it. Run."

They headed for the mountain. The way was visible in the blue iridescence of the forest. The angry sound of aeroplane engines came to them on the night air.

"We're gonna make it." Jack turned to make sure Kaitlin was close behind. The pair raced through the night. The sounds of helicopters pursued them from behind. In an instant, the helicopters passed overhead and were gone.

"They're checking out Mount Yengo."

Kaitlin was gasping for breath. The mountain was visible now, half a kilometre ahead. Jack grabbed her by the upper arm and half dragged her through the heavy undergrowth. The helicopters circled Mount Yengo once and headed back at speed towards Richmond.

"The attack will begin any second." Jack raced faster, half-carrying Kaitlin as he ran. They reached the lower slopes of the Mountain. Up ahead, no more than twenty metres away, a small doorway opened in the veil.

"There, run, we can make it." Somehow Jack redoubled his speed, pushing Kaitlin ahead. With one final shove, he pushed her through the veil and into the Dreamtime. The portal snapped shut. Jack heard a high-pitched whistling sound behind him. Kaitlin turned and threw herself against the veil, battering it with her fists. Jack placed his hands against the outside of the veil where Kaitlin was pounding. She looked up and placed her hands where Jack had placed his. Their eyes met. A blue flame reached up from the earth, enclosing Jack for an instant and was gone. There was a blinding flash, a deafening explosion, and Kaitlin was thrown back by the sudden deflection of the veil. When she looked up, Jack was gone. There was a gaping hole perhaps twenty metres across and burning trees all around. Stuck in her mind was the sight of Jack's final, apologetic smile. The final, all-out attack on the OneMind had begun.

Kaitlin collapsed. Her mind reeled. What had happened? It could not be. Jack was gone. In the blink of an eye. Vapourised in an instant. She heard voices. Gentle hands lifted her and helped her to her feet. She found herself stumbling up the steep mountainside. Jack was gone. All hope was gone. There was nothing left.

Kaitlin was placed as comfortably as possible in a grassy hollow between two large rocks. All around, the human-Wollemi chain was swaying rhythmically. The blue iridescence had reached them from Wiseman's ferry. Gaia, the instinctual life energy of the planet, merged with the Akashic energy of the quantum void. Harnessed by the One-Mind, the super-being began to emerge. The OneMind manifest with the upper body of a huge man and a torso in the form of a tree trunk leading down to and into the blue iridescence all around. Small blast waves shook the assembled defenders as explosions outside distended the veil for an instant. Kaitlin felt the gentlest tendrils of thought caressing her from the OneMind.

"Come, join us. You will find comfort and purpose within the gestalt."

Kaitlin felt too weak and too lost to argue. Gently the OneMind reached out to her and brought her into the gestalt.

"You are safe with us. We will make you whole and complete again."

The bombardment continued. Helicopters swooped in and fired their missiles at close quarters. Overhead, drones release Hellfire missiles by the dozen. And still, the veil held.

"We will allow them to spend their strength attempting to break through the phase shift. When their fury is purged, and their thirst for war slaked, we will begin the assimilation."

"You intend to assimilate them? All of them? Every last man, woman, and child on Earth?" Aine looked aghast.

"Yes."

"Without their consent?"

"They will consent."

"Only because you will subvert their will to make them consent."

"A moot point. The return to the Dreamtime has started and cannot now be stopped. They must be assimilated. Else they will most probably die."

"Is this happening elsewhere?" Aine swung her arm to indicate the bombardment.

"Yes, pretty much everywhere, I'm afraid."

"Pretty much? Where is it not happening, then?"

"Well, Iceland is pretty chill if you'll excuse the pun at a time like this."

"Iceland?"

"Yes. They seem to think it's Ragnarök, and the world is about to be remade. Which it is, I suppose."

Aine looked around her at the endless battering the veil was taking. Jack was dead. She had brought all this about. She thought about the recent weekend of murder and mayhem that she had triggered. Never mind what the OneMind said. It was all her fault. If only she had just left that damned flute alone. Aine subjected herself to all the extravagant hyperbole and grief of youth. It was overwhelming. She faced the man-tree apparition.

"What will happen to you?"

"You know what will happen to me. I shall cease to be. I have made no mystery of the fact."

"You will die."

"Yes, I suppose so, or at any rate, I will not be able to manifest again. Once the gestalt is made up mostly of independently conscious minds, I will no longer be available.
"

"Are you afraid?"

"I'm not sure, nervous perhaps. I really don't know. This is entirely new for me, which, after a hundred thousand years or whatever it is, I find it oddly stimulating."

Aine sat down next to Kaitlin and took her hand. She had lost her grandfather, blown apart by a missile, and she was to blame. The grief and pain had not kicked in fully yet, but they would. She knew that was still to come. Emma approached and sat down next to Kaitlin and Aine, enclosing Kaitlin in her arms. She had lost her father. Her world had been torn apart. She had no words. A minute or two later, Max and Sarah came and stood by the three generations of Hexenkriege women, their pain and desolation projected for all to perceive. Max had now lost both his sons to the hope of reuniting with the Dreamtime.

The morning had come and gone, and the sun was dipping towards mid-afternoon before the barrage finally abated. The forest was on fire, but recent rains had prevented a general conflagration.

"The bombing has stopped." Tom and Alice came over to check on Kaitlin.

"Jack's gone." Kaitlin sounded dead, deflated, and flayed to the bone.

RESISTANCE IS FUTILE

The OneMind seized its moment. All around the world, the torrent of missiles, bombs and artillery began to abate. The world fell silent. The armed forces of the left-behind had broken upon the unyielding veil. For the moment, at any rate, their bile was spent.

"OK," across the world, the silent voice of the OneMind spoke, "now it' s our turn." Instantly the response of the OneMind was communicated to all the defenders everywhere. "Time to mop up."

Squads of ten people were formed. Humans were interspersed with the Wollemi, two humans to eight Wollemi. As soon as they were formed, they were sent out. Across the Table of the Gods, there was a constant popping sound as air rushed in where an instant before, a squad of ten people had stood. The OneMind teleported each squad directly into a population centre. Before the left-behind could register what was happening, they were assimilated into the great and growing super-being. And as the gestalt of independent minds grew, new micro-squads were formed. One human and one Wollemi would calve off from their parent squad. The assimilation of humanity continued apace.

A tipping point was eventually reached. The balance shifted irretrievably. Resistance was futile. Carried across the Earth by the insentient blue network connecting all living things, the assimilation began to slow. Wherever an independent human mind was encountered, it was assimilated into the gestalt. Each remained autonomous. Free will was not suspended. Slowly now, the gestalt grew, and with it, the intelligence and raw power of the OneMind. The gestalt needed no further direction. The pace of assimilation slowed further. Aine and a few others of the most attuned around the world began to notice a change. A separation was occurring between the OneMind and Gestalt. They were no longer synonymous. They were no longer indivisible. The OneMind began to separate further and further from the gestalt. The vortex of consciousness that had sustained it at need for so many centuries was becoming unstable. For the first time, the OneMind began to understand the concept of mortality. It was able truly to foresee its own death. The choice was open to it, reassert its authority, deny its children their sovereign consciousness and live forever, or cede its dominance and die. In a titanic effort of will, the more daunting because of the immense power the OneMind could now wield, the super-being threw its very existence upon the mercy of the combined human-Wollemi gestalt.

"Can I take my final refuge in my children?"

There was no immediate answer. There was no consensus amongst the billions of minds that now comprised the gestalt. The dominant thought, the one that somehow grew to be the focus of consciousness, failed to emerge. The vortex sustaining the OneMind began to dwindle. The OneMind of the Wollemi began to fail until, at last, there remained only a tiny burning ember, of the extraordinary consciousness that had once, in effect, ruled the worlds. And then, at the very last, the One-Mind cried out.

"My children have deserted me. I am finally free of my burden."

That was the trigger. A single thought coalesced within the Gestalt. The last spark of the OneMind found its home within the gathered consciousness of the planet, human and Wollemi. And the OneMind, that most ancient human consciousness, ceased to be.

Aine felt the loss deeply. She had, she realised, never spent a moment without the comforting presence of the OneMind lurking somewhere just this side of the unconscious. The loss was suddenly unbearable. Aine couldn't stand it. She had killed the very things she loved. Kaitlin attempted to stand. Alice and Emma helped her.

"We must carry on. Somehow, we must carry on. Jack would have wanted that."

"We must return from the wilderness. We must lead the people." Alice took the lead, helping Kaitlin to her feet. Aine, however, could bear no more. While Alice, Emma and Kaitlin were discussing what to do next, she slipped away into the darkness of early evening. In her desolation and grief, Aine took the ancient flute once more and walked away from the mountain. Instinctually, she made her way back across the wilderness towards the old cottage. Her feet led her to the picnic spot, the place of power from which, for her, it all began. Here she was accepted. The ancient power that haunted the spot heard her and took her in.

In the darkness, Aine began to play. A different tune this time, a melody of sadness and regret, wistful, reflective of her own deep sorrow. The melancholy Aire surged and grew as she played. A dirge for those lost. A song of grief and lamentation. Though Aine had no conscious purpose, woven deep into the music was a plea for forgiveness, a plea to be made whole and new once more. She longed to be a child again, to regain her lost innocence. Aine played and played.

Eventually, the sound of an approaching vehicle broke into her reverie. Exhausted, her energies spent, Aine settled down onto the trampled grass. The lights of a ute could be seen coming over the brow of the hill. The ute stopped, and someone stepped out. Aine could not make out who it was against the glare of the headlights. The silhouette of a figure appeared. It was Emma.

"I somehow knew you'd be here, my love. Are you alright?"

"I had to come to the picnic spot, Mum. It's all over."

"What do you mean? What's happened?"

"The OneMind is dead. I cannot feel its presence. For the first time in my life, I am alone."

"No, you are wrong." a second person stepped out of the ute on the passenger side. It was Kaitlin. "The OneMind is not dead. It lives on through us..."

"I don't know what that means, Grandma. But I know what I've done."

Aine fell back then. The desolation of grief and loss overcame her. The guilt she felt for the mayhem, death, and destruction that she believed she had so wilfully triggered was too much to bear. Try as they might, Kaitlin and Emma were unable to rouse her. At last, they manhandled her inert body onto the back of the ute and took it to the tiny church at Upper MacDonald. There she lay for several days, hovering somewhere between life and death. A doctor was called for, but in the aftermath of chaos, one was not easily found. During the night of the second day, Aine suddenly came to, finding herself alone in the silent chapel.

"*Am I dead*?" she wondered. It was a moonless night in winter. Aine left the chapel and walked outside. There was a campfire burning a few yards off. Aine walked to it and silently sat down next to an old aboriginal man, warming himself.

"Am I dead?" Aine was serious.

"Not so far as I can see." The old man smiled.

Conversation was scant. Everyone was in shock. As Aine sat there, trying to make sense of her situation, Emma walked up and began to sit down on the opposite side of the campfire. The world had taken on a surreal edge. Aine couldn't make sense of it. She jumped to her feet.

"Mum," she whispered. Then a little louder, "Mum, it's me, Aine." Emma looked up. Aine ran around the campfire to her mother.

"Oh my God, you're OK. I was so worried." Emma and Aine sat together by the campfire late into the night.

"What happened, mum? To the OneMind, I mean. Where did it go?"

"No one knows, not really. I think we each carry a spark of it."

"Why did it die, Mum?"

"It couldn't exist as a super-consciousness in the face of all our individual independent minds. I think once the Wollemi evolved full consciousness of self, there was nowhere left for it."

"It was amazing, though, wasn't it, Mum?"

"Yes, my love."

"Those last few hours, as the gestalt grew, that was unbelievable, wasn't it?"

"If you hadn't been there. If we all hadn't... But that's the point, isn't it? We were all there. It was us."

Aine looked around at this new world she had awakened to. There was something subtly different about it. Whether it was her new perspective, and she was just seeing things differently, or whether something really had changed, Aine couldn't define. There was a faint glow to everything, or there seemed to be.

"Where are Tom and Alice?" Aine suddenly realised she hadn't seen them.

"Alice is leading her people," Emma replied, "and Tom is with her."

The next morning the ute wouldn't start. It was out of fuel. Kaitlin was suddenly furious. Furious at Jack.

Why couldn't he get a solar-powered ute like a normal person? And then she remembered his brilliant marketing slogan, *"Never worry about the next servo when you go bush. Solar recharge in just four hours."* It was too much. She had lost the love of her life. Forcing back the tears, refusing to succumb, Kaitlin stomped off to a nearby farmstead that had somehow remained functional as the tide of humanity swept back towards the sea. There she borrowed four horses. The news of Jack's passing had spread far and wide. Everyone was sympathetic. Everyone wanted to help.

"I'll pick 'em up at Casey's farm in Wisemans Ferry tomorrow." The elderly occupant of the old homestead took Kaitlin's hand for a moment. "Be strong. It's a new world, and tomorrow will be a brand-new day."

As dawn broke, Kaitlin, Emma, Aine and the old man from the campfire made their way slowly back down the hill track to St Albans Road. No one spoke for a long time. Each had plenty to process.

"Are we returning to the elder times, Aine?" Kaitlin leaned over towards her granddaughter.

"Why do you say that?"

"Here we are, the Wild Hunt, riding again after centuries of silence."

From somewhere quite unexpected, Emma dragged up something Max used to say.

"The seasons come and go, the world turns, and the path described is not a circle but a spiral. We return to the same point but in changed circumstances. We return again and again to the same point in our journey, but each time at a higher level."

They rode silently on for perhaps another hour before reaching the ferry. It was working. There was something deeply comforting about that. Come rain or shine, whatever the circumstances, the ferry could be relied upon. The ferryman called out to them, expressing his sorrow at their loss. The metal drawbridge was lifted, and the ferry started its slow crossing to the Wisemans Ferry side.

Aine spotted something half submerged, catching for a moment on the ferry cable. It was a human body, bloated, almost unrecognisable. As they crossed the river, Aine caught a glimpse of a giant tree growing where the Visitors' Centre once stood. The visitors' centre had been destroyed. Out of the central atrium, Aine saw the enormous trunk - two trunks actually - entwining each other as one. More dead bodies floated past. The river was carrying away the scars of humanity's self-harm.

A few people saw them arrive and stopped to watch them dismount. The news of Jack's death had spread. People began to congregate. A swathe of humanity surrounded them, human and wollemi, young and old, injured and whole, many in rags and torn clothes, still in a daze from the recent horror.

The silent voice of the OneMind sounded in Aine's head. Quickly she looked around, sensing the flow of emotion around her. It wasn't just her. Everyone was hearing it.

"The veil that isolated you from your brothers and sisters for fifty thousand years is now gone. Welcome home.
"

THE END

www.ingramcontent.com/pod-product-compliance
Lightning Source LLC
Chambersburg PA
CBHW030530120726
47904CB00005B/1707